Caroline Hazard

Thomas Hazard

son of Robt call'd College Tom. A study of life in Narragansett in the XVIIIth century

Caroline Hazard

Thomas Hazard
son of Robt call'd College Tom. A study of life in Narragansett in the XVIIIth century

ISBN/EAN: 9783337378738

Printed in Europe, USA, Canada, Australia, Japan

Cover: Foto ©Andreas Hilbeck / pixelio.de

More available books at **www.hansebooks.com**

Thomas Hazard son of Robt

call'd

COLLEGE TOM

*A STUDY OF LIFE IN NARRAGANSETT
IN THE XVIIITH CENTURY*

BY HIS GRANDSON'S GRANDDAUGHTER

CAROLINE HAZARD

BOSTON AND NEW YORK
HOUGHTON, MIFFLIN AND COMPANY
The Riverside Press, Cambridge
1893

The Riverside Press, Cambridge, Mass., U. S. A.
Electrotyped and Printed by H. O. Houghton & Co.

To

R. AND M. R. H.

WHO IN THIS CENTURY AND IN THE SAME NARRAGANSETT,

FILL THE HONORED PLACES OF

THOMAS AND ELIZABETH HAZARD,

THIS BOOK IS INSCRIBED BY THEIR

LOVING DAUGHTER.

Tho Hazard son of Robt
Elzabeth Hazard

PREFACE.

Tʜᴇ year following my grandfather's
death, in 1889, after his papers had been
sorted and classified, I began to work
among them, hoping to arrange a memoir.
I soon saw that I should have to begin with
his grandfather, and was led still further
back to the grandfather of his grandfather.
As I worked, the life of the last century
cast a spell over the present, and what I
had undertaken as a chapter has developed
into this volume.

My thanks are especially due to two
Friends, William H. Perry, the clerk of the
Meeting, whose friendship for my grand
parents led him to give me access to
the South Kingstown "Monthly Meeting
Records," which have never before been
examined for historical purposes ; and
Samuel Austin, a descendant of College

Tom's contemporary, who searched the Rhode Island "Yearly Meeting Records" for me. Besides these I owe valuable suggestions to Mrs. Caroline E. Robinson, whose researches in the South Kingstown Records I hope may soon be published.

The details here presented may seem trifling — the accounts of household concerns and neighborhood transactions ; and so they are if they do not inspire a greater reverence for the body which is "more than raiment," and the life which is "more than meat." The problems of that day were different from ours, but the courage required to face them was the same. The men in their homespun and the women in their "camblit" cloaks lived and loved much as we do. And so this little bit of the old life makes a link in the unending chain of life, — that life which is constantly aspiring, ever seeking its divine source.

C. H.

OAKWOODS IN PEACE DALE, R. I.
    October 9, 1893.

CONTENTS.

APPENDIX.

LIST OF ILLUSTRATIONS.

COLLEGE TOM.

CHAPTER I.

THE development of small and isolated communities has long furnished a fascinating theme for the historian and the poet. The scope afforded for original personality is great, and the tendency to follow a natural leader most strongly marked in a society so closely bound together. These two opposing forces working against each other combine to foster the growth of strong individuality. When a community is entirely self sustaining in material things, and independent in intellectual, the old saying might be paraphrased to read "in limitation is strength." Especially was this true in a new country, where the resources of men were taxed to their utmost; and of no part of the new world was this more true than of Rhode Island, and that part of Rhode Island called the Narragansett country. Not from choice, but from dire necessity was Providence planted in the wilderness. To it came not the men Roger Williams would have chosen, but men like himself in peril of their lives from the self-righteous neighbor which shook off what was considered their polluting presence. No common idea bound them together, and though Roger Williams by his force and beauty of character long maintained his natural leadership, it was often a difficult matter. Portsmouth and Newport in the same way were founded by exiles, who soon quarreled among themselves, and the town of Warwick resulted from forcibly deporting some of the turbulent spirits from the Island. As the tide of immigration to Rhode Island came not by sea but from the north, the southern portion, the country of the Narragansetts, was naturally the last to be opened to white settlers. As early as 1634, Governor

Winthrop describes it.   "The country on the
west of the bay of Narragansett," he writes,
"is all champain for many miles, but very
stony and full of Indians."[1]   Except that the
Indians are gone, this is a true description
to this day.   Now we speak of South Kingstown as the Narragansett country, but in
the old days when the Narragansetts were
a powerful tribe their special territory was
bounded on the north by the Cowesits and
Shawomuts, bordering on Greenwich Bay,
and on the west by the formidable Pequots.[2]
The long finger of Point Judith stretches
far out into the sea, giving a long line of
coast, part of it bold and rocky, where the
great sea-bass are still caught, and part with
beaches and shallow ponds full of clams and
oysters.   It is a small bit of country, "this
little corner," as Dr. McSparran called it,
watered by several good streams.   The
Pettaquamscut flows from a charming lake,
not above tide water, and separates the
fertile lands of Boston Neck from Tower
Hill.   Then comes the Saugatucket, which
takes the westerly water-shed of the ridge

---

[1] Quoted in Potter, *Early History of Narragansett*,
p. 16.

[2] *Ibid.*, pp. 1 and 3.

of hills, with their glacial scratches and granite boulders, which make the backbone of Rhode Island. Farther west still, beyond the crest of Little Rest Hill, flows the Chepuxet into Worden's Pond, along the borders of which lies the Great Swamp, and issues from it the Pawcatuck, the little river which figured prominently in the English courts.[1] All this land was granted by a liberal king to two colonies, Connecticut and Rhode Island; for, Dr. McSparran justly observes, "as the geography of this country was hardly emerged into any tolerable light, instead of ascertaining their limits on earth they fixed their boundaries in the heavens."[2] If the Pawcatuck, as the Rhode Island men held, was the stream called Narragansett River, it marked the boundary of Connecticut; if, on the contrary, the bay was meant by that name, the whole country was lost to Rhode Island.

Into this well watered land, with its forests, and "full of Indians," Roger Williams penetrated some time before 1650,[3] and here the persecuted man found a warm welcome. He

[1] Potter, *Early History of Narragansett*, p. 234.
[2] Updike, *History of the Narragansett Church*, p. 500.
[3] Potter, *Early History of Narragansett*, p. 4.

renders thanks "to the Most High who stirred up the barbarous heart of Cononicus to love me as his son to his last gasp."[1]   Here he went to see the little island called Nahigansett, "and about the place called Sugar Loaf Hill I saw it," he writes, "and was within a pole of it, but could not learn why it was called Nahigansett."[2]   Richard Smith had built a trading-house near Wickford, a few years before, and soon took control of the more southerly station which Roger Williams established.   But little progress was made toward opening the country for settlement until the two great purchases, the first in 1657 by John Hull, the goldsmith of Boston, and his associates, called the Pettaquamscut purchase,[3] and the second by the Humphrey Atherton Company in 1659.[4]   The Pettaquamscut purchases extended over a period of several years, and were made with the consent of the colonies, while the Atherton Company, Potter declares, bought their land "in contravention of an express law of the colony,"[5] and, therefore, could not be recognized

---

[1] Potter, *Early History of Narragansett*, p. 4.
[2] *Ibid.*
[3] *Ibid.*, p. 275.
[4] *Ibid.*, p. 58.
[5] *Ibid.*, p. 39.

by the government. The two purchases
covered portions of the same land, and endless strife resulted. Of the seven Pettaquamscut purchasers all except John Hull
were settlers in Rhode Island. Wilson and
Mumford were actually in the Narragansett country, and others came, or were in
Newport, near by. The Atherton Company
seems to have been the speculation of
absentee landlords. The younger Winthrop of Connecticut was one of its rul-
ing spirits. Bradstreet, the Stantons, and
Smiths were of the company. A recent
writer thinks scant justice has been done
these pioneers, whom the Pettaquamscut men
regarded as such intruders, but he says they
were all "anti-Rhode-Islanders in spirit."[1]
Members of this company at this early day
declare that Rhode Island is "a rodde to
those that love to live in order, — a road,
refuge, asylum to evil livers. The public
rolls record what malefactors, what capital
offenders, have found it their unhallowed
sanctuary."[2] And, indeed, from the Connecticut point of view this was quite true, for the

[1] Dr. Edward Channing, *The Narragansett Planters*,
p. 13.

[2] *Ibid.*

founders of the three towns, Roger Williams at Providence, Mrs. Hutchinson and her associates at Portsmouth, and Samuel Gorton at Warwick, were all "capital offenders." In contrast to this Williams nobly expressed what came to be the ideal Rhode Island spirit, when he replied to the demand of Massachusetts to banish Quakers: "We have no law amongst us whereby to punish any for only declaring by words their minds and understanding concerning the things and ways of God as to salvation and our eternal condition." [1]

Both companies undoubtedly expected large results from their land scheme. The Pettaquamscut purchasers bought their first large tract of land from the Indians for sixteen pounds and other considerations.[2] How much the Indians understood of it all is very uncertain; especially of the terms of mortgage, which they did not fulfill. They were stirred to opposition, and in 1662 made a protest to the pretended "title to Point Jude and other lands adjoining."[3] The Pettaquamscut purchasers, holding

---

[1] Fiske, *Beginnings of New England*, p. 184.

[2] Potter, *Early History of Narragansett*, p. 275.

[3] *Ibid.*, p. 277.

under Rhode Island law, were bound to support the royal charter of 1643, giving the land to Rhode Island ; while the Atherton Company maintained the validity of the grant of 1631 confirmed in 1662, to the Earl of Warwick, by which Connecticut claimed it.[1] So hot did the dispute become that two years later the King's commissioners appointed to settle it summarily took the country from both colonies claiming it, and erected it into a separate government called the King's Province.[2] After 1666 the Governor and assistants of Rhode Island took the place of its own officers, which for two years had been appointed by the Crown. All this dissension naturally prevented the rapid growth of the country. A few years later the General Assembly at Newport (1672) appointed four commissioners " to goe over to Narragansett and to take view of such places there and there about that are fit for plantations." They were instructed to inform the English and Indians that " the Collony doth intend such lands shall be improved by peoplinge the same."[3]

[1] Potter, *Early History of Narragansett*, p. 62.
[2] *Ibid.*, p. 69.
[3] *R. I. C. R.*, vol. ii p. 87.

So Rhode Island was taking the matter into her own hands. Instead of sending " assistants " to the General Assembly the Court of General Assembly went to Narragansett. On a May day in 1671 Governor Nicholas Easton, and the other officers of the Colony, met at the house of Mr. Jireh Bull in Pettaquamscut. A courier was dispatched through the country "to warne the inhabitants of this Plantation to attend to-morrow morning at six of the clock,"[1] when among other business transacted Mr. Bull himself, Mr. Samuel Wilson, and Mr. William Hefernan were chosen justices.[2]

To this house in 1672, the following year, came a very different embassy. The Governor was the same and came again from Newport, but with him came a greater than his justices, George Fox, the saintly apostle of the Inner Light. Fox himself describes the meeting, which seems to have taken place at the Bull house, known to have been large and a usual place of assembly.

" We had a meeting at a justice's, " he writes, " where Friends never had any before. The meeting was very large, for the country

----

[1] *R. I. C. R.*, vol. ii. p. 39.

[2] *Ibid.*

generally came in ; and people from Connecticut and other parts round about. There were four justices of the peace. Most of these people were such as had never heard Friends before ; but they were mightily affected, and a great desire is there after the truth amongst them. So that meeting was of very good service, blessed be the Lord for ever ! "[1]   He was asked to come again, but says he " was clear of those parts." However, he " laid this place before " two of his companions, John Burnyeate and John Cartwright, who " felt drawings thither, and went to visit them." So the meeting which had so much influence in Narragansett was established. The house itself in which the gospel of peace was preached by this saintly man had a tragic fate. It stood on the crest of a hill, now called Tower Hill, to guard against surprise, for the country was still full of Indians, and Indians exasperated by ill usage. King Philip's war was already brewing when the saintly man was there. One December night in 1675 the house was attacked, set on fire, and two men and five women and children killed. The news of this outrage

[1] Fox, *Journal*, 1672.

reached the army at Warwick on the eighteenth or nineteenth, and in hot haste they started for vengeance. The Indians were found strongly encamped on the shores of the Great Pond, and the dreadful slaughter of the Great Swamp Fight followed. It seems an especial irony of fate that the destruction of the house from which the purest gospel of peace and long-suffering had first been preached, should have been the actual incitement to one of the most bloody of the Indian battles.

Such was the state of the country; unsafe as to Indians, uncertain as to title of lands,— for the conflicting claims of the two purchases were not settled until 1679,[1] — and unstable as to government. In 1674 Kingstown was incorporated for the amiable reason of "obstructing Connecticut from using jurisdiction in the Narragansett country." They must be strong men who could maintain themselves in such a disorganized society. Each man was a law to himself, and it is small wonder that Narragansett developed men of great individuality and pronounced character.

[1] Dr. Edward Channing, *The Narragansett Planters*, p. 14.

Here it was that Robert Hazard took up his abode. In 1671 he bought five hundred acres from the Pettaquamscut purchasers, bounded north by the road, east by the Saka-tucket," a tract of land lying between Kingston and Rose Hill. He had come from England with his father, and is said to have been four years old when the latter joined in founding the town of Newport in 1638. Who this first Thomas Hazard was no one knows. The times were troublous in the Mother-country, as well as in New England. The Hassards, or Hassarts, took an active part in the siege of Londonderry, having gone to Ireland from Nottinghamshire,[1] and T. R. Hazard thinks the American adventurer was a brother of Robert Hazard of Enniskillen, who died in 1668. However this may be, he came from Boston, where he was admitted freeman in 1636, to Portsmouth, very possibly with Mrs. Hutchinson. On the Island, trouble had already begun on account of the diversity of religious belief. Samuel Gorton, that "proud and pestilent seducer," as he was termed in the language of the day, with his preaching of

[1] J. Hassard-Short, *History and Lineage of the Hassards,* p. 20.

private inspiration and "mystical rubbish,"[1] as Mr. Fiske calls it, arrived in Aquidneck in 1638, sowing dissension among Mrs. Hutchinson's followers; and on the twenty-eighth day of the second month, 1639, Thomas Hazard was an Elder in the new government, which, under William Coddington as judge, agreed "to Propagate a Plantation in the midst of the Island or elsewhere." Mr. John Clarke, Mr. Jeffreys, Thomas Hazard, and William Dyre were ordered to lay out the "meadow growndes lying within the circuit of Newport" and "to proportion it forth dewlie."[2]

The Portsmouth records give a few scant details of the life of this first Rhode Island Hazard. He had two daughters, and in 1658 gave thirty-four acres of land as dowry for his daughter Hannah. In 1675 he filed a paper disclaiming any interest in the property of the widow Martha Sheriffe,[3] whom he was about to marry, and in his will made the following year cuts off his son and daughters with a shilling each, and leaves his wife all his property.[4] Robert,

[1] John Fiske, *Beginnings of New England*, pp. 163–7.

[2] *R. I. C. R.*, vol. i. p. 87.

[3] *Records of Portsmouth*, transcribed by Barclay Hazard in T. R. Hazard's *Recollections of Olden Times*, p. 103.

[4] *Ibid.*, p. 106.

the son, was by this time settled in Narragansett, where he surveyed and divided the land around Kingston, and is called Robert Hazard, Surveyor.[1] In 1693 he signed first of the witnesses to the signatures of the seven purchasers to a paper respecting the allotment of land.[2] He left five sons, the eldest named Thomas after his grandfather, a custom which was continued for seven generations, each eldest son of an eldest son being named after his grandfather, making a succession of alternate Thomas and Robert Hazards. At first blush this would seem to lighten the labors of the student of heredity, but unfortunately for his research, Robert Hazard had not only Thomas for eldest son, but a Robert for third son. His second son George had an eldest son Robert, and also a son Thomas. Though the family rule was adhered to, each son, with characteristic individuality, founded a family of his own, using the names of the older branch whenever he chose. By the end of the eighteenth century there were in this way some thirty Thomas Hazards, of various degrees of

[1] Potter's *Early History of Narragansett*, p. 290.
[2] *Ibid.*, p. 283.

kinship, all calling each other "loving cousin," and distinguished by some nick-name. Updike gives a list of fourteen, headed with College Tom.[1] Bedford Tom, Nailer Tom, Fiddle-head Tom, Pistol Tom, Short Stephen's Tom, are some of the names given in commemoration of some event in their lives, or some personal characteristic.

Thomas Hazard, the eldest son of this first Narragansett Robert, became a great land-holder. He is described as "of Boston Neck in the King's Province or Narragansett Country, yeoman," when on the twenty-eighth of April, 1698, he bought about a thousand acres of land from "Samuel Sewall of Boston, in the county of Suffolk, within the Province of the Massachusetts Bay, in New England, Esquire."[2] The purchase included land on the Saugatucket, probably the site of the village of Peace Dale, land on the Pettaquamscut, and other lands in the Pettaquamscut purchase "lying by the sea side there." In 1710 he bought more land of the same Samuel Sewall, and Hannah his wife, who sign the second

[1] *History of the Narragansett Church*, p. 247.
[2] See Appendix, The Sewall Deed.

deed as firmly as the fine parchment twelve years earlier. This second purchase included land lying on the west shore of the Great Pond and various tracts of both " Upland and Marsh," with sedge rights in Pettaquamscut cove, which were carefully bequeathed by will.

Both the Sewall deeds are beautifully engrossed, — the first upon parchment, the second upon heavy paper. The first is a true " Indenture," the graceful curves in which the top of the deed is cut fitting into the record which was retained by the town clerk. The first deed was acknowledged before John Walley, " one of the members of his Majesty's council for the Province of the Massachusetts Bay." This was Sewall's friend, to whom reference is made in the letter of 1689, in which he is entreated by Sewall " to act on my behalf as you would do for yourself were the case your own as it is mine." [1] In 1692 he was Sewall's attorney at a meeting of the Pettaquamscut Purchasers,[2] perhaps in compliance with this request. He was one of the founders of Bristol, on the east side of the Bay, and a

---

[1] See Appendix, Letter from Judge Sewall.
[2] Potter, *Early History of Narragansett*, p. 281.

man of most liberal mind and high character.[1]

Dame Hannah Sewall, who signs also, was the daughter of the Mint-Master John Hull, about whom the delightful story is told, that on her wedding day her father put her in one side of the great scales, and fairly weighed her down with pine-tree shillings as her dowry.[2]

Judge Sewall himself was born in England in 1652, and came to Massachusetts in 1661. He was the famous witch judge, more famous for the nobility of his confession of penitence for his share in that dreadful delusion than for the error he was led into. He is the typical Puritan of the time, and with his liberal mind and true piety had much to do in shaping the new province.

With the religious zeal of the day, three hundred acres were set aside in 1668 "to be laid out and forever set apart as an encouragement, the income or improvement thereof wholly for an Orthodox person that shall be obtained to preach God's word to the In-

[1] J. L. Diman, *Orations and Essays,* "The Settlement of Mt. Hope."

[2] Hawthorne, "The Pine-Tree Shillings," in *Grandfather's Chair.*

habitants."[1]   In 1695 Judge Sewall gave land to establish a school,[2] a foundation which still exists, and is known as the Sewall School, held regularly at Kingston.   He also gave land, the income of which was to educate youths at Harvard College, " especially such as shall be sent from Pettaquamscutt aforesaid, English or Indians."   Thus early was provision made for the higher education of the Indians; they were also specially mentioned in the provision for the school.   It was he who was among the first to raise his voice for the slave.   " These *Ethiopians* as black as they are; seeing they are the Sons and Daughters of the first *Adam*, the Brethren and Sisters of the last ADAM, and the offspring of GOD; They ought to be treated with a Respect agreeable."[3]   It was with such a man of liberal mind and true piety, but withal a man keen at a bargain, that Thomas Hazard had dealings.   The deeds are drawn and signed in Boston, so he must have made that journey, — probably by the old Pequot trail, which afterward became the high road, — at least

---

[1] Potter, *Early History of Narragansett*, p. 278.
[2] *Ibid.*
[3] 5 *Mass. H. C.* vi. 16.   Quoted by W. B. Weeden.

on these two occasions. The diary of Judge Sewall is very exact as to his expenses and bargaining, and these long and cumbersome deeds doubtless necessitated many a conversation. The money was paid in two installments on the first purchase, five hundred pounds current money of New England were paid down, and the remaining two hundred left on mortgage. The colonies were already in difficulties over their money. One third discount from " Country pay " for money was a usual rate in Massachusetts after 1680.[1] The first paper money was issued by that colony in 1690,[2] and all the colonies were in a similar case, so that the " pound current of New England " had already depreciated from a gold standard.

Land was rented in the English way from Lady Day to Lady Day, and there are deeds of other lands, — one in 1722 " of a certain place called Point Juda and Pettaquamscutt purchase," which in the next year is given to the eldest son, and called " the point Judah neck." It is curious to observe the transitions of this name. The local name is *Pint Judy pint*, with the ac-

---

[1] Weeden, *Economic and Social History of N. E.,* p. 327.
[2] *Ibid.,* p. 330.

cent thrown strongly on the second *pint* in South County speech. The story is told of a vessel sailing in the fog, and nearing the breakers, but unable to shape a course for the thickness of the weather. The captain's wife suddenly exclaimed that she saw land, and tried to indicate upon which quarter. " Pint, Judy, pint!" her husband shouted to her, and as the fog lifted there was Point Judith, which has ever since borne that name. However this may be, the transition from Jude, and Juda or Judah, as some old deeds have it, to Judith was made easy to the Pettaquamscut purchasers, from the fact that Dame Hull, the wife of the goldsmith, bore that name. The ordinary pronunciation of Judy would seem to them a disrespectful abbreviation. If this derivation is correct, it is true in a way that the point was named after Sewall's mother-in-law, as some authorities maintain, but where the first name came from is still a mystery.

A great purchase of land was made in 1738, from Francis Brinley, Esq., and Dame Deborah his wife, which included the whole southern portion of Boston Neck, adjoining a purchase of six hundred and sixty acres made from Samuel Vail somewhat earlier.

There were about eight hundred acres of this land, which was surveyed and divided into four parts in the following year by James Helme, surveyor, and the map carefully preserved with the deed. The price at first sight seems enormous. Twenty-four thousand pounds "Current Lawful Money of New England" were paid for the eight hundred acres. But the depreciation of the currency was already great. Silver had long been current at eight shillings an ounce.[1] In 1738 the rate in Rhode Island had risen to twenty-seven shillings in bills per ounce,[2] making the colonial pound in paper equal five shillings eleven pence silver. Thus the value of the money paid was only £7,100, reduced to the current price of silver of eight shillings per ounce. This was two shillings higher than the sterling value, so that the pounds should be carried at $3.33, making the sum paid $23,600, or about twenty-nine dollars an acre. One of the tracts of land into which the new purchase was divided, in a deed addressed "To all Christian people," is given to Robert Hazard, the eldest son of Thomas, in consideration of "natural love and affec-

[1] Weeden, *Economic and Social History of N. E.*, p. 473.
[2] Rider, *R. I. Historical Tracts*, No. 8, p. 55.

tion." The earliest deed of gift to this son bears his mother's signature also, Susannah Hafzard. She is thought to have been a Nichols, a sister of the Lieutenant-Governor of that name, but no one knows certainly. The black seal she pressed, and the faded paper with her name, are all that remain to bear witness of her.

There are other deeds of gift to his sons, from " Thomas Hazard senior of South Kingstown, etc., gentleman," as he is now called, or as the Narragansett Church Record less respectfully calls him, " Old Thomas Hazard."[1] An amusing variety of spelling in the common surname occurs. There is but one signature of Old Thomas Hazard. All the deeds are signed with a T, and his name written with a double *z*. His eldest son writes his name with a double *s*, or an *s* and a *z*, Jeremiah, his brother, with an *s* and a *z*, and George and Jonathan, also brothers, in the modern way, with one *z*. The Sewall deed of 1698 is the first in which it is spelled in this way, but the indorsement on the back has Hazard with a double *s*. After studying these deeds, it seems proper to find that in his will the

[1] Updike, *History of the Narragansett Church*, p. 274.

aged father leaves the sons five shillings each, "they having all and each of them received their portion already." The pre-amble to this will is touching, in which the testator declares that he is " Ancient and Unwell, but of sound mind and Memory, thanks be given to God," and disposes of " such Worldly Eftate Wherewith it hath pleafed God to blefs me in this Life."[1]   It was a very considerable estate, given to grandchildren and the children of grand-children, with his eldest son Robert as ex-ecutor and residuary legatee. It was signed on the 12th of November, 1746, with a very tremulous and feeble T, and one is hardly surprised to see that it was proved on the 27th of the same month, a fortnight later. The inventory of the will was to the amount of £3745 1s. 9d. in the depreciated cur-rency. It was contested by two of the grand-sons, and appealed to the Governor and Council of the Colony of Rhode Island, who dismissed the protest, and confirmed the will, which is recorded by his grandson Thomas, town clerk that year (1746). There is only one other mention of this Thomas of the T. In 1762 the same grandson

[1] See Appendix, Will of Thomas Hazard.

makes a " Regiſtor of Death."   The record
reads : —

"My Grandfather, Thoˢ Hazard Departed this Life yᵉ 21st day of yᵉ month
call'd November in the year one thousand
seven hundred and forty-six aged 88 or 89
years.   This account taken from a memorandum found amongſt my Father's Papers after his Death.

(Signed)   THOMAS HAZARD,
            ſon of Robᵗ dec'd."

Thomas Hazard had seen great changes.
Where the country was once "stony and
full of Indians," great farms and cattle
ranges had been established.   The preaching of George Fox had borne fruit in the
flourishing meeting held regularly on Tower
Hill.   The "orthodox person" provided for
on the Pettaquamscut foundation was settled,
and had become a centre of influence.   The
Society for the Propagation of the Gospel
in Foreign Parts, after several attempts
finally sent Dr. McSparran, the delightful
Irish divine, so dear to the hearts of his
people.   He found " a field full of briers
and thorns and noxious weeds," he writes,
" that were all to be eradicated before I
could implant in them the simplicity of the

truth."[1] He complains that there are " Quakers, Anabaptists of four sorts, Independents," and that "here liberty of conscience is carried to an irreligious extreme."[2] The Huguenot refugees had left their impress upon the country also. Gabriel Bernon, the most famous of those who came to Rhode Island after the revocation of the Edict of Nantes, himself lived here for years. But the chief stimulus to the intellectual life of the time was the visit of Berkeley. The two years of his stay in Newport mark a golden era in the spiritual life of Rhode Island.[3] Newport was the natural metropolis of Narragansett, and the good dean himself came to Narragansett, to the "Continent," as he calls it. The rough pioneer days were passed, and a time of pastoral plenty begun. The slave trade furnished the laborers for the great farms; ships sailed from Newport to the Guinea coast, and in a few instances brought their wretched captives to the Narragansett shore.

The face of the natural world has changed

---

[1] Updike, Appendix, America Dissected, p. 511.

[2] *Ibid.*, p. 514.

[3] Foster, *Some Rhode Island Contributions to the Intellectual Life of the Last Century.*

but little; the Pettaquamscut still takes its shining way to the sea, and though the Saugatucket turns mill wheels, it still bounds the lands as described in the old deeds of purchase. And among the men who lived here in their absolute independence, freed even from the control of the minister, the growth of strong character and sterling virtues was fostered. The individualism may have been excessive, as in all small self-governing communities. Each man was truly a law to himself, but in listening to "their own teacher in themselves," which George Fox tried to make audible to each soul, there were men who in this liberal atmosphere rose to heights of heroic action.

Newport June the 6th 1702. then received of Mr. Thomas Hazard
Six pounds currant money of New England, it being in full for four
Years Rent of a Lott of Land in the Little neck in Pettaquamscut
from Lady Day 1698. to Lady Day 1702.

pr me Jahleel Brenton

CHAPTER II.

THE writers of the early history of the Narragansett Country all unite in declaring it a favored land, if not literally flowing with milk and honey, at least with abundance of milk, and rich in corn and all the products of a kindly soil. The grass was said to be the richest ever known, the fields the most fertile; one of the enthusiastic sons of the country calls it the fabled Atlantis, the fit home of the gods. And indeed the land is a fair land, diversified by hill and dale, the smiling landscape lit by shining lakes, and every extended prospect taking in the wide blue horizon of the bluest of oceans. Boston Neck lying between the Pettaquamscut and the sea was the most fertile soil, and the earliest settled by the Pettaquamscut purchasers. The corn of the Indians was excellent, even with the rude husbandry of the squaws, and English planters soon raised enormous crops from the practically virgin soil. At the beginning of the eighteenth century the country was taken up by great farmers working their farms with slave labor, either Indian, or negro, or both, and living the life of English squires. Their books and their tea came to them from England direct to Newport, *chocolat* and spices as well, while the West Indies furnished sugar and molasses, with the good rum so much in demand, and occasional " oringes and lemmonds." These apart, almost all the necessities of life were supplied by the great farms, beef, veal, pork, and " dung-hill fowles," corn, potatoes and onions, and wool and flax for the *warsted sarge*, *linning*, and *caliminco*. A life of comparative ease gave ample time for pleasant social intercourse. England was dear to the hearts of her sons, and the pleasant English ways of sports and hunting were adhered to. If we may believe the tales and traditions which have come down to us, the life was of idyllic freshness and simplicity. Peopled as Rhode Island was by come-outers, the most liberal of the liberal, the southern portion particularly was famous for men of pronounced views, and energy of character. The families were bound together by ties of blood or marriage, the welfare of one intimately concerned all, and in times of festivity the whole country-side joined in the jollity, irrespective of church or creed. Especially was this the case at a wedding in one of the leading families. Up from Point Judith, through the bridle-path that led from one great farm to another, divided by stone walls and heavy gates, came the ladies in their *camblitt* cloaks, and the gentlemen in broadcloth and *britches*, with silver shoe and knee buckles, mounted on the Narragansett pacers of famous memory. Colored slaves attended them to open the gates and wait upon them. From Boston Neck the gentry gathered, and from Little Rest, and the farms of Matunuc. Toward Tower Hill they took their way, where, until the middle of the century, the court house dominated the village, for whether in Church or Meeting it was on the high ridge overlooking the bay that the place of assembly was.

In May, 1742, on the twenty-seventh day, a most notable gathering of this kind took place, in the old Quaker meeting-house, on the southern spur of Tower Hill. The oc-

casion was indeed auspicious, for Thomas
Hazard, eldest son and heir of Robert, was
to marry Elizabeth Robinson, eldest daughter of that William who afterwards was
deputy-governor of the State. On the fourth
of the same month (May, 1742), Thomas
Hazard had been admitted a freeman of the
colony, presumably upon arriving of age,
though September 15, 1720, is the date of his
birth, which would make him over twenty-
one years old. As the eldest son of his
father he was a freeman upon attaining his
majority, without the property qualifications
necessary for younger sons.

Robert Hazard, his father, great-grandson
of the first immigrant, is described as " of
Boston Neck, gentleman."   He was one of
the very large owners of property in Narragansett, and it is told of him by his great-
grandson, Isaac Peace Hazard, on the authority of his grandmother, that he had " twelve
negro women as dairywomen, each of whom
had a girl to assist her, making from twelve
to twenty-four cheeses a day . . . one hundred and fifty cows being about the number
he generally-kept. . . . He kept about four
thousand sheep, manufacturing most of the
clothing, both woolen and linen, for his

household, which must have been very
large, as I have heard my grandmother say
that after he partially retired from his extensive farming operations, or curtailed
them by giving up part of his lands to his
children, he congratulated his family and
friends on the small number to which he
had reduced his household for the coming
winter, being only seventy in parlor and
kitchen." [1] He took an interest in public
affairs, and was a deputy to the general assembly from South Kingstown in 1734, '35
and '36, and again in 1738 and '39. In 1756
he was named first of a committee appointed
by the general assembly to run a dividing
line between South Kingstown and Exeter,
and reported the following year. [2]

From his will, dated in 1745 (but not exe-
cuted) a good idea of the methods of living can be gained. He first provides for
his " Dearly beloved wife," and mentions
exactly what she is to have : fifty pounds a
year, " four cows to be kept summer and
and winter yearly and every year," a Negro
woman named Phebee, " one Rideing Mare,
Such a one as She Shall Chuse Out of all my

[1] Updike, *History of the Narragansett Church*, p. 181.
[2] *R. I. C. R.*, vol. v. p. 526.

Jades, with a new Saddle and new Bridle." She was to have an allowance of wood, beef, and pork yearly, the " beef to be Killed and Drefsed, and brought to her into her houfe ; " she was given " Six Dung - hill fowl," and " fix Geese with the privilege of raifing what Increase She Can, but Shall put of (off) all of them to Six by the laft of January yearly."   Her furniture was to consist of one feather-bed, with six chairs, " two Iron pots one brass Kettle, two pair of Pott-hooks, two Trammels," various pewter dishes and platters, some large, some " middling size," pewter Basons, and silver spoons. One piece of *Camblitt* was also given " Saving so much of it as I give to my Daughter Mary to Make her a Cloak ; " of linen the piece " called the fine piece," also a piece of fine worsted cloth, with forty pounds of wool yearly, and a " Linnen wheel, and a Woollen Wheel." She was to have two rooms, " one a fire Room, the other a Bed room Such as She Shall Chufe in either of my two Houfes," and the " Improvement of a quarter of an Acre of Land where She Shall Chufe it to be Well fenced for her Ufe yearly." One wonders if this good dame Hazard enjoyed her garden, that this is carefully mentioned for her. Andirons, fire-shovel, and warming-pan are also given her; the furnishing seems to have been very complete. She was Sarah Borden, the mother of three sons and two daughters. Thomas, as the eldest, by the English custom which prevailed in this part of New England, was the chief inheritor of the estates, and is named as the executor of the will. To his care his mother was left, and though this will was destroyed, long after entries in his note-book occur showing the faithfulness with which his mother's cows were kept.

In a household thus plentifully provided, born the inheritor of large acres, Thomas Hazard grew to manhood. He went to New Haven College for several terms, and from that fact derived the sobriquet of "College Tom." The Yale records of admission previous to 1743 no longer exist. The College had had a troubled existence since 1701, when its charter was obtained, and not till the administration of President Clapp began in 1739–40 did it enter upon its career of prosperity. This is the man of whom Dr. McSparran writes, in speaking of the college at New Haven: "The Presi-

ards, one of whom spells his name in the modern way, the other with a double *s*. They were Governor Robert, own cousin of the father of the groom, and Doctor Robert; the Governor spelling his name with the double *s*, for Esther Haffard, his wife, called Queen Esther, is also there. She was a woman of great force of character. In a lawsuit about her husband's property after his death she was by courtesy allowed a seat beside the judges, where a quick repartee of hers overthrew the arguments of the opposing counsel, and won her case. Stephen Champlin, who married Mary Hazard, a sister of the groom, was there, and John Easton, an uncle by marriage. Rowland Robinfon signs boldly, who then became the brother-in-law of Thomas Hazard. He afterward became famous for his cruel opposition to the marriage of his daughter, the beautiful Hannah, but now was a gay young gentleman, very handsome and courageous, whose own wedding to Anstis Gardner had been celebrated only the year before. William Potter, Thomas Brown, a justice later, and perhaps then, Stephen Mumford and Jos. Hamond, Jr., complete the list of most honored guests.

The wives of these worthies were many of them present. Three Mary Hazards were there, with Abigail Hazard. " Queen Esther," from her fine carriage and strong character, we can imagine dominating the group of women. Lucy Mumford and Hannah Shearman were there, and Isaac and Patience Bull. Four of the Rodmans, Thomas Junior, William, Benjamin, and Samuel were present, and the John Handson who witnessed the will of the aged grandfather some years later. Peckham, Knowles, Greene, and Dyre are some of the other names, with Sheffield, Case, and Battey. Updike and all the writers on Narragansett dwell on the great hospitality of the country. Here was an eldest son, handsome, well educated, and just of age, making a most suitable marriage, and we can imagine the festivities of both families, in spite of Quaker traditions. At the wedding feast which followed, William Robinson is reported to have said, " This day by the marriage of my daughter to Thomas Hazard I have ennobled my family."[1] The narrator of this saying adds that as the families were of equal birth

[1] T. R. Hazard, *Recollections of Olden Times*, p. 109.

and position, it was a personal tribute to the worth of the young bridegroom.   At that early age he seems to have given proofs of the large mindedness and nobility of character for which he was afterwards distinguished.

In accordance with the custom of the times he probably took his young bride home to his father's house.   There is little remaining among his papers to show what happened in the next few years.   Governor Robinson sends him the following note the next year.   The somewhat regal method of summoning the young man to " our Houſe " consorts well with the finished handwriting.

Love: Son

These are to deſire you to come to our Houſe tomorrow morning early as you pleaſe to take home fifty sheep which I have drawn off for you if you will accept of them from yʳ Love: ffather in Law

Wm Robinson.

March yᵉ 22ᵈ 1742/3
(Addressed)

To Thomas Hazard
Son of Robᵗ
at
Sᵒ Kingstown
Theſe

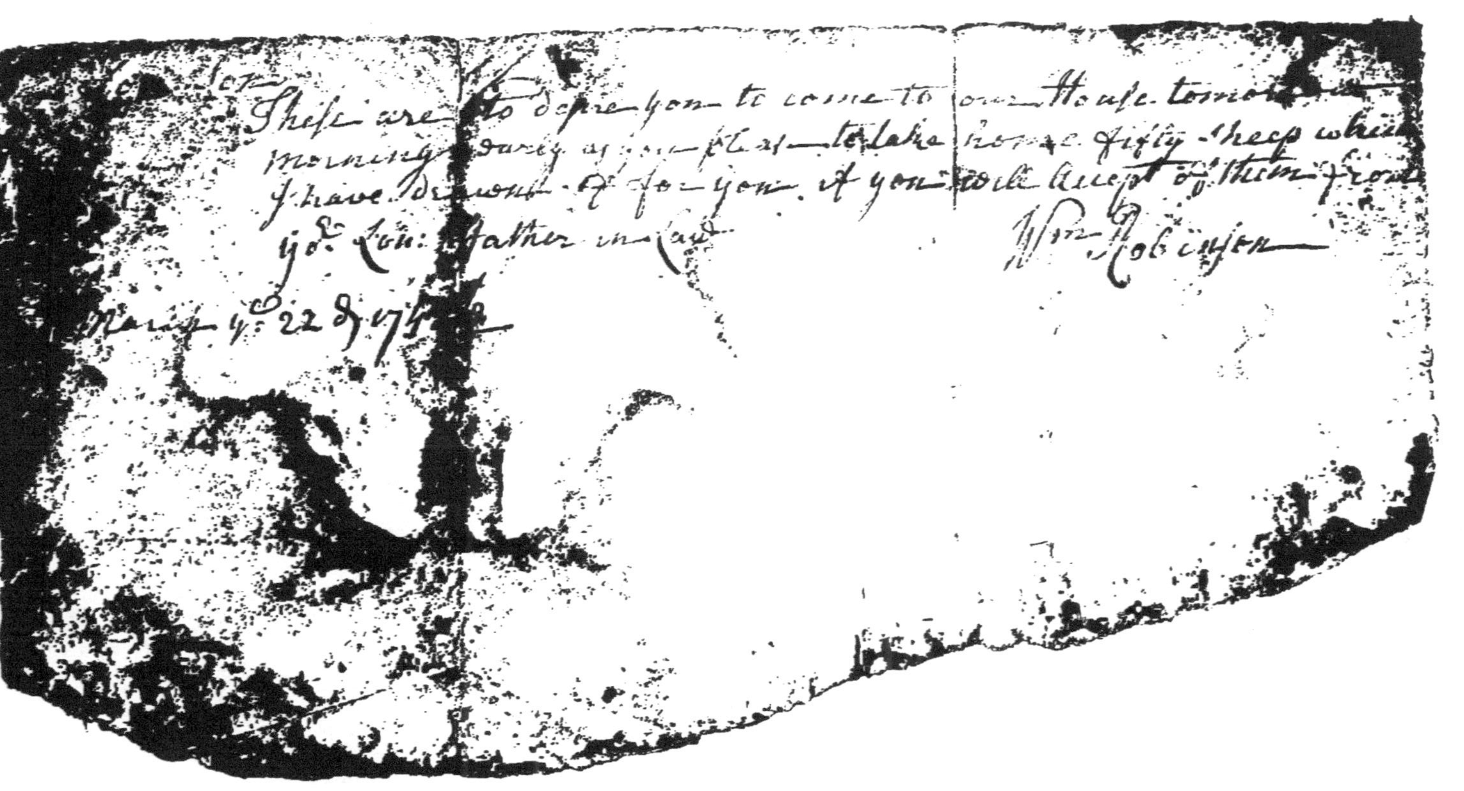

These are to desire you to come to our House tomorrow
morning early as you pleas to take home fifty sheep which
I have drawn off for you. if you will Accept of them from
yor Lov: Father in law
Wm Robinson

Morpeth ye: 22 8br: 75

LETTER FROM WILLIAM ROBINSON

(Endorsed)

Crop the right Ear and a gad under it and a gad under the Left Ear.

So the sheep were doubtless accepted.

In 1744, Robert Hazard makes him a deed of gift of "fforty acres" on Tower Hill, bounded westerly on the high road, the consideration being love and affection. Here it was that Thomas Hazard lived and died. The farm commands a fine view of the bay, with Beaver Tail and Newport lying in the distance, and to the south Point Judith stretching into the sea. The house stood some distance back from the high road, on the brow of the hill. Within a few years the chimney was standing; now all has fallen, and in 1892 a great-great-grandson removed the door-steps of single granite stones which were the last remaining relic of the original house, and has piously placed them in a safe and honorable position, mute witnesses of the past.

In this house the children were born; Sarah, the only daughter, in 1747, who only lived a few years, and four sons. Robert, the eldest, was born in 1753; then a baby named Thomas, who lived four months; and two years later a third son was named Thomas, born in 1758. This was the Thomas afterward called Bedford Tom, because he went to New Bedford and became a merchant, and later to New York, where he was largely engaged in business. Some of his descendants are well-known men.[1] In 1763 the youngest son was born and named Rowland after his uncle Rowland Robinson. He alone of the three sons who grew to manhood has left descendants in Narragansett. His eldest brother went to Ferrisburg, Vermont, and the second to New York as just mentioned. This Rowland had five sons, but of the three who married, only his son Rowland remained in Narragansett. So that the papers which had come down from the seventeenth century in the oldest branch of the family all remained in the possession of the son who stayed at home. Many of them had not been opened since 1827, when they were sorted and dated by Rowland Hazard, until 1889, when his great-granddaughter with reverent touch loosened the old fastenings, and spread them to the light. The deeds of gift or of purchase, the wills, the

[1] Abram Barker, Esq, father of Wharton Barker, of Philadelphia, is his grandson.

accounts and memorandums, of past generations appeared, all the documents pertaining to the things of this life, once lived so much as we live, the husks and externals left behind by the "spirits of just men made perfect."

It is from these papers, stained with damp, and cracking in the folds, that we can gather some conception of the life that Thomas Hazard son of Robert lived, of his farming, of his buying and selling, of his relations to his family, and of his place in Meeting, and glean inspiration for ourselves from the way he served his day and generation.

CHAPTER III.

Thomas Hazard's Awakening to the Evils of Slavery. The Teaching of Dean Berkeley on the Subject. Collision with his Father.

AN interesting story of the manner in which Thomas Hazard became awakened to the evils of slavery was told by all of his grandsons. I have heard it repeatedly from the lips of my grandfather, substantially as his older brother, Isaac Peace Hazard, has related it in the "History of the Narragansett Church."[1] About the time of his marriage, his father wished to establish him upon a farm of suitable size, and give him enough slaves to work it properly. In stocking the farm, young Thomas Hazard was sent into Connecticut, to an old deacon living near New London, in North Stonington, to buy cattle. He arrived Saturday afternoon, and knowing the strictness of the Connecticut Sunday laws, proposed to stay at an inn. But his father's friend, happen-

[1] Pages 322-25.

ing to come to the village, insisted upon
taking him home with him for the Sabbath.
They naturally fell into the religious discussion so common in that day, especially as
Connecticut gave Rhode Island very little
credit for having any religion at all. At
this point my grandfather used to inter-
polate a story of later date of a small boy
who was taken from his Rhode Island home
to visit relatives in Connecticut, and put
through his catechism by the head of the
house. "How many Gods are there?" he
was solemnly asked. "There ain't e'er a
one in Rhode Island!" he promptly replied.
In contrast with this, the story of the visiting Connecticut boy was told, who was
asked the question, "What state do you
live in?" "State of sin and misery, sir,"
was the meek and immediate answer.
With such illustrations of the feeling preva-
lent between the two sections of country,
and knowing the controversial spirit of the
times, we can imagine the long talks of
that Sunday ever memorable in the life of
Thomas Hazard. Finally after discussing
various sects, Quakerism was mentioned,
on which the Deacon exclaimed, "Quakers! they are not Christian People." As

Thomas Hazard was lately from college, and was remarkable for his argumentative powers, and had given some study to the subject, he thought himself able to answer all the usual objections to the Society of Friends. But instead of advancing these, to his surprise the deacon said, " They hold their fellow-men in slavery." He was completely silenced, and from that moment began to turn his thoughts toward the abolition of slavery. He informed his father upon his return of his change of views, and his intention of cultivating his farm by free labor.

King's County — now Washington — had, about 1730, a thousand slaves,[1] who were divided among the great farmers. Robert Hazard is said to have been one of the largest slave-owners in New England, and saw that his son's views if carried out would ruin himself and his neighbors. He endeavored to dissuade him from them, and finally threatened to disinherit him. Fully expecting this, Thomas Hazard persisted in what he believed to be his duty, and began to cultivate his farm with free labor.

They were indeed revolutionary ideas

[1] Updike, p. 174.

which the young man advanced. His
aged grandfather was still living, who had
thought it no sin to own slaves, and the
whole prosperity of the country was founded
on slave labor. All the friends and neighbors held slaves, and two connections even
imported them. Updike mentions Colonel
Thomas Hazard, a cousin of Robert Hazard's, and Rowland Robinson, College Tom's
brother-in-law, as importing them. On the
arrival of the ship at the South Ferry, Rowland Robinson was overcome by seeing the
distress of the poor creatures as they landed.
He is said to have wept bitterly, and taken
home all of his share of the venture, twenty-
eight poor souls, treating them with great
kindness, and refusing to sell any of them.
One woman of great strength of character
called Abigail, afterward at her own request
went back to Guinea, and brought over her
son, Mr. Robinson being at the expense of
the voyage. It is evident that the evils of
slavery were as light as possible, and that
some attempts at freeing individual slaves
were made quite early. In 1729 an act was
passed relating to the freeing of mulatto
and negro slaves, which sets forth that
"great charge, trouble, and inconveniences

have arisen to the inhabitants of divers
towns in this Colony by the manumit-
ting and setting free mulatto and negro
slaves," for the remedy of which it was enacted that a "sufficient security be given
to the town treasurer of the town or place
where such person dwells, in a valuable sum
of not less than £100, to secure and indem-
nify the town or place from all charge"[1] in
case such persons become unable to support
themselves. This act seems to imply that
there were some unprincipled masters, who
manumitted their slaves only when they became useless, but the deposit of a hundred
pounds each made manumission an expensive luxury.

Dean Berkeley, who came from Newport
to the "Continent," as he says, on several
occasions interested himself in the condition of the slaves. He found, he writes,
"an erroneous notion, that being baptized
is inconsistent with a state of slavery."[2] In
this opinion the early settlers showed the
good sense and logical mind for which
many of them were famous. If the slaves
were really chattels, as they held, it was

---

[1] *R. I. C. R.*, vol. iv., p. 415.
[2] Updike, p. 177.

surely as improper to baptize them as it would be their other beasts of burden. Starting from their premise their conclusion was absolutely correct. But the good Dean set himself to enlighten them. "To undecieve them in this particular," he continues, "which had too much weight, it seemed a proper step if the opinion of His Majesty's Attorney and Solicitor General could be procured. This opinion they cheerfully sent over, signed with their own hands; which was accordingly printed in Rhode Island, and dispersed throughout the Plantations. I heartily wish it may produce the intended effect."[1] The Society for the Propagation of the Gospel in Foreign Parts also took the matter in hand, and sent over an address on the subject. "Let me beseech you," a sentence reads, "to consider them not merely as slaves, but as *men* slaves and *women* slaves, who have the same frame and faculties as yourselves, and have souls capable of being made happy, and reason and understanding to receive instruction in order to it."

Dr. McSparran had special services for the slaves, and special hours for instructing

[1] Updike, p. 176.

them in the catechism. He baptized many, and was most humane and liberal in his treatment of them. With his example before them, and the teaching of the church on the subject, in the necessity of the case it could not have been long before the falsity of the position impressed itself strongly on some man. And the man came. If they were chattels, religious instruction was useless; if they had souls, freedom was their right. Thomas Hazard was one of the best educated young men of his neighborhood. Dr. McSparran received young gentlemen, after the manner of his day, to instruct in the classics, and it seems very likely that College Tom's training previous to entering the College at New Haven was received from this learned and liberal divine. With the tendency of the age it is also probable that much attention was given to logic, and the exercise of the reasoning faculty, so that all his study fitted him to accept a conclusion which he had honestly arrived at. The old deacon's words denouncing Quakers, " They hold their fellow-men in slavery," said to him, as they were repeated by his grandsons, with an impressive solemnity, fell into the ground of a good and honest heart, and brought forth fruit an hundred-fold.

Rhode Island early proved a harbor of refuge for the persecuted Quakers of Massachusetts, who found there even more severity exercised toward them than at home. Dr. McSparran says that "emissaries of that enthusiasm were dispatched to the West Indies " in 1654, some of whom visited Rhode Island later. George Fox himself preached in Narragansett on his journey of 1771–73. Dr. McSparran speaks of "the power and number of Quakers in this Colony," and bewails the " heterodox and different opinions in religion, that were found in this little corner."[1] "Quakers, Baptists, Fanatics, Ranters, Deists, and Infidels swarm in that part of the world," Mr. Fayerweather writes in 1760.[2] But the very fact of this freedom of individual belief promoted the growth of the sturdy character, and self-reliance, which could brave opposition and stand firm to honest conviction. It does not seem probable that Robert Hazard was a devoted Quaker, or even a Quaker at all. Neither his name nor that of his father appear in the Friends'

[1] Updike, p. 511.
[2] *Ibid.*, p. 469.

records.   He is described in most of the
deeds referring to him, and mentioned to
the King in council, as will appear, as Robert Hazard, Gentleman — a title his son did
not use and one not consistent with " plain-
nefs."   If he considered his son's religious
opinions extreme, as well as the economic
theories he was advocating, we can imagine
the double exasperation for which the father
considered he had ample grounds.

The exact time of this collision is a little
difficult to determine.   His grandsons used
to say it was about the time of College
Tom's marriage, which took place in 1742.
The deed of gift of land "for love and
affection" from Robert Hazard comes in
1744, and the will of the next year leaves
the eldest son residuary legatee and sole executor.   So the terms on which father and
son stood must still have been good.   Isaac
Peace Hazard says College Tom was a
preacher in the Society of Friends for forty
years before his death.   For a few years
previous to his death in 1798 he was very
feeble, and this general statement hardly indicates more than that he began to preach
somewhere in the fifties.   The will of 1745
is carefully written, duly witnessed, entirely

complete in every way but one. It seems
to have a dramatic story to tell. The lower
right-hand corner, on which the signature
was, is torn off! Was this mutilated docu-
ment used as a final resort to try to compel
Thomas Hazard to abandon his anti-slavery
views ? However it may be, he stood the
test, and it is gratifying to find in the early
fifties entries showing that harmonious relations were again established with his father.
Possibly they gave up trying to convince
each other, and each went his own way.
Robert Hazard is said to have left all his
slaves free by his will,[1] a statement of which
I have copied.[2] Further investigation shows
this to be erroneous. Robert Hazard died
on —

"Ye 20th of ye 5th month 1762 at about
half after One in ye Morning ; after an
illnefs of 10 weeks, 4 days, 11 hours which
he bore with a becoming patience, Aged
73 years."[3]

His will is dated March 11, 1762, pro-
bated May 27, 1762, and the fact that Dr.
Joseph Torrey was one of the witnesses

---

[1] Updike, p. 325.
[2] *Works of R. G. Hazard*, Biographical Preface, p. v.
[3] Appendix, A Regiftor of Death.

seems to imply that he was already ill when it was drawn.   To his wife he bequeaths "my Mulatto Woman called Lydia" and a mulatto boy Newport, with a full furnishing of household goods, silver spoons, " Pewter, Brass, Iron, and Wooden vessels " and allowances of produce to be provided yearly by her sons.   Seven other slaves are mentioned by name in the will, and given to his wife and children; but it is noticeable that while slaves are given to his sons Jonathan and Richard and to both daughters, none are given to Thomas.   The latter is named sole executor and is ordered to sell " all my Cattle and Horſes not herein diſpoſed of, and all my Sheep and Hogs, and all my farming utenſils, and remainder of all my eſtate " to pay the legacies, and to divide the remainder " equally among my sons Thomas, Jonathan, and Richard."[1]

It is difficult to tell what became of the other slaves, as no inventory of the estate or deed of sale can now be found in the South Kingstown records.   Richard, the youngest son, died in the autumn of the same year as his father.   The record is tenderly made by his brother; he —

[1] *South Kingstown Records.*

" Departed this life on ye 30th of ye Ninth month Call'd Septemb^r aged 31 years, 10 month, and Ten days.   He died on ye 5th day of ye Week about 38 minutes after Four in ye afternoon after an Illnefs of twenty days 1762."

This young man's will is dated only twelve days before his death, and the inventory has been found, showing that beside Cudjo, Tom, and Peter, bequeathed him by his father, he had five other slaves to dispose of, two men and three women, whose names are duly given.[1]   It therefore seems probable that these slaves were his third of his father's slaves, which would give fifteen slaves not mentioned in the will of Robert Hazard, making twenty-four the number he had to dispose of.   They were evidently not included in the direction for sale in settling the estate.   Indeed the condition of slavery seems to have been as mild as possible in Narragansett. " You are greater slaves already than our negroes,"[2] Dr. McSparran writes to his Irish cousin in 1752. It seems to have been a kind of serfdom rather than absolute slavery, as the slaves were prac-

---

[1] *South Kingstown Records.*
[2] Updike, p. 530.

tically attached to the soil. To the Christian name as time went on the master's surname was attached, as in the case of Dr. Torrey's man Cuff, and Ned Watson, about whom Shepherd Tom tells an amusing tale of the days of his youth. The old negro, accompanied by the child, on one occasion carried a bag of wet clams upon his back in freezing weather, up from the shore to Tower Hill. To the little boy's great delight, a long icicle, snowy white, gradually formed on the skirt of the negro's short jacket, making a parti-colored demon, stooping under his burden. On being asked to take his turn Cuff Torrey refused to carry the clams for fear of being decorated in like manner.[1] To this day the good names, and often the charming manners, of the old families are found among the colored people of South Kingstown. Far back in the hill country it is a real pleasure to be saluted by a negro of pure African descent, bearing the name of one of the most distinguished of the Narragansett families. Watson, Olney, Gardner, and Helme are all represented in this way. There may be Hazards, but they have taken no prominent part in

---

[1] Rhode Island *Jonny-Cake Papers*, p. 221.

the country life. It is most probable that if they took surnames at all, Thomas Hazard, with his strong feeling on the subject, would have used his influence to give them a name which should be individual.

However he and his father differed upon the question of slavery, it is evident that he was trusted with the settlement of the estate, and took his place at the head of the family. The fatherless son of Richard found in him a faithful guardian,[1] and the children of his sister Mary a wise and peaceful counselor.[2] One longs for some adequate portrait of him, as he was in his fresh young manhood, his young wife at his side, with the world lying before him, and seeking to conquer it by new and untried efforts, which the elders disapproved of, but the sincerity of which won their recognition and respect.

[1] Appendix, Release of Guardianship.
[2] Appendix, Affair of Stephen Champlin.

CHAPTER IV.

ACCOUNT books unfortunately were not written for historical purposes, as Mr. John Fiske justly observes, but in the absence of other record much can be gathered from the book of Thomas Hazard "fon of Robert," with entries beginning in 1750 and ending in 1790. This period of forty years covers the most active part of his life, and from this book, with its full entries and personal details; with its occasional notes still pinned on the written page, a very good idea can be gained of the life of a Narragansett planter. The book itself is a folio volume, eight inches wide by twelve and a half inches long, and nearly an inch in thickness, containing two hundred pages.

The numbering is very confused; it runs smoothly up to the eighty-third page, when the next is suddenly the hundred and sixty-fifth. From that, with the exception that two pages are numbered alike, it runs to two hundred and thirty, and then, as if convinced that was too large a number, drops a hundred off and begins at one hundred and thirty-one. The last fifteen pages are not numbered at all, and a folio sheet of four pages is inserted bearing entries of as late a date as 1789. The cover is of light pasteboard now turned a dull gray. The paper is of good quality, somewhat yellow with age, and the inks used very various, some entries showing clear and black, and others almost indecipherable. It is ruled by hand, sometimes in lead pencil, for £. s. and d., with a fourth column late in the book marked q[r]. These were the quarter pence, or farthings, which were reckoned with "Lawful money." Each page is headed: "*S°. Kingstown In y[e] County of King's County &ct.*," or "*In y[e] Colony of Rhode Island &ct.*"

Opening the book at random it is natural to find entries of various persons who are indebted to Thomas Hazard for cheese, butter, milk, beef, lamb, wool, and all sorts of farm produce, but why they should also be

indebted for shoe buckles, velvet, skeins of
thread, a thimble, and other articles not usually found on a Rhode Island farm is at first
difficult to determine. A little further study
explains it.   In the general scarcity of currency, money seems to have passed through
as few hands as possible. Thus Samson
Will, instead of being paid his wages in
1750 is entered as debtor to Thomas Hazard for "garlix, cambric, and thread of J.
Helme," who was the storekeeper at Tower
Hill, later a judge, and a man of much
influence in the country-side. The money
apparently passed directly to Helme, in this
case.   In another instance one payment
discharged several debts. John Mash, in
1757, is debtor " To thirty shillings in Caſh
Paid to Thoˢ Sweet, Blacksmith ; it was due
from John Nichols to sᵈ Sweet, & from
John Mash to sᵈ Nichols."

A whole series of accounts exist which
are not balanced at all in the usual way, as
in the case of relatives. Latham Clarke,
College Tom's brother-in-law, has the long-
est of these. He has veal, butter, cheese,
oxen at pasture, etc., against which he is
credited with a " Felt Hatt for Dick at £1,
Caſteel Sope, Handkerchiefs at 14 shillings,

Callominco at 18 shillings, Sugar, Indigo, and salt." There is no attempt at footing up, but at the end of the page " Ballanced acco[ts] with Latham Clarke, February the first day, Ann° Dom[i] one thoufand feven hundred and fifty, 1750." Transactions with " Father Hazard " are conducted largely by borrowing and lending, as in 1757 when " Father Hazard had eleven Bushels of Oats of me to Sow for which he is to return eleven Bushels nex year," and entries of Bushels of corn, with no price fixed, "All Paid by my Father."

In studying this record of the life of the last century several points claim the reader's attention. It is a very different account book from any of to-day. No one takes the time now to go so fully into details. What talks and bargaining are indicated in this entry of February 28, 1754: " Thos. Hazard of Newport D[r] To fifty-five pounds promised to pay me in Three months on Swop between Two Horses." Is a sharp bargain always allowable on a horse trade? for fifty-five pounds seems a large sum to pay for a horse, to say nothing of paying it to boot. This brings us to a consideration of the very high prices, apparently, paid for everything, until we remember the unfortunate state of Rhode Island currency. In 1754, £3 15*s.* were equal to one Spanish Milled Dollar, that is, seventy-five shillings of old tenor bills were equal to six shillings silver of 16⅔ cents, or one silver shilling equal to twelve and a half of paper; which reduces our fifty-five old tenor pounds to four pounds, eight shillings, — a much more moderate sum to pay "on Swop." The variability of the currency throughout the book has its own lesson. Rhode Island issued paper money first in 1710. Six other issues followed between that date and 1740, when the bills outstanding of these dates began to be called old tenor. The apparently high prices throughout the book must be discounted according to the value of the paper money, which evidently caused endless trouble, and brought final disaster. Connecticut, New Hampshire, and Massachusetts were in the same difficulty. One "bank" was issued in Rhode Island, to redeem its predecessor, and the bills were to be "in value equal to money." After 1740, the value of the bills was to equal a specified weight of gold or silver. In Rhode Island the issues of 1740 were at 6*s.* 9*d.* per

ounce in silver, or £5 per ounce in gold.[1]
Though at the same time it took twenty-
seven shillings in these bills to equal one
ounce in silver,[2] they soon became current
at the rate of one for four of old tenor.
Hence arose endless confusion.   In 1751, a
year after the first entries in the account
book, the value of a Spanish milled dollar

The Spanish Mill'd Dollar.

was declared by the General Assembly of
June, 1763, to have been £2 16s.   As this
was a declaration of value twelve years after
the fact, made for the use of courts in de-
ciding the many difficult cases which arose
from the depreciated currency, it was of no
service as a basis of value to the struggling

---

[1] Weeden, *Economic and Social History of New England*, ch. xiii., The Period of Inflation.

[2] *R. I. Historical Tracts*, No. 8, p. 55.

accountant. Beside the Spanish dollars there are also mentioned in the book Johannes and half Johannes, gold pieces of the value of eight Spanish milled dollars, and pistareens, and half pistareens.

Such were the difficulties of the currency that primitive methods of exchange had to be resorted to. In Massachusetts from 1720 to 1723 the treasury accepted beef, pork, Indian corn, hides, and other produce at fixed rates.[1] In Rhode Island it does not appear to have come to such a pass, but in the neighborhood transactions of College Tom, he often balances his accounts in this way by barter, or simply enters the items and leaves them unbalanced entirely.

We have seen that the young man and his beautiful bride — for the Robinsons are famous for their beauty—started their housekeeping on the forty-acre homestead, surrounded by the land of Robert Hazard, and that the break with his father did not come till after 1745. Nor could the breach between them have endured as long as tradition asserts. Thomas Hazard was a peacemaker on more than one occasion, and his friendly relations to his father are

---

[1] Weeden, *Economic and Social History of N. E.*, ch. xiii.

testified to by various entries of borrowing and lending. " Father Hazard brought eleven cows to keep" at pasture in 1754. In 1750 College Tom buys a yoke of oxen at £140, — though the pounds sterling mark is out of place, and it should read current money of New England. Most of his horses were probably raised, for few were bought. A three-year-old in 1753 cost a hundred and fifty pounds; a "thirteen-year-old Bay mare with a White nofe" in '54 cost seventy pounds, and an "old black Troting mare," a year later, only fifty-five pounds. A few others were bought, one in 1763, a black mare, at two hundred and forty-four pounds; but the money was just twice as bad as in 1753, the £3 10s. of that date being equal to £7 in 1763, and both only having the actual value of one Spanish milled dollar. In 1766 comes a curious transaction in horseflesh, which shows very plainly the trouble of the inflated currency. Silver had risen still further, so that a dollar was now equal to eight pounds.

1766, 18th 6 mo. George Irejfh To one Dark Coloured Natural pacing Horfe with some White in his Face, at fifty-five Silver Spanifh Mill^d Dollers. I am to take 1 hoggshead of Molaſses, 1 barrell of Sugar at £70, old Tenor per Hundred, the Molaſſes at the value of 36/old Tenor, a Doller being conſidered at the Value of Eight Pounds old Tenor the Remainder in Tea at yᵉ Rate of Eight Pounds old Tenʳ and in Indigo at the Rate of Twelve Pounds, old Tenor; to have one-half of yᵉ remainder in Tea, & the other in Indigo.

This was evidently a Narragansett pacer. The fame of these horses is perpetuated by Updike, and all the writers upon early Narragansett. They were in great demand for export, and were annually sent to the West Indies, and to Virginia. So great was their value that finally all the good mares were sold from out the country, and the old fable of killing the goose that laid the golden egg was repeated in Narragansett. The races on Little Neck beach, now called Narragansett Pier beach, are enthusiastically described by the old writers. Dr. McSparran says he " saw some of them [the horses] pace a mile in little more than two minutes, a good deal less than three,"[1] a wide margin on a race nowadays, when fractions of

[1] America Dissected, Updike, p. 514.

a second are reckoned. They had great endurance, and were capable of carrying heavy burdens in addition to their rider, and many a journey to Boston, or into Connecticut, did they make. This was a valuable animal, for which sugar, molasses, tea, and indigo were exchanged. Tea is first mentioned in the account book in 1750, when it cost £3 4*s.* per pound, and is now mentioned in 1766 at £8 in the highly inflated currency.

In this year the accounts begin to be kept in lawful money, as well as old tenor, but the habit of old tenor prices seems to have been so strongly fixed that often both are given, and the lawful money, on a specie basis, is changed first into old tenor. In 1767 " One old Horse " was sold to Rowland Robinson, for £3 15*s.* lawful money, for which one hundred pounds, old tenor, were paid. The same year William Congdon, son of Joseph, is debtor —

To one Bay Horse five years old @ 500 lbs. & one-half Hundred w*t*. of sugar, such sugar as was Set at 8 Dollers the Hundred, clean & of a bright colour.

Getting his supplies in these large amounts, College Tom seems to have in turn supplied his neighbors in smaller quantities.

The following letter was found between the leaves containing the account of Jeremiah Willson,—

January yᵉ 13 Day 1769

freind Thomas Haſzard. I should been at your houſe before Now but I have been Confined to my houſs with an Very ill turn of Sickneſs but I am much better In health Pleaſe to send me three or four pounds of your Shugare and I Deſire to Pay you In A few Days I have the promis of Money but I Deſire to go this Day where I Expect some from yor friend

Jeʳ Willſon

Two pounds of sugar at thirteen shillings a pound old tenor were sent him the same day, and toward the end of the year the entry comes, —

1769.   I gave a Receipt for the Whole of Jeremiah Willſonˢ account on yᵉ opposite side.

No consideration is mentioned, his " very ill turn of Sickness " probably having settled the debt.   There were two Jeremiah Willsons,[1] son and grandson, of Samuel Willson the Pettaquamscut purchaser mentioned in Judge Sewall's letter.[2]   It is difficult to de-

[1] Potter, *History of Narragansett*, p. 293.   [2] Appendix.

termine which this was, as the younger Willson was born in 1726, and his father might
also have been living in 1769. The Willson
woods, north of Peace Dale, are still called
after the first purchaser.

In 1770 College Tom paid " 25 dollars in
full for a Horse for Rob'," the eldest son,
and the next year occurs a curious entry of
mixed currency and instruction.

1771 9ᵗʰ 4ᵗʰ mo Powel Helme Dʳ

To 7 weeks and six days keeping of yᵉ
Coddington Horse @ 1ˡᵇ of Chocolat per
week

Credit by thy instructˢ my Robert in
the art of Navigation in Part @ 5 shillings 8*d*.

Chocolate is first mentioned in the account
book in 1754 at fourteen shillings a pound,
and in this year, when it paid for the horse's
keep, and offset the instruction in the art of
navigation, it cost forty shillings a pound old
tenor, or one shilling and sixpence a pound
in lawful money. The same year " 1 fatt
Horse " cost forty dollars, or twelve pounds
lawful money, which puts the dollar at six
shillings as we still have it.

These horses had to be shod, and Joseph
Hull was the blacksmith who did it. It would

be interesting to know where he got his iron from. " Iron works for refining " were begun on the south branch of the Pawtuxet by Richard Greene in 1741; the metal used was probably obtained from the bog ores of southeastern Massachusetts.[1]   But however obtained, it was an article a worthy farmer should prize highly, and we find the individual shoes for the horses mentioned, as in the following entries : —

1769 Joseph Hull

One pair of Shoes set on ye hipt Mare and he found Iron for 1 Shoe.

By making ye shoes and shoeing my Bald Mare   I found ye Iron

By Shoeing my old Bay Mare I found old Shoes.

By shoeing my Horſe and my old mare Each a pair of Shoes before.

The same Hull also made a " Hetchel at three shillings old Tenor per tooth 320 Teeth, 16£." A " fire Pann " of his making cost three shillings and 250 clout nails thirty-five shillings.   He sharpened plough irons and made " Snibills for three chests," and " Nib Irons."   In 1770 he is credited

[1] Weeden, *Economic and Social History of N. E.*, vol. ii. pp. 497–500.

with "Shuting my Bucket Hook." This seems to have been almost his last employment, for Joseph Congdon, Jr., soon begins to shoe the horses. In 1774 he sets five pair of shoes on five horses at seven pence one farthing a pair. Also he is credited " By shoeing Rowland's Horse fore only I found the Shoes " at the same price, so it seems probably the shoes were found on both occasions. Rowland Hazard, the youngest son, was born in 1763, and was already established with his horse at the age of eleven. His father soon after allowed him to purchase an acre of land, the deed of which is still in the possession of his descendants. " Tommy's horse " is shod before at 1*s.* 8*d.* ½ the next year.

Another blacksmith who was quite a famous man in his day is not mentioned in this account book, which has scanty entries after 1770. Thomas Hazard, son of Benjamin, " Nailer Tom," as he was called, in his diary has constant references to dealings with " Cousin Hazard," for College Tom was his own cousin, the eldest son of his father Benjamin's eldest brother, so that there were thirty-six years between them. Nailer Tom's mother was Mehitable Redwood of Newport, and having lost both parents early, he was apprenticed by his guardian to a blacksmith, and became an excellent one. A journal of his, covering the period from 1778 to 1781, is in the Redwood Library in Newport, and has been published.[1] Constant mention is made of Cousin Hazard. He often dined with him, quite regularly after meeting, apparently. He "held the harrow for Cousin Hazard," "made stone wall for him," hoed corn for him, and on June 13, 1779, "Went to Providence in Cousin Hazard's Chaise." This is said to have been the first chaise in Narragansett.[2] Nailer Tom also "*Drawed* rods," made nails, "fixed Cousin Hazard's chaise," made buckles, bits, and *sturrups*, and put irons on the toes of his shoes. He also shod horses, as in August, 1781, when "Cousin Hazard finished mowing. Shod Watson's young mare, She hurt my hand."[3]

Horses were perhaps the most important of the domestic animals, since they not only worked the farm, but were the means of locomotion. There were few roads in

---

[1] *Narragansett Historical Register*, vol. i. Nos. 1–4.
[2] *Ibid.*, p. 295.
[3] *Ibid.*, p. 284.

the South County in the middle of the last
century, but bridle paths led from one great
estate to another, through endless gates, the
survivors of which may still be found in the
"hill country" of Matunuc.   But the farm
could not be properly worked without oxen,
in our ancestors' opinion, and the account
book has an early mention of a yoke bought
in 1750 for £140.   A horse the same year
cost only fifty pounds, which seems to show
the relative value, though the horse is not
described as to age, or merits.   Two years
later, when potatoes had just doubled in
price, a milch cow and calf cost £160, and
a three-year-old-horse £150.   So a ratio
is difficult to establish.   In 1755, a yoke
of oxen cost £130 and an old black trot-
ting mare £55.   Few oxen seem to have
been bought, probably most of them were
raised on the farm.   The spring ploughing,
was done by oxen then as now, and the sea-
weed brought up from the beaches in the
autumn.

The teams and carts were also let to
neighbors. In 1766, Adam Gould is debtor
   To my Team & one Hand to cart stones
   ½ day 4*s.* 4[d] Lawful
   To Two pair of oxen to help him Plough

Two days each pair at 2*s*. 3ᵈ Lawful per
day
Andrew Nichols has in the same year —
   My Team & Cart & man to cart wood
   four days at one & half Doller per day
   £1.16ˢ Lawful
This again reckons the dollar at six shillings, and the six dollars (thirty-six shillings)
is carried out directly in pounds and shillings.   The following entry is also interesting : —

         1770.   13ᵗʰ 6 mo. Josʰ Torrey ᴰʳ
To the Mash on Spectacle Island, To
my four hands besides Thoˢ my Son &
Team assisting in mowing Raking &
Bringing off 7*s*. 6ᵈ
To Carting of it to thy house beside Assist. work that afternoon £4 old Ten. =
3ˢ Lawful
1773   To carting one Load of Cole from
Ministerial Farm 9ˢ
Nova Scotia coal had been brought for
many years to Boston, and this most probably came in at the South Ferry, or at Robert Hazard's wharf on Boston Neck.   Powel
Helme had —
   1 pair of oxen three times to ye ferry &
   to Littlerest.

And Dr. Torrey had —

> My Cart & oxen going up to George
> Gardners Mill for Boards,

for which service as early as 1750 he paid £2.

With horses in constant use saddles were of course necessary. In 1753 a man's saddle cost thirty-three pounds. Three years later a new pillion cost six shillings, a bridle fifty shillings, and mending a side-saddle twenty-three pounds, five shillings. Stirrup leathers cost one shilling and four pence. The leather was all tanned and dressed near home. Constant entries occur. In 1757 beef hides sold at five shillings a pound. The largest transactions in leather are with Colonel John Potter, and a third seems to have been a very usual rate for the tanning.

James Rodes was an early tanner, and in 1757 "Drefsed to y^e halves" the skins sent him. The following year they were to be dressed at the same rate, " or 5 shillings per Pound old Tenor to be at my Election when done." In 1759, " This year $\frac{1}{3}$ for Drefsing & 2 Sheep Skins." Colonel John Potter also took the skins, as in the following entry, with its pleasing liberty of spelling : —

> 1764   John Potter Coll^l

The 4th 7th month. To one ox hide,

one bull hide, one Heifer Hide and one
Calve skin all which he brought from
Jeremiah Brown's Tan-yard, and six
Cave skins his Boy Carried from my
Houfe, He to have one third for Tan-
ning the Beef hide and Tanning and
Currying the Calve Skins.

In 1777 Paul Green was the tanner. To
him were delivered —

Ten calves skins Two of them eat much
with Rats two Swine skins four Beef
Hides all to be Tanned and the Calves
skins Curried for one third the Hoog's
skins to be Dressed for Saddle Leather.
1778.   4th mo 3.

Sent by Tommy to Paul Green Five
Beef Hides & one Horfe skin in all Six
skins of Creatures of full groth; Two Veal
Calve Skins & one Skunk Skin much eat
by the Doggs he is to Tann & Curry
the Calves for one Third.   5th 11th day
Carried Two Veal Calve Skins to Pay sd
Green

William Little was the shoemaker in the
fifties.   In 1756 he made " Shoes for son
Robt making 1 at 25s., he found the Sole
Leather, the other at 20s;" an odd way of
reckoning the individual value of each shoe.

He also made heels for women's shoes. Why heels should have given trouble is difficult to imagine, but Nailer Tom in 1781 records that he "fixed the heels of Cousin Hazard's Shoes."[1]   Three years later shoes were six pounds a pair. In 1768, John Sherman makes twelve pairs of shoes for twenty-four pounds, and seems to have all the shoe-making of the house to do.   He is paid, —

1768   For Making and Repairing Shoes for ye Family ye year Past and his find[g] some Women's Heats (hats) amounting to the sum of £75.00.00

As with the large quantities of sugar, so with the leather, Thomas Hazard's neighbors had the advantage of his stores.   Various entries occur of pieces of leather such as this, —

1781   John Torrey D[r]
To part of a Calve Skin enough to cut out a Pair of Shoes at 3*s* Lawful

A large reduction in price from 1763, when "Leather for a pair of shoes" cost £5. The farm must support itself, and not only in life must the "creatures" serve their master, but their usefulness still continues after the riding and ploughing is done.

[1] *Narragansett Historical Register*, vol. i. p. 177.

CHAPTER V.

IF horses were important to the early
farmers in Narragansett, and oxen were
essential to the work of the farm, it was
more truly the cows which brought in the
revenue, and were the main dependence of
the country. The climate of Narragansett
is well suited for cattle, the mild winters
demanded comparatively little shelter for
them, and the fodder was excellent. Marvel-
ous stories are told of the hay crops grown
upon Boston Neck. The grass was said to
be waist high, and more luxuriant than at
present in the new fields of the far west.
Under these favorable conditions the prosperity of the country rapidly increased. In
1748 we find that John Gardner[1] of South
Kingstown prays the General Assembly to
grant him the liberty of keeping a ferry

[1] *R. I. C. R.*, vol. vi. p. 242.

between South Kingstown and Jamestown, as he is provided with "a good wharf and Pier situate in a convenient and commodious place." He represents to the Assembly "that the inhabitants, trade, and commerce of this colony have so far increased of late that the ferries established on the Narragansett shore, and the boats employed in that service are not sufficient to transport with convenience the numerous passengers, their large droves, various effects, and merchandise; the boats often being crowded with men, women, children, horses, hogs, sheep, and cattle, to the intolerable inconvenience, annoyance, and delay of men and business." This urgent petition was duly granted.

In 1750 hay sold at £20 a load, at which rate seven loads of hay would pay for a yoke of oxen in the same year. There was an exceedingly dry season all through New England in 1749, which may have affected the price. In 1755, when prices had risen, it was still £20 a load, and a yoke of oxen cost £130 only. Little hay was sold; but few entries of it occur. Probably only enough for home consumption was raised. Herd's-grass seed was twenty-five shillings a quart in 1764. In 1760 Henry

Shearman is debtor "to one load of good Hay for which he is to mow 13 days in next season of Mowing." Nor was much beef disposed of from the farm. Beef hides have been mentioned, and the roasts probably appeared on the family table. In 1765 beef was sold at 4*s.* 6*d.* per pound, and five years later at five shillings. In 1778, when the currency was on a specie basis, it is reckoned at 3*d.* per pound, while pork is three farthings higher, and cheese at 5*d.* It was evidently not held in great esteem as an article of food. Perhaps the oxen were too hard worked. Veal is a shilling a pound more, and pickled pork three times as much as beef. " A neat beast " sold at £65 in 1768, but that was only £2 8*s.* 4¼*d.* lawful money. Milk sold at a shilling a quart in 1752, and continued at that price for some time. Four years later it was sixpence more. Butter was 5*s.* 6*d.* a pound in 1750, and rose to seven shillings the next year.

But cheese was the important product of the farm. College Tom does not seem to have disposed of it himself, but sold his cheeses to some one person who exported them. For several years James Helme was the man. In 1754, 3627 pounds were made which sold at three shillings the pound, bringing £545 17*s.* The next year only 2769 pounds were made, which sold at the same price per pound. The quantity made decreases as the price goes up. In 1756, 2496 pounds sold at five shillings, and in '57 1909 pounds at 6*s.* 6*d.* In 1763 there is more made again, twenty-eight cheeses of 2830 lbs. weight, which brought ten shillings a pound.

The 4th of ye 7^m 1759 had in ye Cheefe House 46 Cheefes new milk with them in ye Prefs & 8 Cheefes made every other day at first & one we have eat. In 1765 occurs this entry:—

4th 6th mo. Numbered the Cheefes made this year and there were in ye Cheefe House of new milk cheefe new made 22 and 2 in ye Prefses & one amaking the whole number 25.

4th 6th mo. Cut one cheese. One cannot help hoping that it proved to the good farmer's liking.

In 1766 there was an effort by the General Assembly to force a return to a sound currency, and in this year the cheese is reckoned at twenty pounds weight for a Spanish milled dollar. Twenty-four hundred weight of cheese was made this year. The year following, Rowland Robinson, the brother-in-law of College Tom, took a hundred and nine cheeses of about the same weight at the same price. The old tenor bills were firmly rooted, however, and the next year John Dockray has the product of cheese, some twenty-seven hundred weight, at eight shillings, old tenor. Two years later, 1770, still another rate is used, three thousand odd pounds being sold to David Green at 4*d.* ½ lawful money. Nineteen years later, 1789, one of the last entries in the book has cheese at the same price.

The presses for these cheeses were made near home. In 1772 Daniel Dye is credited with four days' work, " Made 1 Cheese preſs and 1 Coffin Phillis. £4."

So life and death are mixed ! How often must Phillis have filled the presses, for she is doubtless the prototype of that ancient negro of famous memory whom " Shepherd Tom " has celebrated as his grandfather's never-to-be-forgotten cook. It was a common name among the Narragansett negroes, and in College Tom's household she would be well cared for, and was evidently decently buried. The Phillis of " The Jonny-Cake

Papers " could not have been this one, as she died more than thirty years before " Shepherd Tom " was born.

Several interesting purchases of cows were made, as when Jonathan Hazard, of Newport, in 1762 bought

1 Winter Milch Cow & Calf @ £150.
He is credited By 11 Dollers @ £7   £77.
By Seventy-Three Pounds old Iron   73.
                        £150.

A pound of iron, and a pound with the delusive sterling mark evidently were of equal value.

In the same year —

Rec^d of Thomas Robinſon of Newport to the Value of one Hundred & forty Eight Spanish Mill^d Dollers in Gold & Silver as Calculated by Doct^r Robt Hazard from Whoſe Hand I Rec^d them.

7th mo 1762 Jos^h Congdon gave his note of Hand for 100 of s^d Dollers as he had ye same to Buy Cows in Cuttnecticut & myself gave note for forty & 8.

In 1664 when corn was at eighty shillings, old tenor, per hundred, and a pair of shoes cost nine pounds, occurs the following entry: —

Rec'd of Jos^h Torrey by the Hand of his

wife 14 Spanish Mill[d] in gold & Silver to buy a cow for him in Connecticut. Returned 8 dollars some cop[r] 1 cow to s[d] Torrey.

That is to say, the cow cost a little less than six dollars in actual money. A journey into Connecticut is evidently indicated for the purchase of cattle, perhaps to the same farmer near New London visited in the early days.

Mention has already been made of Joseph Torrey. In 1770, —

31st 1st mo. Settled accounts with Doc[r] Joseph Torrey and there is Due to me upon Ballance the full Sum of Seven Pounds six shillings 9[d] old Ten[r] having first Deducted his acct[s] both for Phisick and the Labour of his man Cuff.

This Dr. Torrey was an interesting man, a physician both for the body and the soul. He came from Boston to Narragansett, and was married by Dr. McSparran in 1730 to " Elizabeth Willson, at the house of Jeremiah Willson in South Kingstown." [1] She was probably the daughter or sister of the friend who wanted "*Shugare*," as before noted. The following year four gentlemen wrote to Bos-

[1] Updike, p. 117.

ton to have Dr. Torrey settled among them as minister, and on May 17, 1732, he was ordained by the Reverend Samuel Niles.[1] He is called the " first incumbent of ordination." He immediately laid claim to the ministerial lands, and a long and tedious lawsuit was the result. The gift of land for the support of an " orthodox person " in 1668 has been already mentioned. It seems the phraseology of the gift was left purposely indefinite. The purchasers at a meeting in 1692 wanted to assign it for the use of the Presbyterians, but Jaleel Brenton, Esq., argued that it would damage them in estimation " at home," that is, England, if they gave so much to the Presbyterians and nothing to the Church; " and therefore," he said, " if you will be ruled by me, we will not express it to the Presbyterians, but will set it down *to the ministry* and let them dispute who has the best title to it!"[2] The dispute did not come for thirty years, but when it did, was long and pertinacious. As the land lay unclaimed, in 1702 Henry Gardner entered upon twenty acres of it, and James Bundy

---

[1] Potter, *Early History of Narragansett*, p. 123.

[2] For a full account of this controversy see Potter, *History*, p. 123, and Updike, p. 70 and following.

upon the remaining two hundred and eighty, which he sold to George Mumford in 1719. Upon the arrival of the Church of England missionary, Mr. Gardner promptly surrendered the twenty acres he held. Mumford retained possession of the larger tract, in spite of various suits for the recovery of it. In 1732, after being twice defeated in court, Dr. Torrey, who laid claim to the whole tract in virtue of the confirmatory grant of 1679, appealed to England, and obtained possession of the two hundred and eighty acres, which he conveyed to six trustees who leased it " to Robert Hazard, gentleman," and Dr. McSparran brought suit against him as terre-tenant. The original grant of 1668 having come to light, Dr. McSparran wished to have " one real suit upon the whole title." In his defense, Robert Hazard put in as answer "two pleas in abatement, three pleas in bar, and finally on the general issue of Not Guilty." It was in making these pleas that his manuscript copy of " Coke on Littleton " and the fine edition of Dalton's " Country Justice " probably helped him. After various suits and counter suits it went to the King in council, and finally on the 7th of May, after more than thirty years of litigation, Dr. McSparran was defeated, and the lands confirmed to Dr. Torrey.[1] This lawsuit, in which College Tom's father had so active a part, no doubt had its influence in forming the wish to educate him for a lawyer. Dr. McSparran complains that there are " a vast many lawsuits " in the colony, "more in one year, than the county of Derry has in twenty."[2] He himself was not loath to engage in them, as we have seen, and in a new country the troublesome question of boundaries always occasions them. As late as 1722, when the dividing line between North and South Kingstown was run, the line is described, "and so continuing said course as near as we could for the badness of the way."[3] Such boundaries were not conducive to clear titles, and endless confusion often resulted. Beside his preaching Dr. Torrey practiced medicine, and had also some farming. The " Mash " on Spectacle Island was his, as before noted, and from his long association with Robert Hazard the friendship between the families seems to have been close.

[1] Appendix, Paper in this case, Affidavit of Foxcroft and Chauncy.

[2] Updike, America Dissected, p. 515.

[3] *R. I. C. R.*, vol. iv. p. 316.

Shepherd Tom, in his interesting " Recollections of Olden Times " recalls hearing of the good doctor in his young days. He lived, he says, in a house that stood about a mile from the village of Tower Hill, on the south side of the road leading west, still called the " Tory lot."

" I the more particularly remember old Parson Torrey," he continues, " from a uniform way my father used to tell me, when I was a small boy, the old Presbyterian had of reproving his son, a very naughty boy, to whom he would say with great emphasis when he behaved amiss, ' Why! I am ashamed of you, John! I am ashamed of you !' "

This son of Dr. Torrey's also appears in the account book, —

1781.   Settled accounts with John Torrey (for weaving) and there is due him the Ballance of Seven Pounds Fourteen Shillings at the rate of four Pounds p^r bushel for Corn

These were old tenor prices again, with corn at eighty shillings the bushel.

Rowland Robinson, who took the cheeses for several years, was a man of marked ability, hot tempered, and hasty, " a man of violent passions, but of a noble benevolent nature," one of his descendants remarks. He had constant quarrels with his neighbors, but was really most generous. In his later years he quarreled with his nephew and namesake Rowland Hazard, and threatened to cut him out of his will, but ended by leaving him much of his land. The tragic fate of his beautiful daughter Hannah has been fully told.[1] From their fine house, still standing on Boston Neck, she managed to run away with her lover, a young French gentleman. Soon after her marriage she began to pine for a reconciliation with her father, the more so as her husband proved a man of light and fickle character. She was finally carried back to Narragansett upon a litter, only to die in her father's house, who bitterly mourned her loss, which his harshness had certainly done something to occasion. She is still spoken of as the unfortunate Hannah, and this bit of tragedy rises from the leaves of the old account book, associating itself with the name of Rowland Robinson more closely than his generous deeds, or broad acres.

The pasturing of cattle also added to the

---

[1] T. R. Hazard, *Recollections of Olden Times.*

income of the farm.   There are only one or two mentions of a man famous in local history, — Geoffrey Hazard, " stout Jeffrey " as he was called. The first is very early in the book, with the date unfortunately obliterated:

> 4th of 6th mo Carried my oxen to Jaffeory Hazard to Pafture   Carried my cow y[e] 16th of 6th month   Carried 3 Heiphers 21st of y[e] 6th month

Apparently they were not well cared for, for —

> 9th of ye 9th mo one of y[e] Heiphers was in my upper Pafture & Harry told me he saw her some days before in y[e] Training Lott.   Drove her to Pafture again the 13th of the Same Month.

This Geoffrey Hazard was famous for his strength. He is reported to have lifted two-year-old colts, and to have been able to drink from the bung-hole of a barrel of cider, holding it above his head. A great stone lay for many years where he lifted it and threw it down. The story is that some slaves were building a wall, and had this stone on skids, but were unable to move it. Seeing Geoffrey Hazard come riding by, they called to him for help, as his strength was famous throughout the country-side. But he was displeased at their familiarity, and lifting the stone off the skids, threw it on the ground, where it lay until brought to Peace Dale by Rowland Hazard. It is now in front of the house at Oakwoods, inscribed:

> Stout Jeffrey Hazard lifted this stone
> In pounds just 1621
> In South Kingstown he lived and died
> God save us all from sinful pride.

But the usual records in the account books are of cattle brought, not sent, to pasture. In 1762 " Peleg Peekham brought 9 Cattle to keep," and " Andrew Nichols brought his Father's Cow to keep by ye week @ £3 p^r week." Samuel Willson, Eber Shearman, and many others brought cows to keep, among them College Tom's mother. Robert Hazard died in 1762, and the sons were left to care for their mother. Her accounts came regularly,—

> 1765, 20th 5th month Mother Hazard Took away her Cows & left her Calf with me to keep.

In December of the same year College Tom " Took a Black Cow to keep for my mother," and in 1766 " Settled acc^{ts} with my mother Hazard & took a Receipt for her annual legacy." Then after a few years comes the entry, —

> Sarah Hazard Widow
> Job Took away Mother's Cows ye 7th day
> of the 2^d month 1772.
> The 7th 6th mo 1773   Settled this acc^t as
> alfo for Mother's Coffin with Brother Job
> Watson.

This was "Sister Sarah's" husband, with whom "Mother Hazard" seems to have lived, though Shepherd Tom says she died in Newport.   There is only one other mention of this lady; in the Regiftor of Death.

> Sarah Hazard widow of Robert Hazard late deceafed departed this Life the 1st day of the 2nd month Call^d February 1772 about half after Eight o'Clock in the evening being the 7th day of week aged 77 years the —— of the Eighth month Call^d August 1771.

So it was a week after her death that her cows were taken away.   They were probably the wide-horned, red-skinned cows of Devon extraction which have come to be the native of Rhode Island, giving milk rather scanty in butter-making properties, but excellent for the cheese which Narragansett became famous for.   Upon their meek heads a large part of the prosperity of the country was built.

CHAPTER VI.

IF the details of the early Narragansett
life seem somewhat hard and prosaic, when
we turn to the sheep there is an atmosphere
of pastoral simplicity, an air of leisure
and contemplation, that surrounds the great
flocks. The country, with its hills and dales,
its fine grass and abundant water, was well
fitted to support the timid creatures who
contributed so much to its comfort. Sometimes in severe winters they suffered greatly.
Dr. McSparran, writing in 1752, says that he
had seen the Atlantic "froze as far as the
human eye could reach." [1] In 1780 there
was a cold season long remembered, when
the bay was frozen over, and not a ship
moved in Newport harbor. In one of these
cold winters a great flock was snowed in,
in the little ravine on the east side of Tower

[1] Updike, America Dissected, p. 525.

Hill, near where the Tower Hill House now stands, which is still known as Dorothy's Hollow. The story is that their shepherdess braved the storm to try to rescue them, but perished herself with her sheep. Tales are also told of a flock edging into the sea, the exposed sheep taking refuge behind the others less exposed, till all were drowned. But such winters were the exception, and little shelter was usually provided for the flocks. At Anthony's on Point Judith the wall of a sheep-fold of the old pattern can still be seen. It is a high stone wall, running east and west, and not long ago still had its roof. The fold was open entirely at the south, except for the timbers that supported the roof. Such rude shelters were common, — perhaps not unlike the places where shepherds watched their flocks by night centuries ago. In the early days there was still need for watchfulness. The Wolf Rocks beyond Kingston were occupied by their first inhabitants until quite recent years. Dogs, however, were not the trouble they are now. In fact, the sheep were so much more valuable than the dogs, but small consideration could be given any dog who developed worrying instincts.

The great farmers all had their own flocks, each sheep with a distinctive ear mark. The South Kingstown records contain pages registering the different ear marks, and Nailer Tom duly mentions a change in that used by College Tom. Dr. McSparran mentions "butter, cheese, fat cattle, wool, and fine horses," as the principal products of Narragansett. Again he says, " I mentioned wool as one of the productions of this Colony, but although it is pretty plenty where I live, yet if you throw the English America into one point of view there is not half enough to make stockings for the inhabitants."[1] He adds that he wishes "Ireland were at liberty to ship us their woolens, which we shall always want." The poor Doctor complained bitterly of the weather: "We are sometimes frying, and at others freezing," he says, and he evidently longed for his own Irish homespun.

Thomas Hazard did not sell very much wool apparently, but raised enough to clothe his household. One hundred pounds is the largest sale, recorded in 1766, when it sold at $14\frac{1}{2}$ pence lawful. This must have been a particularly fine lot, for the

[1] Updike, America Dissected, p. 516.

same year another sale was made at nine-pence a pound. The following year " Old wool and Dagg Locks" sold at fourpence half-penny a pound. This dag-locks, as we should write it, is an interesting word, from the Scotch " daggle," a drizzle of rain, hence anything daggled was moist, or draggled, and dag-locks were the long skirts of the sheep's fleece. In March, 1769, a man is paid for " one day's Work at Daging Sheep." The use of this word suggests the presence of Scotch shepherds in Narragan-sett. The prices of wool mark the depreci-ation of the currency very clearly. The first year of the account book has it at eight shillings old tenor. It rises to twenty-eight shillings, three and a half times as much, in nine years. After the spasmodic effort after specie payments in 1766 and '67, in 1768 it is at thirty-two shillings old tenor. The entries of prices of wool are infrequent, however, as most of it was for home con-sumption.

Hind-quarters of mutton were often sold; and a saddle of mutton was a favorite roast, which must often have appeared on the home table. In 1750 a few sheep brought forty shillings each, and in 1767, twelve pounds old tenor, or nine shillings lawful. Some efforts were made to improve the breed, which degenerated somewhat from the original South Down stock, and Rowland Robinson imported a fine South Down ram. His anger can be well imagined when he discovered that a lazy negro, who was in the habit of helping himself from his flock, had killed this valuable beast to furnish a roast to his family. There were also a few of the short-legged "creeper" breed, which were prized by their owners. South County mutton is almost as famous as its turkeys, as the sweet grasses and broken surface of the country are particularly favorable to sheep.

Of the shearing there is no mention, though Nailer Tom records both washing and shearing sheep for Cousin Hazard,[1] but the wool was often combed at home, as in 1778, when Valentine Ridge is credited—

By combing at my house 40 lbs. of wool

By combing at thy house 33¾ lbs.

He also combed *warfted* at fourteen shillings old tenor a pound. Dr. Torrey's son John was a weaver as before noted, and this wool comber was very probably a son of

---

[1] *Narr. Hist. Register*, vol. i. p. 280.

Master Ridge, the Irish schoolmaster of Tower Hill, a man noted for his strong character and courtly bearing. Shepherd Tom thinks he probably left Ireland for political reasons, and he would naturally in coming to the new world select the place where his countryman, Dr. McSparran, was settled. In a new country each man must count as an individual, and there seem to have been few of the social lines drawn which exist in an older community. The doctrine and practice of the Friends on this point was doubtless not without its influence, and there was no apparent descent in the social scale from a physician to a weaver, or a schoolmaster to a wool comber. Those who knew the older generation of Narragansett men will recognize that they were truly no respecters of persons; a man was a man, no matter what his surroundings, and to be treated with a respect the degree of which was measured only by his character.

The wool thus combed was spun on the "woolen wheels," smaller and stouter than the linen wheels also in use. Hannah Greenman, widow, in 1761 is credited with "30 skeins, 4 knots of Worfted spun for

us at six shillings per skein." She also
spun *Linen* yarn at the same price. Daniel
Knowles, "son of Daniel late deceased," in
1776 spun both worsted and *Lining* yarn.
In that year he spun thirty skeins of *Kersey*
yarn at eight shillings. James Carpenter
of West Greenwich spun *Linnen* yarn, and
also carded and spun *Tow* yarn. He was
also a weaver of tow cloth diaper, but in
general the spinning and weaving seem to
have been done by different persons.

Robert Martin is the earliest weaver
mentioned, who in 1753 wove " 30 yards of
Linning Cloath, at seven shillings, and 22
yards of *Ticking*" at the same price. If the
varieties of linen corresponded with the spelling, they must have been numerous! The
ticking was for the great feather beds, so
universal in all the comfortable houses,
and so valuable that they were mentioned
in the wills of the period. Eber Shearman,
Jr., of North Kingstown, was an accom-
plished weaver. He wove *Sarge* cloth at
six shillings, tow cloth at four, *linning*,
striped cotton and *linning*, plain cotton and
Linning, Flanning, sarge worſted, blue cloth
Sarge, and half *Duroy*. This last is interesting. We still have corduroy, and the

sixteen and a half yards of " half Duroy," woven in 1755, would doubtless make a stout riding suit. " Gardner ye weaver at Tower Hill," Benedict Oatley, and Joseph Jesse have a share in the weaving for the household from 1756 to 1760. The price in 1757 is fixed at twenty shillings a pound for wool, which they received of Thomas Hazard " to be paid for in weaving at the rates following: Tow at 3*s.* 6*d.*, *Flanning* 3*s.*, Worfted at 5*s.*, and other cloths at the same rate." Benedict Oatley, in 1760, wove " about twenty-six and three-quarters yards of Tow Cloth, about One yard of Which was wove Kerfey." He also could weave striped cloth and wove " one piece Chex." William Taylor, in 1756, is paid " for Scouring and fulling one piece of Cersey," and " dyeing scouring Pressing & Shearing one piece of Sarge." The Indigo for dyeing cost a dollar and a half per pound in 1766. Some was obtained the same year in barter for the pacing horse at £12 old tenor a pound, a dollar being reckoned at eight pounds.

But Martin Reed[1] was the prince of weavers of the old time. The first mention of him is in 1763. After that the entries are

---

[1] Updike, p. 283.

frequent. He is called of North Kingstown, for his house was near the old St. Paul's church, of which, for many years, he was the devoted clerk. He was left an orphan at the age of seven, and just before the death of his widowed mother was apprenticed to a diaper weaver. According to the old custom this apprenticeship lasted till he was of age, and he only had one quarter's schooling. But he was ambitious, and determined to excel in his work. He studied at night, and eagerly read all the books he could find upon his chosen work. At the end of his apprenticeship he married the daughter of a diaper weaver, and with a single loom began his career, which was one of continued prosperity. On June 14, 1761, he was baptized by Mr. Fayerweather, and is called in the record " Martin Reed, the Parish Clerk, an adult." He was a most devoted attendant on the church services, and had the care of the church building for many years. He led the singing, and under Dr. Smith's direction, with Martin Reed as leader, it is said, the " Venite " was first chanted in America. When the church had no rector, in the troubled days of the Revolution, it was he who read morning prayers, and the funeral service for the dead. His piety and sense stood him in good stead when Jemima Wilkinson, hearing he had called her a blasphemer, came down from her house at Little Rest, clad in her robes of state, and went to his house to overawe him, as she had many others. "Claiming to be the Son of God, she threatened that if he did not repent and humble himself, she would put forth her mighty power, and blast him and his family. He answered that he entertained no gods like her in his house, and that if she did not forthwith leave he would *turn* her out; on which she troubled him no more."[1] He used his musical ability in a practical way by constantly singing when at work with his journeymen and apprentices. The songs were Irish, Updike says, and he knew a great number, or if he did not sing he uttered " their airs by a melodious whistle, to which the workmen became so accustomed that it became to them a relief to their toils." In this primitive work-room, with its few hand looms, with the swift shuttle thrown ceaselessly to the accompaniment of the master's

1 Updike, p. 285.

voice, not only flannel, striped and plain, worsted, tow-cloth, and linen were woven, but broadcloth, and *Caliminco*. This last, which we are instructed to spell calimanco, was a glossy woolen satin-twilled stuff, checkered, or brocaded in the warp, so that the pattern showed on one side only. It was in use for dress occasions, and gentlemen of the old school had calimanco morning gowns. In 1766, Martin Reed wove twenty-three yards of it at sixteen shillings a yard for Thomas Hazard, and other entries occur. He also wove two "coverlids" that year, at eight pounds each. Thirty-four pounds four shillings were paid for weaving a " Piece of Broad Cloth, 57 yards."

Updike calls Martin Reed the first manufacturer in Narragansett, though there was a much earlier establishment of a woolen industry. Colonel George Hazard, a brother of "old Thomas Hazard," in 1719 gives to Thomas Culverwell for love and good-will "a Little part of my farme belonging to my now Dwelling house. . . . More Especially for ye Promoting of ye Wooling Manufactuary which may be for my benefit and the Publick Good." The bounds of this half acre are duly given on " the Saquetucket," and Henry Gardner for the same reasons joins in giving full power to make a dam. " The land that shall be Drowned by making of ye said Dam " was given to Culverwell; " Which Dam is to be made for ye fulling of Cloth, and to ye Promoting of a fulling Mill." The deed expressly provides that if Culverwell "shall neglect to Keep and maintain a Good fulling mill," the lands and rights are to return to the grantors.[1] This first dam upon the Saugatucket was upon Colonel George's homestead near Rose hill. Two years later Culverwell receives " one hundred pounds in Curr* paſsable money of New England " from George Hazard for a portion of this land with its buildings,[2] and June 6, 1723, the whole was bought back from Culverwell, the land being specified as the same land Culverwell " purchased some time past of the Aforesaid Hazzard, . . . with all houses out houses Mill or Mills there on standing or being with all the waters and Water courses thereto Belonging." " Levery and Seizen " of this land was given by " Turf and Twigg," before witnesses who duly sign the memorandum.[3] January 8,

---

[1] *South Kingstown Records*, vol. i. p. 101.
[2] *Ibid.*, p. 197.   [3] *Ibid.*, vol. iii., New Series, p. 5.

1725, Colonel George gives it all to his " Beloved Son Thomas Hazard Cloather," for " Natural Love and Tender affection," " With the Houfings Mil'es Prefses Shears and other things which may tend or Belong to the Cloathing Trade &ct." It is most generously given, " from henceforth as his own proper Estate and goods absolutely without any manner of condition." [1]   So it was a great-uncle of College Tom who started the woolen " manufactuary," with his naïve expression of hope for his own bene-fit as well as the public good.   No mention of this mill is made in the account book. There were the plain hand weavers, but Martin Reed seems to have been the best in the country-side.   All the gentry came to him, and he seems to have been the only one who could weave calimanco.   Benedict Oatley, in 1767, weaves worsted plain, and *Sarge*, also " 12 yards plain Broad Cloth," for which he took in payment some mutton, corn, and ten and a half pounds of *gammon*, at twelve shillings a pound.   This word comes from the French *jambon*, and we trust the good weaver enjoyed his salted and smoked pork.

[1] *South Kingstown Records*, vol. iii., New Series, p. 136.

Nicholas Brags wove linen, Benedict Oatley also, both fine and "cors," and Martin Reed as well. The flax was apparently grown upon the farm, and doubtless much of it spun at home under the eye of the mistress. The last entry in the book, 1790, records, "Rutter the old Black man Drefsed for me flax." In 1761 Hannah Greenman, widow, spins "linnen yarn" at six shillings the skein. Some is spun by the weaver James Carpenter, in 1768, at eight shillings, and woven into diaper at ten shillings a yard. He also makes a charge for "boiling and washing the yarn that made S^d Cloth." In 1775, John Gould "took $2\frac{1}{2}$ lbs of Flax to Spin 8 Scains to y^e pound." It was his wife who did it, as a subsequent entry shows. Astress Crandall was a famous spinner of both linen and worsted. She spun "card-work" as well, and has a special entry for "spinning doubling and drefsing 1 skain of stocking worfted three double." Her account for spinning for the two years ending in 1778 amounted to over a hundred and eighty-seven pounds, old tenor. The friendly relations of the good farmer's household to their humbler neighbors is shown in the following entry, —

1776 John Smith Paid ye above Charg of 1 & $\frac{1}{2}$ bushels of Corn in his Wifes Whitening linnen Cloth for my Wife when they settled

" Debb," doubtless a colored woman from the absence of a surname, spun yarn for stockings and mittens, and then knit "said stockings and mitts at 4 pounds 18 shillings, old Tenor." She was carefully paid 1st mo 20th day 1778. This was six years before the emancipation act. Stockings are seldom mentioned; a pair in 1756 cost 35 shillings, and a " Linning Handkerchief " in the same year 22 shillings.

The tailor who made the cloth into suits of jackets and breeches was Andrew Nichols. Eunice Nichols, probably his wife or daughter, is called tailoress, and she doubtless visited in the great houses, making the gowns for the good dames. Andrew Nichols had the constant work of the house apparently; for he is first mentioned in 1757, and last in 1779. At the earlier date, —

1757 Paid Andrew Nichols for making one jacket, and mending one Pair of breeches, 55 shillings.

He seems to have been a man fond of reading, a good Friend, as the records show, and to have cut the coats of broadcloth in the proper shape.   In 1769 he is debtor —

To one book entitled the Principles & Precepts of ye Chriſtian Religion &ct at 10ˢ old Ten. $= 4^{d}\frac{1}{2}$.

9ᵗʰ 12ᵗʰ Settled Accounts with Andrew Nichols, turning our accounts into old Tenʳ, and his amountˢ to one Hundred & thirty-nine Pounds old Tenʳ and there is the Ballance of 11*s*. $8^{d}\frac{1}{2}$ in old Tenʳ due to Andrew Nichols.

As early as 1751 comes the entry of all the necessaries for a suit, presumably sent to Andrew Nichols to make.   Richard Hazard, College Tom's brother, has it, — very probably the half of an importation of the *Devonshire Cerſey* and trimmings.   The account reads —

Richard Hazard   Dʳ

1751. To one Three year old Horſe £105
6 Yards of Devonſhere Cerſey @ £6.   36
½ yd of Shalloon @ 24/
¼ yd of Fuſton @ 34/
¼ yd of ozenbridgs @ 12/
⅛ yd Cotton Velvit @ £7
4 yards of Tape @ 6ᵈ
To Two dozen of Buttons @ 10/
To 2 ſtiks of Twiſt @ 5/
½ oz of silk at 40/

I have been unable to determine what ozenbridgs were. They are mentioned only once again in 1763, when Jane Nash had "$\frac{1}{4}$ $\frac{1}{8}$ & $\frac{1}{10}$ of *ozenbridges* @ 38s." From the fact that it was sold in such small quantities, and used by both men and women, it would seem to be some kind of stiffening, for the collar possibly. Years later College Tom's grandson manufactured a very coarse cotton and wool cloth which he called Osnaburg. Was it possibly from a remembrance of this word in his childhood?

In 1770, Andrew Nichols is credited with

$4\frac{1}{2}$ days Work at Tailoring 2^s 3^d

5th 5mo By Cutting 3 Pair of Trowſers for my boys & 1 p^r for Wm Pratt @ (blank)

By 2 days Work making my jacket

& 5 days y^e same month making

Cloths for the children.

This account is paid by pounds of veal, butter, beef, lamb, mutton, and " corn 1 Bushel when thou Paſs^d from P^t Judith." In another account Andrew Nichols has a thimble at six shillings and a saddle cloth and white sheep's skin. The thimble was doubtless a commission, for as College Tom went to Newport or to Providence in his chaise, we can fancy him stopping along

the road, and with the courtly air his grandsons inherited inquiring if there were "any
commands."

Some of the latest entries in the book
relate to Andrew Nichols. In 1777, when
money was on a better basis, and corn at
three shillings a bushel, he is credited —

> By making one pair of breeches for
> Tommy 6 shilling 9 pence
> By making one pair for myself 9 shillings
> 1779 To making a great coat and close
> body coat 15 shillings

In the matter of clothes the country was a
thoroughly self-sustaining one. Every step
necessary to the production of clothing was
taken in the immediate neighborhood, from
the shepherd who *dagg'd* the sheep, the
wool comber who combed the wool, the
spinners who spun, and the weavers who
wove, all went in regular order till Andrew
Nichols made the cloth up, and Thomas
Hazard went to meeting clothed in a suit
made from wool of his own growing.

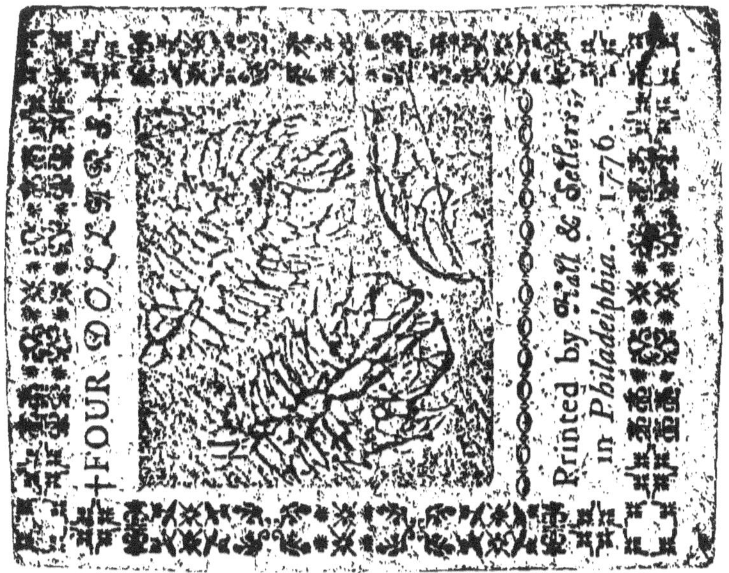

FOUR DOLLAR BILL

CHAPTER VII.

WHO that has seen a great field of corn waving in the summer sunshine can fail to be impressed with its beauty? When it is in tassel, and the tufted plumes nod and bow to their neighbors, as the light breeze rustles through the leaves, it is indeed a fair and stately sight. The year is at its prime during the hot August days that bring its perfection. Beautiful as a great field of wheat or barley is, with its ripples of light and shade, like the play of an inland sea, yet the corn, with its stately height, its luxuriant sabre-like leaves, its blossoms fringed with pendulous anthers, and its silky tassels sheathed in satin wrappings, has an individuality of its own, a pride and dignity of growth befitting the native of a new world. From the time when Squanto taught the early Plymouth colonists to cultivate it, this stately plant, so bountiful and so beautiful, played an important part in the history of New England, and often furnished both food and a medium of exchange.

Narragansett from times immemorial was celebrated for its corn. John Oldham brought five hundred bushels from there to Boston in the Rebecca in 1634. " The Indians had promised him one thousand bushels, but their store fell out less than they expected." [1] A couple of years later this hardy trader was killed on Block Island, and an embassy was sent to Canonicus to treat about the murder. They were " entertained royally," the old account says, and the first huckleberry pudding on record was made for their feast. The Indians boiled " pudding made of beaten corn," we read, " putting therein great store of blackberries, something like currants." [2] If for *blackberries* we read " black berries, something like currants " we have a good description of the huckleberries which still abound in Narragansett as they did in this late July or August of 1636.

---

[1] Winthrop's *Journal.*   Quoted in Potter, *Early History of Narragansett,* p. 16.

[2] Johnson, *Wonder Working Providence.*   Quoted by Potter, p. 18.

On Broad Rock Farm, some of the land owned by College Tom, and still in his family, two of the Indian *caches* for corn can still be seen. They were small hollows in the ground roughly lined with stone, not more than a foot deep at present; perhaps three feet long and two wide. Here the stores of corn were buried, or as in the Great Swamp fight, put in baskets and tubs and set in the wigwams. The destruction of this supply in the fight was one of the severest blows to the Indians. During this very summer parched corn has been picked up on the site of this battle, now more than two hundred years gone by. The fire, which destroyed so remorselessly, charred these tiny grains, which are preserved just as they were when it smouldered and died so long ago.

The virtues of Rhode Island jonnycake have been celebrated by College Tom's grandson, Shepherd Tom,[1] as he delighted to call himself, and when he says Rhode Island, it is usually Narragansett he means. The reader is instructed just how the corn should be ground, at what rate the stones

[1] The *Jonny-Cake Papers*, by Shepherd Tom. Published by S. S. Rider, 1882.

should revolve, and what kind of stones they should be. The baking is seriously considered; the middle board of red oak from the head of a flour-barrel is indispensable to bake it on, and the fire before which it bakes must be of walnut logs. Hasty pudding, porridge so good that it was respectfully mentioned in the plural as " them porridge," dumplings, and a store of other dainties, all excellent and wholesome, are treated of with the romantic remembrance of a joyous youth full of health and high spirit.

The corn that furnishes these homely dishes has its own history. There is something fine in its stability, while financiers and legislators experimented with the currency and ran through the whole period of inflation with its worthless fiat money. A bushel of corn still furnished just so much food, and instead of being measured in value by the money of the day, often became itself the measure of the value of the currency.

As early as 1630 efforts were made to regulate the price by arbitrary methods. It was at that time twenty shillings a bushel.[1] The following year it was made receivable for debts in the Plymouth Colony unless

---

[1] Weeden, *Economic and Social History of N. E.*, p. 98.

beaver or money were mentioned.[1]   From
1637 each year for several years the rate
was fixed at which taxes were to be paid in
it.   Three shillings was about the normal
rate, with variations either up or down according to the season, until the period of
inflation began.   Indeed it had already begun, as the Spanish piece of eight, the
Spanish milled dollar of our acquaintance,
was set at the same time at five shillings.[2]
A century later the colonies were all suffering from a debased currency.   Massachusetts, as we have noticed, received " country
pay " again for taxes, in which corn was received in lieu of money.   Rhode Island was
issuing one bank after another, and the
currency steadily depreciated as the credit
of the colony declined.   In 1751 a Spanish
milled dollar cost £2 16s. in old tenor bills,
and College Tom sold his corn at 25 shillings a bushel.   Then it steadily rises.   Six
years later it was 35 shillings, and in 1759
had reached 60 shillings, touching 100
shillings in 1762 — the highest price mentioned at all.   The next two years must

[1] Weeden, *Economic and Social History of N. E.*,
p. 101.

[2] *Ibid.*, p. 142.

have brought better harvests or the local demand must have varied, as it is quoted at 90 shillings and 80 shillings, while in '65 it was at 100 shillings again. The spasmodic effort to reduce the currency to a specie basis in 1766 only resulted, as before noticed, in making two sets of prices, and corn is quoted in the 9th month at 90 shillings old tenor, or 3 shillings lawful money, after harvest, that is, while three months before it had been at 100 shillings or 3*s.* 8*d.* Then it seems to have settled at 80 shillings old tenor, or 3 shillings lawful, for a number of years, recalling the price in the early days. This seems to have been the normal rate. In 1778 College Tom makes an agreement with Sier Averit, an Indian, who very likely was baptized by good Dr. McSparran as Josiah, setting forth what work he is to perform, and the payment for it, forty dollars for the term of eight months for which he is engaged; " *The value* of which money is hereby agreed on between the Parties." Pork was to be at 3¾ pence per pound, beef at 3 pence, cheese 5 pence, and Indian corn at 3 shillings a bushel.[1] This agreement is signed by the Indian, the

[1] Appendix, Contracts for Labor.

same man who a couple of years later had ten dollars for his " sickness and trouble."

Not many transactions in corn are recorded. In 1767, Adam Gould was paid for fourteen and a half days' work, four of which were days' mowing done by his sons, seven bushels and three pecks of corn, one "Fatt lamb," and one Spanish milled dollar. In 1784, some debt seems to have been paid in corn, and the entries are carefully made of its disposition. About twenty-five bushels are accounted for : —

1784 Corn measured out of the Corn I had of Joseph Collins in ye 1st mo.

4 bufhels to Carry to Mill.

1^{b} $\frac{1}{2}$ and & 3 Quarts took by Robt.

2 bufhels for John Shearman.

2 bufhels for Nicholas Holway.

2 mo. 4 bufhels sent to mill for the Family.

3rd mo. 2 Bufhels sent to mill for the Family.

20th. 4 bufhels sent to mill for Ditto.

$\frac{1}{2}$ a bufhel & 4 Quarts exchanged for onions.

20 one Bufhel Paid Nicholas Gould.

20 three Pecks & 4 Quarts paid Nicholas Gould

29 Two bufhels for ye Family ufe.

This Joseph Collins was the good Friend who wrote a beautiful hand, and whose transcription of the " English book of Discipline" is among the precious volumes belonging to the South Kingstown Meeting.

There were several mills near by to which the corn was taken to grind. Benny Rodman's mill was on the Saugatucket, where the Peace Dale dam now is, shaded by the big buttonwood tree, which tradition says was once his horsewhip, and which has grown where it was thrust into the ground. The stones, of native granite, of this mill, were said to be good, — far better than the stones of Coon's mill, lower down the stream, which were coarse grained and made " round meal " instead of " flat."[1] But the best meal was ground at Hammond's mill, at the head of the Pettaquamscut, and it is probable that the corn sent to mill for " ye Family ufe," went on old Baldface's back, and was carried by *The Mill boy*, much as described by Shepherd Tom.[2] Nor need this worthy have stretched the truth when he declared to the five-year-

[1] T. R. Hazard, *R. I. Jonny-Cake Papers*, p. 3.
[2] *Ibid.*, p. 49.

old boy that he had performed the same office for the father, and the grandfather of his grandfather. The child naturally regarded him as a miracle of antiquity; but a man of seventy in the first years of the present century could easily have performed the pleasant service of riding with a grist, over the charming country to the head of the lake, for "old Thomas Hazard," who died in 1746, and it is even possible that a man then living could have ridden for Robert Hazard, the first Narragansett settler, though when we are asked to believe that old Baldface had also served so many generations, we must have doubts respecting the longevity of the horse if not of the negro.

Beside the corn that was so important a factor in the colonial life, there are records of rye, which in 1756 was exchanged bushel for bushel for corn, oats at half the value, and barley at about ten shillings less. Of vegetables, potatoes and turnips were about half as valuable as corn, while onions in 1767 sold at the same price per bushel. Apples were plenty, and cost half as much as corn in 1759, while one bushel of white beans in 1776 would buy two bushels of corn. They seem to have been rare, for they are first mentioned in the previous year.

The agreements with the men who worked the farms which raised this produce are carefully made,[1] and indicate very clearly the embarrassment of the currency. If our surmise is correct there were half a dozen negroes at least who had descended with the land, and were dependents upon the estate. Early in the book comes the entry, —

> Priamus a Negro Boy Came to live with me at my Houſe the week after ye General Election Held at Newport for General officers for the Colony of Rhode Iſland, in the year one Thouſand Seven Hundred & fifty seven, being six years old the Octobʳ following the sᵈ Election which was held in May before.

This boy had a life of adventure, as will appear, but lived in Narragansett until he came of age, in this respect following the old method of apprenticeships. Another "Negro boy," Oliver Smith —

> 11ᵗʰ month 27ᵗʰ day, 1781 came to my house with his Mistreſs Elizabeth Smith

---

[1] Appendix, Contracts for Labor.

age 8 years the 7th of the 8th month this Prefent year, who is to work for me for his Bringing up until he may have an advantageous opportunity to go apprentice.

Even this last memorandum was made three years before the emancipation of slaves in Rhode Island. In 1789, an agreement is made with "Jack Sanford a Black man to Labor with me at Hufbandry." He was to be paid "the value of Three Dollars p^r month, in articles and Produce off the farm." Corn is set at 3 shillings per bushel, cheese at 4$\frac{1}{3}$^{d} per pound, "and other articles at a proportionable Rate in the old way, & in Cloathing as may be agreed if He needs any"

One man in 1759 came on trial for a month, for which he was to receive "Thirty Shillings Lawful Money it being Connecticut Prock so called." Four years later it was agreed with Henry Hill to "Labour for me at Husbandry," for a term of ten months at the end of which he was to receive the "sum of 400 pounds old Tenor or the Value thereof in any kind of Bills or money current at the s^d time." In settling his account there is an interesting entry which throws light upon the customs of the day. He is debtor to half a quire of paper at thirty-four shillings, and "to 10s. Paid Fox the scribe." What letters did "Fox the Scribe" write for him, and how often was he employed in such ways, one wonders? Hill had also shoes, wool, and other things entered against him, and at the foot of his account is entered, —

> Settled the above acc^t with Henry Hill when I Paid him for his Ten months Work done in the year 1764.

Early in the book there seems to be a list of laborers : —

> Taken out of ye Hampshire money Rec^d from Jeffrey Hazard —
>
> £2 to Lowes. (The "Lowes Jakeways Spinster" who will appear later.)
> 4 Shillings to Jo Mash.
> 30 Shillings to Robin
> £6 to John Daniel
> £18 to Patter
> £150 to Father
> £51 to John Dock^y.

The last two of course are not laborers, John Dockray being a connection by marriage. One of these men who frequently appears in the book is recorded : 1764 16th of ye 1st mo

as having "left my Businefs & was Worf
than his Bargain with me."

Jeremiah Auftin, as he writes his name,
appears frequently. A long account in 1765,
in which he is credited " By 8 days mowing in his own person " and by the mowing
of his sons, and by seven days and a half
raking, is not footed up at all, nor any
prices given, but "sixteen Pounds old Ten^r
in Cash " are paid, and in the following
spring, —

> Settled all accounts with S^d Auftin &
> paid him ye Ballance for which I took a
> Receipt in full of this date & is now
> amongft my Receipts.

In 1673 Michael Dye agreed to work for
eight months. He was to receive "400£
old Tenor, or an equivalent in Dollers at
£7 p^r Doller, to be at my election." The
next year, 1764, a man was hired for seven
months at £360, old tenor, " or the equivalent in any other medium Current in the
Colony of Rhode Ifland." The set of
agreements make very instructive reading,
and one regrets the loss of " the other
book " referred to in this one, which may
have contained more, and thrown still further light upon the workings of the vari-

able currency. As we have noticed, it was the produce which furnished the most stable values, and corn became a measure for other values.

A useful man came to work in 1762, who not only worked at husbandry, but made shoes in wet weather, "if it shall beſt agree with my conveniency," the agreement says. In addition to his wages a horse was to be kept for him during the term of his stay. Another man in the following year was to " labor at Carpentry " in wet weather. A curious agreement occurs in —

1778. Jacob Barney Came to my Houſe the 19th of y[e] 5th month and went to work the Next day at Hatting (viz.) on the 20th and is to Work four months @ Journey Work, and he is to teach my Son Tommy the Hatter's Trade & alſo another Lad if I require it & Provide one and I am to Pay Him the Common journeyman's Wages in the uſual way (according to the N° of Hatts he Shall make in s[d] Term) by the Hatt, and to find him his Board for his inſtruction of the Lad or Lads as aforeſ[d]

This was in the early years of the Revolution, in the terribly disorganized

state of the country, and it was like the
thrifty Friend, a hatter having come in his
way, to have some one profit by learning
what could be learned from him. Hats had,
of course, fallen in price from the time one
cost £40 in 1763, but it is interesting to
trace the old system of journey-work.

John Dye, "ye gardner," had higher wages
for his more skillful work than the ordinary
laborer. He worked at three pounds a day
in 1764, and is debtor —

> 26th 4th mo. To one Ten shilling Bill
> Lawful Money dated ye 12th of ye 5th
> month 1760 Turned into old Tenor £14.
> Credit by 6½ days work at Gardening
> £19. 10^s.

This makes each shilling of lawful money
count for twenty-eight of old tenor.

But few farming implements are mentioned. Rakes, to rake hay, have been noticed. In —

> 1769 sent to Abijah Babcock's on y^e
> Tower Hill one Dozen Sythe Sneads
> to sell. Wm Dyre bought 2 ye same
> year. 1770 Jeffry Watson bought one.

Husbandry is defined as consisting of
" Howing, Ploughing, Walling, Ditching,
Fencing, Mowing, Haying and Milking

&ct." and also as " any kind of bufinefs to be done at Farming," which is even more inclusive.   It was this business, which is the foundation of the wealth of a country, that engaged the labors of College Tom.   Hampered as they were by the evils of the currency, the produce of the land yet supported a prosperous people, until the final crash came, brought on by the political as well as financial difficulties, and the fine farms once so flourishing and productive were left to revert to their primeval condition.   The people as well as the land became impoverished, till in due time from the wrecks of a purely agricultural community manufactures took their rise.

Cousin Thos. Hazard
please to Let Brother Enoch Hazard
have Three Bushels of Barley on my
Acct.
Hazard

Stonington The 16. May 1768

CHAPTER VIII.

THE record of the life of the feminine part
of College Tom's household is far less full
than that of the men. Some of the great
houses are still standing in which the mistress
of the last century lived, and ruled her small
kingdom. Many a house was built with a
fine gambrel roof, giving good attic room, into
which the slaves were locked at night. The
house often had two chimneys, built quite
near together in the middle, taking up what
in modern times would be used for a hall.
One of these chimneys was the kitchen
chimney, with its great open fireplace and
brick oven built into the side of it. College
Tom's house had only one main chimney,
but that was twenty-three feet wide at its
base.[1] Pewter dishes, brass and iron pots,

[1] *Narragansett Hist. Register*, p. 293.

and " pot hooks and trammels " by which
the pots for boiling were hung, were valuable enough to be bequeathed by will. Robert Hazard, the father of College Tom,
mentions twenty-one silver spoons in his
will ; " the largest silver spoons," silver " salt
spoons," and " other silver spoons," he calls
them.   Sarah, his daughter, who afterward
married Job Watson, has half " of all my
Pewter Brass Iron and Wooden vessels "
left her, " two feather beds with furniture,"
with one half of the tables and chairs, and
also of " Cupboard, Desk and Chests." She
is to have the privilege of living in the man-
sion house with her mother until her marriage.   Isabel and Phœbe, two slaves, are
given her, and a thousand pounds old tenor,
within a year of her father's death.   The
married daughter, Mary Champlin, having
probably had a wedding portion, has only
silver spoons, and five hundred pounds.[1]
Ten years later Stephen Champlin, her husband, died, and there seems to have been
some trouble over the will, which Thomas
Hazard settled.   A farm was left to a
younger son, Robert Champlin, which had
still two years' lease to run. Stephen Champ-

----

[1] *South Kingstown Records.*

lin, who is called the "Son and Heir at Law,"
and also the executor and residuary legatee,
in consideration of a lease made to him by
his mother, "and for the Love, Goodwill
& affection which I have and Do bear towards my said Brother Robert Champlin ...
and for Promoting & efstablifhing a lafting
Peace unity and Harmony throughout our
Whole ffamily," relinquishes his share of
the rent for the two years the farm is still
let. This paper is drawn by College Tom
himself, in his hand throughout, and witnessed by himself and his wife. It seems
to give indication of much family discussion,
and one looks with interest to see the other
lease. It also exists, written in the same
hand, bearing the same date, February 5,
1772, — a lease of five years from Stephen
Champlin to his mother of a portion of a
house situated in Point Judith, "under the
yearly rent of one Pepper Corn to be paid
unto the said Stephen Champlin, his heirs &
afsigns always upon the 25th day of ye third
month in every year of the said term."

This is the old date of Lady-day for
leases, though the consideration is somewhat unusual. Poor lady, she only lived to
pay the peppercorn one year, for before the

second 25th of March came round, she had joined her husband, having died on the 17th of that month, 1773.

In a farming community the women always have an important part of the work to perform. They looked after curing the feathers which composed the much valued feather beds. The dairy with all its labors was their care, to say nothing of preparing the food for the hungry farm hands. The account book of Thomas, " son of Rob'," gives only scanty details of the work done by these worthy women. In 1756 Sarah Pugh, as she is sometimes called, or Pew at others, worked for nineteen weeks at twenty shillings a week. The kind of work is not specified. In the same year Lowes Jakeways, spinster, worked ten weeks at the same price. She is charged with —

$\frac{1}{4}$ yard Linnen Cloth at 28 shillings
$\frac{1}{2}$ skein of Thrad at 1 shilling 3 pence
To 20 shillings in caſh when she went to the New Light meeting.

This is a reference to one of the sects spoken of by Dr. McSparran as abounding in Narragansett. The Friends meeting records have several mentions of them, and they evidently gave a good deal of trouble

to the orderly minds of Friends. One man
as early as 1748 is denied his membership
because he suffered Friends meeting " to be
disturbed & broken up by the afores[d] Wild
& Ranting people, which meeting was in
his own houfe."[1] Twenty years later they
were still flourishing, and a Friend is cast
out, as he had joined himself in communion
with " the people Called New lights and
pretended to Juftifie himself in being Dipt[d]
in outward water."[2] They are called a
" Diforderly people," and are apparently of
" dark and erroneous principles." A paper
is on record where a good Friend condemns
his conduct as follows : —

" I did sometime past Inconsiderately attend a meeting of the people called New
Lights and so far joined with them in their
worship as to pull of my hatt which incon-
siderate conduct of mine I freely condemn."
It seems a little strange that a woman working for College Tom should have been
allowed to attend a meeting so much disapproved of by the society, but it is another
instance of the strong individuality fostered
in Narragansett. In 1757, Sarah Bent did

1 *South Kingstown Monthly M. R.*, vol. i. p. 269.
2 *Ibid.*, vol. i. p. 199.

some work at twenty-five shillings a week. The wages increase with the depreciation of the currency, as before noticed, and in an agreement of 1759 comes an interesting provision for furnishing shoes at much less than the usual rate. There may have been a shoemaker in the house, as there was in 1762, for in the year of this agreement some shoes cost six pounds a pair. Women's shoes of the last century were, however, much thinner than those worn by the stronger sex.

6th of 1st Mo A: D: 1759 Mary Dick began to Work and is to Work until ye 1st of ye 4 mo @ 30/ pr Week & from that Time until ye end of ye eleventh month @ 40/ pr Week that is to say 8 months of ye year at 40/ & 4 at 30/ And she is to have Two pair of Shoes in ye Year at £4 the Pair, she to do the Houfehold work & ye Dairy both Butter and Cheese and other Bufsiness when Necefsary.

Martha Nichols, probably a relative of the worthy tailor, has 20 shillings for "making 1 Gound." *Sempstry* is done by " Joanna Dugglass Single woman," who in 1764 worked eleven weeks at seventy-two shillings a week. For quilting she had eighteen shillings a day, and we can imagine the busy quilting bees at which she presided. The one in this year lasted ten days. Two years later Mary Chase agreed to work for one year "at the Value of 50 shillings old Tenor p[r] Week for the Summer Seafon & forty for the Winter Seafon. She is to work at Houfewifery Spinning &c."

Sarah Crossman is mentioned as doing tailoring in 1761, and Eunice Nichols, tailorefs, has a long account in 1776;[1] Jane Nash was another workwoman, and Amy Shearman has in 1755 "one pound in Cafh to pay for making her Bonet." Sarah Pugh already mentioned has "2 Shillings in Cafh to buy a Comb," and in 1761 "£8 in Cafh out of Pigg money." The following year "14th 7[mo] Sarah Pugh left us." These women's accounts are entered thus minutely, and the money paid often directly to James Helme. One woman has "Eight pounds in Cash to go to Tower Hill," which a woman in our day would prefer, leaving her at liberty to buy what she wanted at the country store; though another apparently has given notice of her

---

[1] *Appendix*, Accounts of 1776.

intended purchases, for she is charged with money, " When She Went to James Helme's to buy her a Skirt &c." Lowes Jakeways' account is " Difcounted with James Helme " directly, she apparently having little to do with it.

Death entered the kitchen, and took the kindly workers, as in the case of Phillis. "Venibee departed this Life the 3rd of the 1st month 1759," we find, and then comes an entry in quite a different part of the book : —

> Borrowed of Thos Brown 53 feet of pine Board to make a Coffin for Venibee which he seemed willing to part with.

Written across this is Paid ye Boards.

Beside these experienced women there must have been the children of the old slaves who were useful in the household.

Thomas Hazard, Jr., writes to Rowland Hazard : —

NEW BEDFORD, July 8, 1803.

Patience, that our father and mother brought up has been here about ten days. She is very much deranged and so troublesome in our house, that I was obliged to apply to the authorities and have her sent to the work-house where she now is, as we do not know in what town in the state of Rhode Island she belongs. I shall be much obliged by thy informing me immediately on receipt of this, what town has to maintain her so that our selectmen may take the necessary steps to get her where she belongs, and to be clear of the expense and trouble of her. We are all as well as usual. With much love to dear Mother, thy wife and children in which mine join,

Thy affectionate brother,
THOMAS HAZARD, Jr.

It would be interesting to know the life which this " dear Mother " lived in the early days of her marriage. She had the sorrow of losing her oldest child, her only daughter, at the age of six years, in 1753, and a baby boy who only lived four months. Robert, the oldest son, was sent to school at a very tender age. A record in exceedingly faint ink tells us that —

Betty and Robert began to go to school to Rachel Nichols the [obliterated] 6 mo

A : D : 1758 Rob' went but 2 weeks.

Which one can hardly wonder at, as he was only four and a half years old. Again we find, —

Robert left off School the 4th of Octob[r] y[e] 7th day of ye week 1760.

There were no Saturday holidays, evidently.

One longs for fuller details of the visits which were made to the hospitable farm. What a winter journey that must have been when —

Richard Smith of Philadelphia Came to my Houfe 23rd of y[e] 12th mo Set out for boston the 26th 1757

Doubtless there were other visitors, but no record of them is preserved.

In 1771, there was a question before the meeting which must have interested the women, and sounds to us very modern, for it is the same question England is still discussing, of the propriety of marrying a deceased wife's sister. A year later the matter was referred to the quarterly meeting, and with the fairness of Friends the question was put, —

"Query to be able to marry a deceased wife's Sister or Deceafed Husband's Brother and what is necefsary to be done in such Cafes."[1]

Was it some special case which excited

<hr>

[1] *South Kingstown Monthly M. R.*, vol. ii. p. 267.

this action? One can fancy the long discussions of it, in those days of ample leisure, on the long afternoon visits to the great farmhouses. Good dame Hazard seems to have taken little share in the women's meetings, or even in the festivities. She is at Nailer Tom's wedding, but many of the marriage certificates upon which the Thomas Hazard, son of Robert, is found, have no Elizabeth Hazard near it. Her farm, her garden, and her children would keep her busy, while from her house on Tower Hill she could look into Newport Harbor, and count the ships as they sailed in and out. When her grandchildren, the children of her youngest son, Rowland, were born in her house, she is said to have been tenderly anxious over them, and especially devoted to the second boy, who was named after her husband and her father, Thomas Robinson. The reminiscences of Shepherd Tom, as in later years he liked to call himself, have often been alluded to in these pages. No passage is more charming than that in which he describes his efforts as a five-year-old boy to cut a log for his grandmother's fire, beginning early in the morning and finally rolling it in triumph into her sitting-room

at dusk.   Many were the approving glances
which followed him during the day, and the
intervals of rest, in which kisses and dough-
nuts played an important part.[1]   In the
early life of this good lady, Tower Hill was
still the seat of the court house and the
centre of the social life of the country.   It
was here that Judge Helme lived, the Chief
Justice chosen by the general assembly in
1767, who distinguished himself for capacity
and application.[2]   With the versatility of the
time, he united several pursuits, — he kept
the country store and for a year or two took
the product of cheese from the farm.   His
wife, Esther Powell, the granddaughter of
Gabriel Bernon, must have been a charming woman; "the dearest, the best, the ten-
derest wife," her bereaved husband calls her,
when in 1764 she died of "a pain in her
breast, with great difficulty in breathing,"[3]
for which the modern name would be pneu-
monia.   The letters of her husband are
most beautiful in the expression of his deep
attachment, to this "dear dead partner"
who has "left not her equal behind her."
The whole family circle must have been a

----

[1] *R. I. Jonny-Cake Papers*, p. 234.
[2] Updike, p. 336.   [3] *Ibid.*, p. 136.

delightful one. It was Judge Helme himself who plotted the Boston Neck purchase
for old Thomas Hazard; his son Powel instructed Robert Hazard (son of College
Tom) in " the Art of Navigation in part," as
before noticed, and was credited for his
teaching against pounds of chocolate. The
horse which played a part in that transaction is called "ye Coddington Horse,"
which belonged to Mrs. Helme's uncle, as
Colonel Coddington married Jane Bernon,
a daughter of Gabriel Bernon. A sister of
Mrs. Helme's was the wife of Mr. Seabury,
the clergyman at New London, and the
stepmother of the first American bishop,
who may have been the nephew who visited
Mr. Helme at Tower Hill.[1] The Helmes
seem to have been very liberal in their religious beliefs, and it is pleasant to see that
in spite of the lawsuit going on about the
ministerial lands, Dr. McSparran and Dr.
Torrey must have been on good terms personally. Dr. Torrey married James Helme
and Esther Powell in 1738, while Dr. Mc-
Sparran baptized the first child, with Colonel
Coddington, his wife, and daughter as sure-
ties, a couple of years later. Some years later

[1] Updike, p. 138.

still, Dr. McSparran baptized two more children and read the visitation service for Mrs. Helme's mother, who shortly after died, and he preached her funeral sermon in Dr. Torrey's meeting-house.[1]

Mrs. Torrey lived a little below the hill. It was she who brought the Spanish milled dollars for the purchase of a cow in Connecticut. She was a Willson, of the family of the Pettaquamscut purchaser, and a relative of that Jeremiah who wrote the note asking for sugar, after his "very ill turn of sickness." Across the Pettaquamscut on the Robinson estate lived Anstis Gardner, the charming wife of Dame Hazard's brother, Rowland Robinson. There is mention of money in Rowland Robinson's account in College Tom's book, which "my Wife lent his Wife, in her last sickness." There were many connections on both sides of the family, in South Kingstown, Conanicut and Newport. Latham Clarke married Martha, the sister next youngest to Elizabeth Hazard, and in 1752, in spite of Quaker principles, there is a —

Memorandum in the affair carried on by Latham Clarke and myself against

[1] Updike, pp. 165, 166.

Mother Robinson. The Expenses to be equally Borne between us Viz[t] — to a fee in s[d] affair.

To Mathew Robinſon to engage as attorney for us   £12. 00. 00

To £4 to David Richards as an attorney for us   4. 00. 00

The next year the case was continued and forty shillings were paid —

to Augustus Johnſon at Providence for drawing and entering reaſon of appeal (on the acc[t] of admi[n] on the eſtate of W[m] Robinſon, late dec[d]. preſented to y[e] Town Council of So Kingstown and allowed by them, & appealed from by us to the Governor & General Council, which sat at s[d] Providence.)

This "Mother Robinson" was the step-mother of the two ladies. She had been the widow of Caleb Hazard, originally Abigail Gardner, daughter of William Gardner of Boston Neck, a sister of Mrs. Dr. McSparran, and aunt of Rowland Robinson's wife.[1] So closely were all the families of Narragansett connected that this affair must have made some commotion, and given endless food for gossip over cups of strong Bohea tea.

[1] Updike, pp. 125, 126.

William Robinson left to each of these two daughters seven hundred pounds in bills of credit of old tenor, one good bed and bedding and a silver porringer,[1] but their step-sisters each had twelve hundred pounds and a negro girl, so that may have been the cause of complaint against " Mother Robinson." The Friends Meeting Records contain no mention of it, though Friends are often appointed to deal with those who go to law, and the lawsuit of " Tommy Hazard the Blacksmith " and Nicholas Easton is fully detailed upon its pages. So it was probably with the advice and consent of various Friends that this step was taken.

The ladies of the neighborhood had their tea and chocolate at enormous prices; the tea at from three to six pounds a pound, and the chocolate at forty-two shillings. A little velvet is mentioned in 1768 at £13 a yard. Binding for a *Pettycote* in 1761 cost fifteen shillings, and buttons were a shilling apiece. Thread, a little earlier, was one shilling and sixpence a skein. In the kitchen things were very expensive also; pepper was twelve shillings an ounce in 1753, with nutmeg at the same price. A flask of

---

[1] *S. K. Records,* William Robinson's Will.

oil in 1755 cost twenty-six shillings, and raisins were eight shillings a pound shortly before.

It is delightful to find the charming family relations which existed, and the devotion of her sons to Elizabeth Hazard. In 1801 Thomas, the second son, writes, " I hope my dear mother has ere this received her flannel, and that the quality of it is such as suits her, it being the finest I could find in the town of Boston where I procured it." She had a hard trial to go through with the illness and failure of her husband, but was aided and sustained through it by her daughter-in-law. The changes of the time must have been hard for her also, for the whole country became greatly impoverished in her latter days, and she lived to see a new order of things.

Under date of South Kingstown, November 13, 1796, her daughter-in-law writes to her husband, Rowland Hazard, at Charlestown : " Thy mother desires her love to thee, my father's and brother's families, and says she wishes thee would come home. She thinks if thee were here everything would go on easy. I have no doubt it would relieve her mind of a great deal of anxiety."

The son did come for part of each year, both the older brothers having left home, and the grandchildren continued to be her pleasure and comfort. She survived her husband, and died in 1803, beloved by all who knew her.

CHAPTER IX.

FROM the study of the account book of Thomas Hazard son of Robert, it is evident that agriculture was the main business of his life, as was the case with all the Narragansett planters. His homestead farm, which by will he leaves to his eldest son, ran from the " county Rhode," that is, the Pequot path of the early days, eastward till it was bounded by the Pettaquamscut River and cove. The sedge rights are also bequeathed with this farm, which is called about one hundred and fifty acres. To his youngest son he leaves a farm on the west of the road of about the same size. These are the only farms mentioned especially, the rest is spoken of as " all the Remainder of my Lands and real Estate." He had his grandfather's love of land, and beside what was left him by his father and grandfather added to his estate by purchase. In 1764 he bought land in Westerly and "Charles Town" and later some in Cranston and Dartmouth. The price of land near home was very variable. In 1778 one acre was bought from Peleg Peckham for £21, and ten years later Jeremiah Willson sold thirty-seven acres for ninety pounds.

Beside the land in South Kingstown, Thomas Hazard and his brothers Jonathan and Richard were left joint heirs to their father's interest in the "Susquehanna Company" in which he is called a proprietor. This company held its meetings at Hartford, or at Windham in Connecticut, and in 1768, Thomas Hazard made a journey to the latter place to transact business, on his brother Jonathan's account as well as his own, and also for S. Hazard, — probably one of the many Stephen Hazards, — who gives a power of attorney to "my Friend Thomas Hassard, of South Kingstown." Richard, the third brother, died in 1762 as before mentioned. His son Robert's affairs seem to have fallen into some disorder, for in 1776 he signs a release of guardianship to Thomas, his uncle, "not meaning hereby

Received of Robert Hoszer Esq[r] of
South Kingstown in y[e] Coloney of Rhodisland
two spanish Milled Dollars in Complyance
with y[e] vote of y[e] Susquehannah Company
at their meeting Held at Hartford
November y[e] 21st 1754

Received p[er] me   Sam[l] Grayson.

to discharge my former Guardian Enoch Hazard for any demands I have against him." [1]

But the money of the time presented great difficulties. As early as 1747, there were those who saw that the country was standing on treacherous ground. Among the papers is "a copy of a Letter from Quebeck," written from a French point of view and addressed to " Pr. M——r in France," dated October 11, 1747. [2] The " fmall petty Colony of *Rhode-Island*," is declared to have "200 Sail of Veffels belonging to it and if the Governments are fuffered to go on making Paper Money, they will drive us out of this Part of the World, without any Help from their Mother Country." The making of paper money enabled the New Englanders to send home " vast Quantities of Gold and Silver," the writer continues, " having no use for the fame, so long as Paper Currency anfwers for a Medium of Trade." But the " Farmers and Tradefmen have put their Land in Pledge for the Paper Money they fit out fo many Veffels with," so this

[1] Appendix, Release of Guardianship.

[2] Appendix, Letter from Quebeck. A copy of this paper is in the John Carter Brown library also.

wily pamphleteer advises sending large con-
signments of goods to friends of France,
who will take only cash; "and by this
Method procure all the hard Money that
is ſtirring amongſt them," at the same time
petitioning Parliament to put a stop to the
issue of paper money by the Colonies. " If
this Method, great Sir, is induſtriouſly and
faithfully purſued and carried on we ſhall
unavoidably impov'irſh, diſtreſs, and confound them: All the lower Claſs will no
more be able to pay for Clothing from their
Mother Country, but muſt be contented to
live as they did of Old, to wander about in
Sheep Skins and Goat Skins and to dwell
in Caves and Dens of the Earth; and thoſe
of the higheſt Claſs will be obliged to leſſen
their Trade, ſell their Veſſels, and no more
be able to ſend Home to their Mother
Country ſuch Quantities of Silver and Gold.
Then no more *New England* Invaſions,
no more beating down our walls at *Cape
Breton;* and when we have another War,
we ſhall not only have their Money, but
their Veſſels, and their Men being poor
muſt ſeek Shelter in ſome foreign Land."

How widely this paper was circulated, or
with exactly what intent, there is no means

of knowing. The whole subject of inflated currency has been ably treated,[1] and our effort here may be confined to tracing the effects of the legislation on the prosperity of the community we are chiefly interested in. Numberless examples have already been given of the complexity of accounts. Finding the burden intolerable, in 1766, the General Assembly, meeting at South Kingstown the last Monday in February, passed an act, reviving the act of 1764 for the "Speedy calling in and sinking of all bills of credit . . . called the Ninth Bank . . . let out upon loan; and likewise for putting a final end to the name of Old Tenor throughout this colony."

As there was a considerable sum of these bills of credit outstanding, this act was to "continue in full force until all the said bills of credit emitted in the year 1750 be brought into the grand committee's office."[2] This act accounts for the double prices which begin in this year. The habit of old tenor prices seems to have been too firmly

---

[1] Rider, *R. I. Historical Tracts*, No. 8. Weeden, *Economic and Social History of N. E.*, ch. xiii., The Period of Inflation.

[2] *R. I. C. R.*, vol. vi. p. 482.

fixed to be altered suddenly, but a proper effort to comply with the law was made.

The following year the account book has this entry : —

> The Act of the General Assembly for Fixing and afcertaining of Interest & for preventing excessive usury in the Colony and also for shortening ye Time for the Redemption of mortgages was made at the Session held in the 6th mo 1767 to Take place 3 months afterwards.

The country was full of lawsuits about mortgaged land. In the absence of banks each land-holder became a lender. The variety of coin used also complicated affairs. An entry in —

> 1758 £21 - 10s. Lawful money turned in old Tenor at £5 10s. the doller —

makes a complicated sum. In 1766 comes a credit —

> To 3 Pistereens at 7^{d½} Lawful

Peleg Peckham, the good Friend who took cheese, sends in part payment, by his wife, as duly entered, —

> 1 piece of Gold of ye Value of 8 Doll^rs and 4 Dollers in Dollers by ye Hand of thy Wife

In 1768, also for cheese, Rowland Robin-son pays —

> 13 half Johannes equail to 104 Span.
> milled Dolers one was Light

The "one was Light" should be read in parenthesis, for clipping coin was not unknown. This is a puzzling entry, for the Johannes in the same year is carried out —

> Two Johannes in Gold to ye Value of
> 16 Spanish Mill^d Dollers £4. 16. 00

which counts eight dollars to the Johannes and six shillings to the dollar. The former entry counts the half Johannes at eight dollars also. It may be a slip of the pen, the word half being written by mistake.

In addition to these coins *coppers* are also mentioned : —

> 1774 10th mo Jeffrey Watson Jr D^r To
> 1 Vol of Sewels Hiftories at 18 Shilings
> & four Coppers expenses on it 2^d $\frac{1}{2}$
> Rec'd Two Dollars and four coppers of
> Jeffrey Watson jun in full 12^s, 2^d, $\frac{1}{2}$

which makes a copper equal a halfpenny and an eighth of a grain, and eighteen shillings of paper equal twelve of silver. This was one of the books subscribed for in Friends meeting, for which College Tom was appointed to take subscriptions.

College Tom lent money to his neighbors ; and a few records of such transactions are found. John Nichols was the son of the tailor, and one wishes the account of his journey was presented in fuller detail than in the following meagre entry: —

1760 6th of ye 4th mo Lent John Nichols four Spanish Mill^d Dollars, his Brother Andrew present. Said John Nichols had at y^e Same time four Spanish Mill^d dollars, five Piftereens & Six half Pistereens, for which he is to acc^t for with me when he returns from Bofton, being about to set out on that journey.

9th 6th mo. C^r, By 2 dollers, & acc^t of Expenses on a journey to Boston, 3 & a $\frac{1}{6}$ more.

1769 30th 11th mo By four Spanish mill^d Dollers & $\frac{1}{3}$ & $\frac{1}{10}$ of a Doller it being in full ffor y^e Dolers mentioned above together with his expenfe mentioned above.

There were various dealings with "Cousin George Hazard," who was in reality College Tom's nephew, but in the old fashion is called cousin. In this respect the Narragansett families were very clannish, and remembered the cousinship to a remote degree. Indeed it sometimes happened that cousins of the same name were more closely related on the

mother's side, so frequent were the inter-
marriages. In 1776 comes the entry, —

Lent Cousin George Hazard 35 dollars, £10. 10*s*.

Then in —

1778 8th month 4th day, Cousin
George Hazard, son of Richard, borrowed
of me 37 paper dollars.

1779 3rd month 9th day.

George Hazard, son of Richard, entered
and occupied part of my house above the
road, and is to give me $9.00 per annum,
to be paid in labour at Hufbandry the next
season, at 3 shillings per day for mowing
and 1 & 6 for Howing and Haying

The money lent or borrowed is often specified, as in 1764, when Thomas Hazard —

Rec^d of J^as Helme by the hand of his
Son Powel y^e sum of Eighteen Pounds &
five Shillings Lawful money so Call^d of
1759 date Exclusine ye interest.

This was returned in one month, as duly
entered. Later in 1785, —

3rd mo 10th Lent Peleg Peckham Six
Silver Dollars in the old meeting Houfe
the day Danl Cafs was there.

To add to the difficulties of the bad
money, lotteries were in great favor. The

General Assembly granted the privilege of having one for all sorts of purposes, both public and private. In 1770 one was granted to build a meeting-house in Cranston, for some Baptists who complacently declare that they are " willing to devote part of their time to the public worship of God." [1] They were granted to build roads, to repair bridges, to build wharves, or to help people who had lost their property.

These were the " days that tried men's souls," and the South Kingstown meeting was shaken by them, as will appear, but the account book gives no evidence of it until a later date. Rowland Robinson was a deputy to the general assembly, in the early seventies, and in 1776 went to Block Island bringing off beef hides. Block Island gave the government much uneasiness. " The peculiar situation of Rhode Island and the extensive sea coast had not escaped my mind," General Washington writes to Governor Cooke; " I well know the enemy have it in their power to do it considerable damage unless there is a sufficient force to repel their attacks." [2] April 1, 1776, three large ships were seen off Conanicut, and Gov-

---

[1] *R. I. C. R.* vol. vii. p. 21.   [2] *Ibid.,* p. 505.

ernor Cooke sent his son "express" to Washington at Cambridge with the information.

Jonathan Hazard, College Tom's brother, to whom one half of the land west of Worden's Pond was left, part of the original purchase of 1710, seems to have moved there, for in 1776 his son Jonathan was deputy from Charlestown, and in that year was sent to Block Island to apprehend John Wright for furnishing supplies or intelligence to the king. His instructions are "that Mr. Hazard earnestly exhort the inhabitants of New Shoreham to remove off from the island."[1] He is paid his expenses to Block Island to "apprehend disaffected persons," £3 7s. 6d.[2] He is also appointed one of a committee to examine suspected persons, with power to view "all desks, chests, or other suspected places under lock or otherwise."

Thus actively were members of College Tom's family engaged in the cause of liberty. His principles of non-resistance, however, were very firm ; there is no indication that he took any part in the struggle, except as an exhorter to quiet endurance, and a distributer of aid to the suffering.

[1] *R. I. C. R.*, vol. vii. p. 541.   [2] *Ibid.*, p. 577.

Matters were going from bad to worse with the finances of the colony. The Colonial Records are full of reports on the state of the money. The bills as they became due were burnt by the proper officer, but fresh ones took their place. A table of value of Spanish milled dollars is given in an act fixing the depreciation of continental bills for each month after January, 1777.[1] One hundred Spanish milled dollars at that time were worth a hundred and five in paper. The price rapidly increases till three years later, in August, 1780, they were worth seven thousand paper dollars, and May 30, 1781, sixteen thousand in paper. It was made obligatory to accept this depreciated paper in exchange for land, and the general distress can be imagined. During the summer of 1786 all business was at a standstill in Providence and Newport, and the farmers allowed their produce to decay rather than sell to the merchants at the heavy discount they demanded. The forcing act was brought to the test and declared unconstitutional, in September.[2] But the ruin

---

[1] *R. I. C. R.,* vol. ix. pp. 282–424.

[2] Fiske's *Critical Period of American History*, pp. 173–177.

was already widespread. I have been told
by the youngest granddaughter of College
Tom, that she had heard her mother relate that her grandmother used to say she
saw the money go out of the house in baskets full of gold and silver, and come back
in bundles of rags. Not every one in
South Kingstown accepted the " rags," as
the spirited protest of William Knowles
proves : [1] —

Henry Potter and John Segar both of
South Kingston on oath say that on the
twenty-sixth day of Febr'y last past they
saw Col. Samuel Segar make a tender of
the sum of two thousand one hundred dollars unto M^r. William Knowles of s^d South
Kingston to discharge two bonds & a note
said Knowles had against said Segar, but
the s^d Knowles refused to take the same,
saying that he would not take such trash
as that was, but if s^d Samuel Segar would
pay him & in the same sort of money the
said Segar had of the said Knowles he
would take it.

(Signed) HENRY POTTER.
JOHN SEGAR.

[1] Now in the Hazard Memorial, Peace Dale, with the
paper money tendered.

Kings County to wit South Kingston March 11th 1780 Henry Potter & John Segar subscribers to the above Deposition made Oath to the Truth of the same in order to perpetuate the same.

Before CARDER HAZARD, J. C. Pleas.

S. PERRY, Jus. Peace.

William Knowles
cited but did not attend.

(Endorsement on back.)

Evidence of HENRY POTTER & JOHN SEGAR inter SAML. SEGAR & WM. KNOWLES.

In April, 1780, money was at 4000 paper dollars for 100 silver, and it is small wonder it is called " such trash."

But Thomas Hazard carried out his Quaker principles. He enters his Rate bill this year and the following, and makes the entry for his son as well: —

Rate Bill 1780 Signd by Robᵗ Potter Town Treafurer for Raifing Continental Soldiers, Silver money £8 8s. 3d.

Clafs Bill the Same year Sign^d by the above Thos Potter &ct [*sic*] the above named committee £5 7*s*. 0*d*.

1781. Rate Bill 3rd mo 4th day, signed by Thos Potter, John Gardner, Robt Brown & Saml Babcock.

Clafs money Silver	£15	4*s*.	6*d*.
Rowland Hazard	0	1	6
State Tax Silver money	18	15	4
	£34	1*s*.	4*d*.

Dated 18th 1st 1781

Sign^d by Jos^h Clarke gen^l Treafurer.
1781. Continental money tax 1781 warr^t from the General Treafurer   £1176. 6. 0
Continental Town Tax signed by Robt Potter, Town Treasurer   238. 10. 0
Rate Bill, dated —— of —— month, A. D. 1780 warrant sign^d by —— demand   £2. 9*s*. 6*d*.
Taken by Timothy Peckham Collect^r one yearling bull price £3 12*s*. 00*d*. hard Money, and one yearling Heipher price £3 00*s*. 00*d*.

The distrained cattle show how he carried out his convictions, and suffered their loss rather than support the "carnal war and fightings" which disturbed the meeting so much.

Some of the latest entries in the book find him still submissive, —

One cow taken by Dan¹ Shearman, 9th month 4th day 1782 I know not his Demand by inquiry it appeared He did not come to yᵉ Houfe, but spoke to Robᵗ in the field.

A fortnight later —

The 20ᵗʰ 9th mo, 1782 Willson Pollock Collector Took Four of my best Cows all giving milk he said that he had several Taxes againft me amounting to £33 & upward hard money But shew no warrant or order from authority I accidentally saw him with the Cows as he drove them up the Lane that leads to the Highway westward from my Dwelling House.   (Signed) Tʜᵒ Hᴀᴢᴀʀᴅ.

So he put himself on record as suffering for conscience' sake. In 1789 Rhode Island finally signed the constitution, having run through almost all possible evils with her currency. She was the last of all the colonies to yield to the common good, — her excessive individuality having been at once the source of her strength and her weakness.

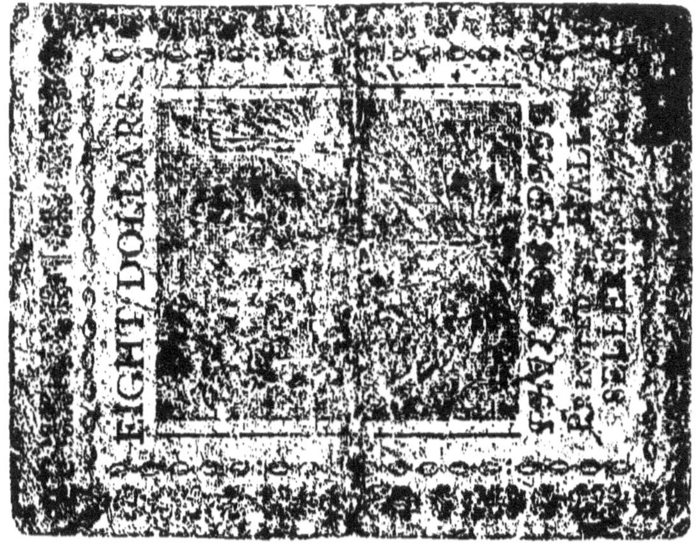

EIGHT DOLLAR BILL

CHAPTER X.

BEFORE me, as I write, lies a fine leather covered book, of two hundred and eighty quarto pages, closely written, in the hand of the last century, and inscribed on the inside cover, —

The Monthly Meeting of South Kingstown[s] first Book of Records y[e] 9th of y[e] 5th m[o] 1743 No 1.

This is the first of the eight volumes now extant belonging to the meeting, for the early records which would possibly contain some mention of George Fox himself, and Chalkley, and the early founders, were destroyed by fire many years ago. Fortunately for the reader who desires to follow the life of Thomas Hazard, it is quite early enough for him, and his marriage in 1742 is duly recorded in the proper place. Here are hidden away records of the scandals of the country-side, the " dealings " with Friends for dishonest behavior, the discipline, and papers of denial which were solemnly read in meeting. And with these serious offenses against the " Light of Truth " are those which were quite as severely dealt with, though now they only cause a smile. One young man was brought to a sense of his misconduct and presented " a paper of Condemnation . . . concerning his outgoings in dancing in a Light & airy Manner ; "[1] and going to an entertainment " Subsequent to a Marriage at which was Muſick Dancing and vain mirth "[2] is a cause of offense for which John Rose is dealt with by Thomas Hazard and Peleg Peckham, who are appointed for that service. But the young man was obdurate and appeared " not in a Dispoſition to Condemn his outgoing." The young people gave a good deal of trouble, as they would marry out of " Unity " and had to be disciplined. Occasionally the young

---

[1] *S. K. Monthly Meeting Records*, vol. i. p. 140.
[2] *Ibid.*, vol. i. p. 101.

man apologized, as in the following entry. How the bride took it is not mentioned.

To the Monthly Meeting of friends now in being at So. Kingstown. I through Inattention to the Light of Christ have Married a wife out of the good order of Friends neither was she a member of their Society. Therefore now being Sincible that their Rules and orders therein is Confistant with truth and Seeing the error of my doings am sorry for my Transgresfion therein and Defire friends to pass by my offence and Still Continue their Care for me Defiring I may be preserved to walk according to good order for time to come.[1]

The poor fathers, too, had hard times, as when William Robinson, son of the old Governor, in 1768 allowed his daughter's marriage, but on being waited upon by a committee of Friends, "said William told them that his Daughter was married out of our Society & that he allowed her to be married in his houfe but said he had rather it had been otherways."[2] This confession was not received as "satisfaction" by the meet-

---

[1] *S. K. M. M. R.*, vol. i. p. 225.
[2] *Ibid.*, vol. i. p. 203.

ing, and he presents a paper condemning
his conduct for allowing it, and for having
" vain mufick and Dancing." [1] Good Peleg
Peckham is indignant at one wedding which
he was appointed to see "orderly carried
on." He reports that he "expected to
have been entertained at s[d] Martha's appart-
ment but contrary to it was at s[d] William's
who not being a member of our Society
I thought was an Imposition." [2] Some of
the weddings to which friends were sent,
were apparently only "in the main orderly
carried on," and some "Pretty orderly
carried on, confidering the Concourfe of
young people," [3] and one wonders if it was
at such time the young fellow fell, as he
confesses : —

> Whereas I took more Strong Drink
> than was Commendable and also afsisted
> my Brother Amos in gitting married Con-
> trary to friends Rules without acquainting
> my father therewith I therefore freely
> Condemn it and Defire friends to Con-
> tinue me Under their Care.

Stoneingtown y[e] 18th of 10th mo. 1767. [4]

People lost their tempers too, then as

---

[1] *S. K. M. M. R.*, vol. i. p. 208.   [2] *Ibid.*, vol. i. p. 104.
[3] *Ibid.*, vol. i. p. 53.   [4] *Ibid.*, vol. i. p. 199.

now ; but the watchful care of Friends was over them, and one respects young Caleb Hazard, who declares that he " has of late so far given way to the pafsion of anger as to Strike & fight with Coon Williams " which transgression he " freely condemns." An old man and his sons are also interesting. He is the father of the young man before mentioned, and states his case plainly. A man, he says, —

Come to me in my field and tho I Desired him to Keep off yet made an attempt to beat or abufe me to prevent which I Suddenly and with too much warmth pushed him from me with the Rake I was leaning on Which act of mine as it did not manifest to that Christian patience and Example in Suffering Tryals of every Kind becoming my profefsion I therefore Freely Condemn it and Defire that I may be enabled for the future to Suffer patiently any abufe or whatever elfe I may be Tried with and alfo Defire friends to Continue their watchful Care over me. For the monthly meeting to be held at Richmond y[e] 31st of y[e] 8th mo. 1767.[1]

---

[1] *S. K. M. M. R.*, vol. i. p. 197.

We get a glimpse of the roads, too, when Mathew Allen is summoned to appear, but sends excuse "he being an ancient man, and the Distance so far to ride," and another who cannot come, "as the weather has been Difficult and he lame."   But our chief concern is with Thomas Hazard, and his connection with the meeting. His first recorded service was on "ye 29 Day of ye 1st mo 1753," when a minute declares that at the request of "ffriends" he had "Tranfcribed a copy of the yearly meeting minutes and prefented to this meeting." [1] A committee are appointed to "compair them with the original," and make report at the next meeting that "they are a true Copy."   This service is recorded when he was only thirty-three years old, and in a few years he is appointed a Representative at the various monthly and quarterly meetings, at first with Thomas Rodman, an aged friend. He goes to Westerly and Richmond, and as early as 1757 is appointed "to audit the accounts with Thos Rodman the meetings Treafurer." [2]   Two years later "This meeting adjourns till next fourth day week to meet at Thomas Hazard's Son

---

[1] *S. K. M. M. R.*, vol. i. p. 55.
[2] *Ibid.*, vol. i. p. 77.

of Robert at the 9ᵗʰ hour." At the adjournment he was appointed on the committee "to Draw & Sign an Epistle" to the next quarterly meeting, and to attend that meeting.[1] Almost every month for a number of years has some record of him, as representative, or on various committees to deal with "Disorderly walkers," or to advise in the settling of the "temporal affairs" of some distressed friend. It is he who is on the committee with Joseph Congdon "to stop yᵉ leak" in the old meeting-house, and to "make such small repairs as they shall find needful at prefent."[2]

The question of slavery was already before the meeting. John Woolman, whom tradition speaks of as College Tom's friend,[3] visited Narragansett first in 1748. He journeyed through Connecticut, and after three days' riding, he says, "we came amongst Friends in the Colony of Rhode Island, and visited them in and about Newport, Dartmouth, and generally in those parts."[4] The "Monthly Meeting Records" unfortunately contain no mention of his preaching, but Thomas Hazard and his friend Jeremiah

---

[1] *S. K. M. M. R.*, p. 97.　　[2] *Ibid.*, p. 103.
[3] Updike, p. 324.　　[4] Woolman's *Journal*, p. 75.

Austin, who had freed his single slave, his only inheritance, and worked himself at day labor,[1] must have taken great comfort in this visit of the devoted preacher, and taken courage to continue their work in an unpopular cause. The general conditions of slavery in Narragansett have been mentioned. A recent writer alludes to the " Slave code of Rhode Island supplemented by the by-laws of South Kingstown," as by no means a mild one.[2] He does not speak of the provision for manumission on deposit of £100 security in 1729. In 1750 a law was enacted declaring that no person shall "presume to sell, give, truck, barter, or exchange with or to any Indian Mulatto or Negro servant or slave any strong beer, ale, cider, wine, rum, brandy or other strong liquor by what name or names so ever called or know." A fine of fifteen dollars was to be paid for each offense. No slave was allowed to be abroad after nine o'clock at night, with a penalty attached for each offense of being " publickly whipped by the Constable ten stripes." The owner as an alternative was allowed to pay a fine of three dollars. Indians, mulattoes,

[1] Updike, p. 326.
[2] Dr. Edward Channing, *Narragansett Planters*, p. 10.

and negroes were not allowed to be entertained without consent of master or mistress, with "dancing, gaming, or diversion of any kind." In South Kingstown a by-law forbade the "keeping of creaters" by negroes.[1] On the other hand a slave could not be sent out of the country without his own consent, and a certificate from two justices of the peace was required to this consent to make transportation legal. If the slave was "notoriously unfaithful," proofs could be given at a court of General Sessions, and the owner could be authorized to send him to any other part.[2] When we consider the terms of an apprenticeship at about the same time these restrictions do not appear quite so severe. In a regularly printed form filled out for one of young Richard Hazard's sons, it appears that the apprentice binds himself to serve faithfully his master and mistress, "their secrets keep their commands obey At Cards Dice or any other unlawful Game he shall not play;" he shall not absent himself "by Day or by Night" from his master's and mistress' ser-

[1] *South Kingstown Records.* Quoted by Dr. E. Channing.

[2] *Public Laws of R. I.,* Revision of 1798, Act of 1776.

vice without their leave; or "haunt Alehouses Taverns or Play houses." This cut off the apprentice from all diversions as effectually as the slave. For his service he was to be taught his trade, and to " read, write and Cypher as far as the Rule of Three " and his wearing apparel was to be furnished for the sum of £400 old tenor, paid by his guardian.[1] The times were strict, and the slave laws must be read not with our modern views of liberty, but in accordance with the spirit of the days before the Revolution.

The various meetings were again stirred by John Woolman in 1760. He and his companions held five meetings in Narragansett, where he says he went " through deep exercises that were mortifying to the creaturely will. In several families in the country where we lodged, I felt an engagement on my mind to have a conference with them in private concerning their slaves."[2] He speaks of this as an " unpleasant task assigned him." In Newport he found that a large number of slaves had been imported from Africa and were then on sale by a

---

[1] Appendix, Paper of Apprenticeship.
[2] Woolman's *Journal*, p. 161.

member of the Society, upon hearing which his appetite failed and he was sorely distressed. After many inward difficulties, he presented a petition to the Legislature for the meeting to approve and present, which would forbid the future importing of slaves. This was approved by the meeting, and a minute was also made and sent to several quarterly meetings to discourage participation in lotteries among Friends. After the Yearly Meeting was over he had private conferences with members of the society who held slaves.[1]

As early as 1757 the South Kingstown monthly meeting puts itself on record on this question, when —

This meeting Received a paper of Richard Smith as his Teſtimony against Keeping Slaves and his Intention to free his negro girl which paper he hath a mind to lay before the Quarterly meeting all which is Referred for further consideration.[2]

One of the Rodmans, a few years later, was in trouble over a slave. He was condemned by his own meeting, but appealed

---

[1] Woolman's *Journal*, p. 167.
[2] *S. K. M. M. R.*, vol. i., p. 82.

to the quarterly meeting, which confirmed the judgment of the monthly meeting given against him, "on account of his buying a negro slave" and "it is the mind of friends that there ought to go out a publick Teſti-mony & Denial"[1] of the purchaser, which was accordingly done, and a solemn "paper of frd^s Teſtimony of Disowning" was read at the end of a First-day meeting. Stephen Hoxfie, the excellent clerk of the meeting, through whose care the records are so legible now, was appointed to draw it up.

But the famous slave case was that of the Rathbuns, father and son, which is fully detailed, and must have brought opinion to a focus upon the whole question. This case was before the meeting eight years, dur-ing the latter part of which it was reported upon at every monthly meeting. At first Thomas Hazard was not formally con-nected with it, but as it became more com-plicated he was added to the committee[2] to deal with the offenders, and report from month to month. Having bought a slave, Joshua Rathbun is brought to confess his error as follows :—

[1] *S. K. M. M. R.*, vol. i. p. 131.
[2] *Ibid.*, vol. i. p. 252.

Wefterly the 27th of ye 12 mo 1765
To the monthly meeting of friends to be
held at Richmond next

Dear Friends.   I hereby acknowledge
that I have acted Disorderly in purchas-
ing a Negro Slave which Disorder I was
Ignorant of, at the time of the purchase.
but having conversed with Several friends
upon the Subject of Slavery have gained
a knowledge that heretofore I was Ignorant of, both as to the Rules of our Society,
as well as the nature & inconfiftancy of
making Slaves of our fellow Creatures,
am therefore free to condemn that Incon-
siderate act and Defire Friends to pafs
it by, hoping that I may be preferved
from all conduct that may bring Un-
easinefs Upon friends for the future am
willing likewise to take the advice of
Friends both as to the bringing up and
Discharging of the Afores^d negro.

JOSHUA RATHBUN.[1]

This expresses very clearly what must
have been the general feeling of the day
in regard to slavery, and sounds like an
honest change of heart.   Nevertheless on
the 28th of 1st month, 1771, —

[1] *S. K. M. M. R.*, vol. i. p. 171.

Joshua Rathbun appeared in this meeting and informed that he had signed over a bill of Sale to his son of that negro garl he purchased (and give incouragement to take friends advice in order to Discharge his duty towards her) now friends think it necefsary that something be done in that affair.

A committee was appointed to deal with him and a further note comes, —

Whereas our last monthly meeting condefended to appoint a meeting to be held at the said Joshua Rathbun's houfe for the space of three months but since it has appeared to this meeting that said Rathbun did not stand Clear in his Teftimony for the caufe of Truth as he ought to have done against that of Slavery, therefore that meeting appointed at his houfe is Discontinued.[1]

The son was then dealt with, and this entry follows, —

30th of 12mo. 1771.

Friends appointed last monthly meeting to Treat with Joshua Rathbun y⁰ 3rd and his father Joshua Rathbun y⁰ 2nd Concerning their Dispofing of a Negro

---

[1] *S. K. M. M. R.,* vol. i. p. 238.

Garl as a Slave report as followeth that
they have treated with them on that acco[t]
and find by inquiring that Joshua y[e] 2nd
who had a bill of sale of said Negro girl
afsigned s[d] bill of Sale over to his Son
Joshua Rathbun y[e] 3rd for a Consideration of fifty Dollars which Dollars the
said Joshua y[e] 3rd told us his Father
made up to him another way and that as
the s[d] negro girl Cost him nothing he
promised his father Joshua Rathbun y[e]
2nd that the Girl should have her freedom at a Suitable time if she Lived not-
withstanding he (that is Joshua Rathbun
the 3rd) had Sold her and she was sent
out of the Country without (as he told
us) his father's consent nor do we find
that Joshua Rathbun y[e] 2nd did afk the
advice of Fr[ds] refpecting said negro girl
at the time he conveyed her to his son
or ever made any Complaint of his Son's
Conduct in that cafe to friends until they
was other ways informed thereof. The
consideration of which is refer[d] to our
next mo[ly] meeting.[1]
After long waiting the son is denied[2] be-

---

[1] *S. K. M. M. R.*, vol. i. p. 249.
[2] *Ibid.*, vol. i. p. 260.

cause he "encouraged the Deteſtable practice of enſlaving mankind," and the father
advised in 1772 to —

. . . preſs it on his Said Son to Redeem
Said Slave and if his Said Son Should
refuse or neglect so to do that he Commince and proſecute an action at Common Law against his son for the Recovery
of Damages Upon a promis made by his
said son. Frds to assist him, & the sum
recovered to be used for the redemption
of the girl.[1]

" Thos Wilbur, Joseph Congdon, Nicholas
Bragg, and Thos Hazard of Robert" were
the committee, and one wonders if a trace
of College Tom's early law training appears
in the advice to "Commince and proſecute."
The father did not take it, however, and
was still further dealt with by the meeting. One has some sympathy with the poor
man, who was denied the comfort of the
meeting in his own house, but Friends were
inexorable, and the record shows how well
they cleared their consciences : —

1st of 3rd mo. 1773.

We the Subscribers according to the
appointment of Last Mon[ly] meeting have

[1] *S. K. M. M. R.*, p. 261.

Inspected the holding a meeting at Stonington Harbour as a meeting of ffriends and find that Such meeting hath been held on first days at Joshua Rathbun y[e] 2nd and that he hath frequently appeared as a preacher therein. We Treated with such as are members and with Joshua in perticular and defired him and them to defist therefrom S[d] Joshua says he Should be glad to take friends' advice but hath peace in holding said meetings apprehending it as he said as his duty.

SOLOMON HOXSIE.
JOHN COLLINS.
JOSEPH CONGDON.

Amos Collins is appointed to inform those friends that live thereaways that said meeting is held out of the Unity of Fr[ds] and that unlefs they defist from attending it they who have will be proceeded against as disorderly walkers.[1]

Three months after the old man was denied his membership,[2] and so the episode of the " Negro garl " ends as far as the records show. Indeed, it is to be feared that

<hr>

[1] *S. K. M. M. R.*, vol. i. p. 276.
[2] *Ibid.*, vol. ii. p. 7.

the good showing of Friends in 1773 as to their "clearness" on the Slavery question was made in much the same way, not by convincing so many slave-owners, as by turning out those who were unconvinced. John Knowles and Stephen Richmond in 1771 "Appears of a disposition to comply with friends rules in liberating their slaves." Three friends "discovers something of a Difpofition to comply," while four "Did Shew the Contrary Difpofition." They were informed on the 29th of 7th mo. 1771, that all who did not free their slaves may "expect to be Denied Memberfhip."[1] Two months afterward a sturdy Friend appeared in meeting and "saith that he shall not comply with the Rules of the Society, Refpecting his Slaves to Liberate them," and he and three others are therefore denied membership.   On the

28th of 6th mo 1773

Frds Appointed to Visit Slave Keepers made report that they don't find their is any held as Slaves by Frds and there are some yt are set at Liberty and no proper mannamifsion given therefore said committee are continued to see that they are

[1] *S. K. M. M. R.*, vol. i. p. 243.

mannamitted and make report thereof as soon as they conveniently can.[1]

So the main work of the committee appointed in April, 1771, was finished. The men who did this service, a service which must have tried them sorely at times, and divided families and neighborhoods, were Thomas Wilbur, Benjamin Hoxsie, Joseph Collins, John Robinson, and Stephen Hoxsie.[2] Their work was continued until all the slaves had proper papers.

One such paper is recorded, —

26th of the 2nd mo. 1774. These may certify that about 25 years ago I had several negroes which upon an agreement between them and me set at Liberty which Liberty I have seen to be my duty to confirm from me my Heirs and afsigns the Negroes are York, Betty, Zilpah and Zadock York is since Dead but the other Three I still confirm their liberty according to the good order of Friends from me

HEZEKIAH COLLINS.[3]

Witnefs THOMAS WILBUR.

---

[1] *S. K. M. M. R.*, vol. ii. p. 1.
[2] *Ibid.*, vol. i. p. 238.
[3] *Ibid.*, vol. ii. p. 18.

In these local concerns Thomas Hazard seems to have taken a less prominent part than in earlier years, but he is constantly sent to quarterly meeting, and added to committees, as in the Rathbun case when it became complicated. He was also on various committees to transact the business of the whole society. In this very year, 1773, the London yearly meeting is informed that Friends' " labor for the freedom of the Enslaved Negroes is still continued," and " that we have appointed our friends T. Hazard Isaac Lawton Philip Wanton and Jacob Mott Jr of Rhode Island a committee to correspond with our correspondents in London." [1]

This year of 1773 was a year of special activity among Friends. Joseph Wanton, of the old Quaker family, was the governor of Rhode Island. He was the son of Governor William Wanton, who left the Society of Friends on his marriage. The lady's family were strict Congregationalists, and as his family were Quakers, religious objections were made to the marriage, upon which he finally said, " Friend Ruth, let us break from this unreasonable bondage; *I* will give

---

[1] *R. I. Yearly Meeting Records*, 1773.

up *my* religion, and *thou* shalt *thine*, and
we will go over to the Church of England
and go to the Devil together!"[1] It was
the son of this ardent lover who came to
the head of colonial affairs, a few years
before the Revolution, and who would
naturally have some sympathy with the
Society his father left. Among the papers
of Thomas Hazard is a letter from Judge
Mathew Griswold, of Connecticut, to this
governor of Rhode Island, dated June 10,
1773. It is evidently in reply to one from
Rhode Island on the subject of slaves.
They are "Esteem^d with us," Judge Griswold says, "as the Proper Objects of the
Care and Protection of the Government
in common with Other Inhabitants. If
any outrage undue Violence or Inhumane
Severity is used it is Esteem^d the Duty
of the Informing & Peace officers of the
Colony to interpose and give Relief upon
proper Application made to them." But
Judge Griswold is not clear as to manumission. "Those Things are not greatly
Favour^d in Law: by People of Consideration here," he says, "Inasmuch as the
Negroes who have been Manumitted in

[1] Updike, p. 296.

this Colony : being Ignorant of the Art of Honest living have Frequently become Strowling vagrants have United with Thieves & Burglars and proved very Troublesome and Dangerous Inhabitants. I sho[d] be Concerned that any People sho[d] be oppressed by unlawful holding in Servitude. Justice ought to be done to Every one."[1] The presence of this letter among the papers seems to indicate that Thomas Hazard's interest in the question was not only well known, but that he was on terms of friendship with Governor Wanton. This was the year (1773) that Stephen Hopkins was disowned by the Society because he would not liberate a slave woman, and the year that Moses Brown liberated all his slaves, preparatory to joining the Society in 1774.[2] This excellent man, who did so much for the Society and for the infant manufactures of the State, was apparently a quarter of a century behind Thomas Hazard in his convictions on the subject of slavery.

In 1774 Thomas Hazard was appointed on the committee to " use their influence at the General Afsembly of Rhode Island or with

---

[1] Appendix, Letter from Judge Griswold.
[2] *Moses Brown, A Sketch*, by Augustine Jones, p. 15.

the members thereof that such laws may be made as will tend to the abolition of slavery, and to get such laws repealed as any way encourage it."[1]   This committee presented an act which was passed by the General Assembly. The fact that the men who petitioned the Assembly for this purpose were themselves all "clear in their teſti-mony" as to slavery must have carried great weight. The noble opening sentence read: — "Whereas the inhabitants of America are generally engaged in the preservation of their own rights and liberties, among which that of personal freedom must be considered as the greatest; as those who are desirous of enjoying all the advantages of liberty themselves should be willing to extend personal liberty to others,"[2] it is therefore enacted that no negro or mulatto slave shall be brought into the Colony.

The whole of New England was soon plunged into trouble with the disasters of war, and little further action was taken until peace was restored.

The negro called in the account book

---

[1] *R. I. Yearly Meeting Records*, 1774.

[2] *R. I. C. R.*, vol. vii. p. 251.

Priamus will be remembered. Among the papers is a long letter from John Pemberton of Philadelphia, so characteristic that it is given in full. This excellent Friend, "our dear John Pemberton," as Mrs. Elizabeth Drinker in her diary calls him, was the clerk of the meeting for sufferings in 1777, in Philadelphia, and was arrested and imprisoned for refusal to bear arms.[1] He traveled in Ireland a few years later, and finally died in Germany in 1795.[2] He had evidently been in Narragansett, as his charming message of "my Dear Love in thy freedom to such who may enquire," and his mention of "my friends in your parts" indicates.

Philad^a, 5 mo 15, 1780.

Dear Friend Thos Hazard

There is a negro man here, whofe Case claims Commiferation, and having lived with thee 15 or 16 years, as he tells me I hope thou will use fome endeavors that Justice be done him & he fet free. His Name is Primus, after leaving thy Service he lived about 7 years with Wm Barden

----

[1] Hodgson, *Historical Memoirs of the Society of Friends*, p. 342.

[2] Mrs. E. Drinker's *Journal*, p. 264.

who he allows was his master, & who
agreed with him, that if he would go three
Voiages in a Privateer he fhould be manumitted, he went two & returned fafe, the
third Voiage he was taken & Came hither
with the British, fo that he performed
what had been required of him. The
Privateer he went in was a floop called
the America, One Dennis Com^d and William Cranstead Lieutenant. These two
were Present when his master entered
into this Contract with him. If these
men can be found and will Certify what
he afserts to be true I fhould hope proper
steps may be taken to Clear the poor
man. if the said Wm Barden cannot be
prevailed with, without such procedure
He remained here after the British left
this place, & has been taken up by one
Joseph Knary or Connary, who says he
purchased him of one Rice of Hartford
in Connecticutt. The few months he
lived in this City before taken up he
behaved well, as far as I have heard.
Knowing that these poor People are
often greatly imposed upon I undertake
to represent his Case & hope thou will
be diligent & speedy in doing what thou

can for his relief. I should be plesed to hear of thy Succefs in this application, for it would be Distresfing to him and Cause perhaps deep & Sorrowful Reflection to his Old Master, if he should be sent into Cruel hard bondage which may probably be the Case if not foon relieved. He has been fold thrice this Winter and suffered much from want of Cloathing, the persons who had him being doubtful of their right to detain him. But it is much a Custom for hardened Worthlefs men to purchase these poor people and take them to the fouthward & sell them where there's none to plead their Cause, and where they suffer much. He walked to this City in the beginning of 3ᵈ mo last, near 50 miles bare foot.

I often remember my friends in your parts with much Sympathy and love, & desire they may be kept & preserved in Faith and patience and In Integrity & Uprightness of heart. My Dear Love in thy freedom to such who may enquire & with same salutation to thee & thine remain thy Affectionate Friend.

JOHN PEMBERTON.

if a Certificate could be produced from
Dennis & Cranstead of the ab° ment[d]
agreement, I expect wee may be able to
secure the man from his oppresſion.

No further record of this man has been
found, but the letter exists to show the spirit
with which John Pemberton and his friends
worked for the oppressed slaves.

In December, 1783, a Committee of the
Legislature was appointed "to take into
consideration a petition preferred unto this
Assembly by a committee of the people
called Quakers respecting the Abolition of
Slavery,"[1] and directed to report. This
was the petition of the old committee which
had held over through the war, of which
Thomas Hazard was a member.[2] In February, 1784, two months later, the act he had
labored so earnestly for was finally passed.
The preamble recalls Thomas Jefferson's
famous Declaration, so lately written. It
reads,—"Whereas all men are entitled to
life, liberty, and the pursuit of happiness,
and the holding of mankind in a state of
slavery, as private property, which has gradu-

[1] *R. I. C. R.*, vol. ix. p. 735.
[2] *R. I. Friends Yearly Meeting Records*, 1784.

ally obtained by unrestrained custom and the
permissions of the laws, is repugnant to this
principle, and subversive of the happiness
of mankind, the great end of all civil government,"— therefore it was enacted that
no person born after the date of the act,
"negroes, mulattoes or others" were to be
considered slaves.   The children were to be
instructed and might be apprenticed by the
towns in which they were born ; they had
the right to be supported in case of inca-
pacity, the towns and not the owners
assuming the support and education of all
children of slaves.[1]   Good as this was, three
years later an additional act was required.
"Forgetful of the danger which then im-
pended, and inattentive of the principles of
justice . . . a renewal of the African trade
for slaves has been entered into by divers
inhabitants of this state,"[2] the act reads.
A penalty of a hundred pounds for every
slave imported was fixed, or a thousand
pounds for every vessel engaged in the
trade.[3]

[1] *R. I. C. R.*, vol. x., p. 7.

[2] *Ibid*, vol. x., p. 262.

[3] There is some reason for supposing this act to have
been drawn by Thomas Hazard, but I have not been able
to satisfy myself of the fact.

A little later, following the passage of the Abolition act, the *Providence Society for Abolishing the Slave Trade* was founded. A copy of what is apparently the original constitution of the society is printed on a folio sheet, and preserved among the papers, but has no date whatever. In drawing up this constitution Thomas Hazard had a hand. The proceedings of the society set forth that on the 29th of the 1st month called January, 1789, "a meeting of citizens of the town of Providence and parts adjacent was called for the purpose of establishing a Society for Abolishing Slavery." David Howell was chosen moderator, and a committee of seven, including Judge Howell, Moses Brown, Arthur Fenner, Thomas Hazard, Thomas Arnold and two others was appointed to "draw up a system of regulations and government and report at a meeting to be held on the 20th proximo at the Friends' Meeting House in this town." At this meeting the constitution drawn up by the committee was adopted, a copy of which is the paper referred to.[1] David Howell was chosen President, John Dorrance, Vice - President; Moses Brown,

[1] Appendix.

Treasurer; Thomas Arnold, Secretary; and Thomas Hazard was put upon the standing committee of seven. The society includes the names of most of the distinguished men in the State; Daniel Lyman, James Burrill, Richard Ward Greene, and other distinguished lawyers were the counselors of the society. Among the corresponding members were Jonathan Edwards, the Elliots of Boston, Judge Sullivan of Massachusetts, and William Rotch of New Bedford. Samuel Hopkins was a member; Anthony, Foster, Bartlett, Buffum, Almy, and other excellent men were active in it. Thomas Robinson of Newport, brother-in-law of College Tom, was an active member, untiring in his efforts to release slaves, and to prevent the importation of any into Newport.

Thus in his old age the great object of College Tom's life was attained. Freeing first his own slaves, he lived to influence his own Monthly Meeting very strongly, and from that meeting was sent to the larger Yearly Meeting, where his sincerity and ability won recognition, and with the foremost men of his day he labored for justice and liberty, against the "deteftable

practice of enflaving mankind." Through
a long life he kept this end in view, and
whatever may have been his private griefs
and losses in the troubled times, the attain-
ment of this great object gave comfort to
his last days.

CHAPTER XI.

THE advanced position which the South
Kingstown Monthly Meeting took in regard
to slavery would lead us to expect other
good works from it. Nor are we disap-
pointed in a search for them. "We catch
virtue from ourselves as well as from others,"
— and with a few leaders such as Thomas
Hazard, Joseph Congdon, and Stephen
Hoxsie, the meeting was sure to advance.
A good share of the business of the meeting
was transacted by College Tom, when he
was still a young man. He is "defired to
send up to the Yearly Meeting Treafurer"
the subscription to the yearly meeting stock
in 1761.[1] He was on the committee with
Stephen Hoxsie and Thomas Wilbour to

[1] *S. K. M. M. R.*, vol. i. p. 118.

draft a paper stating the duties of the overseers of the First-day and week-day meetings in the same year.[1] A little later the
overseers are charged to suppress all " Slep-
ing and other indecencies " in meeting. He
has constantly to prepare the report for the
Quarterly Meeting, and is sent to that meeting often. In 1763, with Peleg Peckham,
Benjamin Rodman, Joseph Congdon, and
Thomas Wilbour, he is instructed " to take
a deed of the old meeting houſe and lot at
South Kingstown "[2] and has a constant
oversight of the building from that time.
The account book has the full memorandum of repairs which he and Joseph Congdon were ordered to make in 1761 : —

4th 8th mo   To Sixteen Pounds in Cash
to Buy Boards
    Joseph Knowles took it as he went to
      Newport   £16. 00s. 00d.
    Joseph Knowles returned
     s[d] £16 Pounds again to
     me   £16. 00. 00
    To 2500 Shingles @ £30
     as by Sam[l] Greens Rec[t]
     dated 12th octob[r] 1761.   75. 00. 00

---

[1] *S. K. M. M. R.*, vol. i. p. 122.
[2] *Ibid.*, vol. i. p. 142.

To 199 feet of pine Board
@ 1*s.* 6*d.*   14. 17. 06
To Freight of s⁴ Boards &
Shingles 1 20/   6. 00. 00
To Carting s⁴ Boards &
Shingles @ £10   10. 00. 00

and the account is presented to the meeting, "which is allowed."[1]   At the same time he was appointed with Joseph Congdon "to Receive the book at Newport prepared for to Tranſcribe the Engliſh book of Diſcipline in and procure the same done."   Two years later the committee reports that they have " Compleated & presented it the Cost thereof being fifty Pounds old Tenʳ."[2]   This book is among the books of the Meeting, a fine large quarto, beautifully written, entitled *Christian & Brotherly Advices Given forth from time to time By the Yearly Meeting in London.   Alphabetically Digested under Proper Heads.   Transcribed by Jos: Congdon.*

The meeting also subscribed for books. In 1763 a " proposal for Printing George Fox's Journal in one vollom by subscription was received "and Stephen Hoxsie appointed to take subscriptions.   " Barclay's Appoligy now printing at Philadelphia " is also to be

1 *S. K. M. M. R.*, vol. i. p. 135.   2 *Ibid*, vol. i. p. 125.

subscribed for in 1774, and Thomas Hazard and John Collins are to take subscriptions "for William Sewel's History propofed to be printed at Philadelphia." A minute from the Philadelphia Yearly Meeting gives further light upon this.

From the Extracts 9 mo. 1774.

It having been under the consideration of the meeting for sufferings to reprint the apology by our ancient friend Robert Barclay for which they have encouragement from Friends in *New England* — this meeting willing to promote it, recommends to the several quarterly and monthly meetings to promote subscriptions for the purpose as speedy as they can.

N. B. The price of the books to subscribers is not to exceed 5*s.* 5*d.*

The account book has two entries in reference to it —

1774 10 mo 20 day

6 shillings sent to Philadelphia when subscriptions were sent there —
and another a little later. The Sewel Histories also are mentioned, with their exact cost. But well as the meeting looked after its own affairs, our chief interest is in its

position on the larger questions which even then had appeared, questions which the next century has had to grapple with, and some of which it will bequeath to its successor. On the rights of man we have seen the strong and fearless position that was taken, and it is delightful to find that in the rights of man, those of women were included. The signature " Thomas Hazard Clerk this time " occurs frequently, but one can imagine no occasion on which it was signed with greater vigor than to the following minute which he is instructed to draw up. The Nine-partners Monthly Meeting had sent " lines " strongly intimating that it is not according to their practice to receive women Friends unless their certificate is signed by at least the Clerk of the Men's Meeting : —

Therefore in Condefention to our friends of the monthly meeting at Nine-partners we do hereby direct the Clerk of this meeting to signifie to sᵈ monthly meeting that we have neither precedent nor Difcipline amongst us for such a practice, neither do we think it Convnant So far to Degrade our women's meeting, But to Let them have the Ufe & Exerfise of our Difcipline as occasion may call for it

in Conducting the affairs of their meeting
not Defiring the Preheminence where
Truth admits of none But believing that
both male & female are all one in Christ
Jefus.

Thomas Hazard Clerk this time.[1]

1st day of ye 4 mo 1771

Something of the indignation of the
courtly gentleman at the offered indignity
to the women he has treated with such
respect all his life seems to breathe in this
minute, as well as his conviction of the true
equality of the sexes. Thus on another of
the vexed questions of to-day, College Tom
spoke his word with vigor and decision.

Nor was he silent on temperance. It is
interesting to trace a bit of early legislation
on that subject directly to the South Kingstown meeting, and to College Tom himself.
In 1768 occurs this entry: —

There being many Disorders committed near our annual General Meeting
at South Kingstown by Rude Libertine
Disorderly people Black Tawnies &
others Some of whom expofing Liquor
and Cakes to sale by means of which
Liquors some are Drunken &c greatly

[1] *S. K. M. M. R.*, vol. i. p. 235.

to the Scandal of Religion therefore
friends are Defired to find out and prose-
cute such meafures as may remove said
grievences   29 of y⁰ 8 mo 1768.[1]

The next month the matter was referred
to the Quarterly Meeting, and Thomas
Hazard sent as representative. From this
quarterly meeting he was appointed with
Thomas Steere, Ephraim Congdon, William
Redwood and Joseph Congdon to present
a petition and act to the General Assembly
to prevent the selling of liquor and the
playing of games on the days of the General Meetings near the places of assembly.
The act contains many of the phrases of
the minute and was doubtless drawn by
Thomas Hazard, as the following letter from
William Redwood indicates. It is written
in a beautiful copperplate hand addressed

     To

       THOMAS HAZARD Son of Rob⁰
          in
           South Kingstown.

     NEWPORT 2ⁿᵈ mon. 21ˢᵗ. 1769.

Efteemed Friend

        Thy favour of 17ᵗʰ
Insᵗ with the Petition & Act of Afsem-

[1] *S. K. M. M. R.*, vol. i. p. 207.

bly came to hand yefterday. I have Signed the Petition, and shall enquire what number the Committee confifted of, if they are not all inferted in the Act, I will insert them, with the day of the opening of the Sefsions, and forward them as soon as pofsible, agreeable to thy request.

I Remain with much Efteem
Thy Afsured Friend
WILLIAM REDWOOD

THOMAS HAZARD.

From the preamble of the act an idea of the holidays of the time is gained. Play-ing at quoits, wrestling, and exercising in any other games, with running horses, are forbidden, within a proscribed distance of the meeting, with the sale of "cakes, beer, cider, rum, or any other spirituous liquor by retail."[1] This act seems to have been among the earliest temperance legislation in the Colony. Slaves are specially men-tioned in it, the owner having to pay the fine in case a slave is the offender.

The account book contains only a few entries mentioning the meetings. "Oringes

---

[1] *R. I. C. R.*, vol. vi. p. 578.

and Lemmonds " were sent for to Newport on one occasion when the meeting was held in Narragansett, but they were not obtainable, and Latham Clarke, who had the commission, brought back the money.   In 1770 Peleg Peckham is charged with " shoeing thy mare in ye Journey," and " one shilling eight pence p^d when we pafs^d ye ferrys to Newport."   As Peleg Peckham was clerk of the meeting, they were presumably going to a quarterly meeting in Newport. In 1775 comes an entry —

> 7mo 7th day   To one large Veal Calve skin ye day I set out for the Quarterly meeting.   Sent per Rowland

and later another mention

> 1778   6^m 9th To three Ditto (calf skins) when I went to ye yearly meeting
> 7th mo 8th day   To three Ditto when I went to ye Quarterly meeting.

A few copies of the minutes of the meeting are found, one with a list of the members of the meeting for sufferings.[1]   Nor were Friends unmindful of the importance of education.   As early as 1780 a committee upon which Thomas Hazard served, appointed by the yearly meeting, reported upon the need of capable teachers to carry out the views

[1] Appendix.

of the Society respecting the education of youth, and suggested the appointment of a further committee to take the matter into "solid consideration." Thomas Hazard, Moses Brown, Elisha Thornton, William Rotch, and others were appointed to consider plans for erecting a school, for the education not only of the children of the Society, but to train teachers, and provide instruction for poor children.[1] On the 8th of 11th month, 1784, this school was opened at Portsmouth and continued four years. In 1785 the South Kingstown meeting sent £7 2s. as a subscription to the stock of " the yearly meeting school,"[2] which closed for want of funds the next year. After a four years' interval Thomas Hazard was again on a committee "weightily to consider in what way the fund (gradually increasing, but still inadequate to maintain a school) might be most beneficially applied consistently with the intention of the donors."[3] This school, through the fostering care of Moses Brown, one of the original com-

---

[1] *R. I. Yearly Meeting Records.*

[2] *S. K. M. M. R.,* vol. ii. p. 255.

[3] *Samuel Austin.* Thomas Hazard, son of Robert (unpublished).

mittee on its foundation, opened again in Providence, January 1, 1819, and has become the now famous Friends' School.[1]

Once before Thomas Hazard had been interested in the foundation of an educational institution. The act of incorporation of Rhode Island College, passed in 1764, names him as one of the incorporators, and he was appointed one of the original Board of Fellows at the same time.[2]

But the Revolutionary question was the absorbing one of the time, and the Friends of South Kingstown bore noble testimony against "Carnal war and Fightings." This is a phrase of College Tom's, who signs himself Clerk of the day, upon which the minute containing it is drawn up. The handwriting of the Narragansett men of the last century is very similar. Peleg Peckham, Joseph Congdon, and Thomas Hazard all wrote very much alike, but I am inclined to think after careful comparison, that the Thomas Hazard, Clerk this day, is his own signature, and the first hundred and seventy-five pages of the second book of Records, as well as several marriage records, are in

[1] *Augustine Jones.* Moses Brown, p. 24.
[2] *R. I. C. R.*, vol. vi. p. 386.

the same hand. He and Peleg Peckham are appointed in 1778 to transcribe "the several Rules or Minutes of the Yearly Meeting,"[1] and throughout his life his pen seems to have been at the service of the meeting, from the time in 1753 when he presented his first copy of minutes at the request of Friends. It is an excellent clear hand, both strong and flowing, and ends in 1781, in the middle of a sentence, which is continued by a different person. All through the war this same hand records the minutes, and very often Thomas Hazard is instructed to draw them. The sufferings of Friends ramified in a way we should hardly think of. Not only were they subjected to hardship by the distraining of goods when they felt obliged to decline the payment of their rates, but they must not be concerned in any of the profits of war. We can hardly blame the good Friend who in the scarcity of reading matter bought what came to hand, but he is dealt with because he "purchafed some Books at a Vandue that came on Shore in a Vefel & fold as plunder taken in War."[2] The money itself

---

[1] *S. K. M. M. R.*, vol. ii. p. 108.

[2] *Ibid.*, vol. ii. p. 120.

became a difficulty to a tender conscience. At an adjournment at Newport, 13th day 1st mo. 1776, there was some —

Advice to F^ds in regard to receiving and paſsing the late paper Currency that is made and paſsed in these Colinies Iſsued Exprefsly for the purpose of carrying on war it is recommended to friends Serious Consideration and Obſervation and that each Particular meeting have a coppy thereof to read publick.[1]

Numberless Friends were disowned for being concerned in military matters, even so far as to hire substitutes, and the young men who enlisted themselves, " the offence being so repugnant to Truth," were summarily denied.

Friends were advised by the meeting for sufferings at Providence of 8th mo. 13th, 1776, to " enter deeply into themselves & not implicitly follow the sentiments of others, but see that their proceedings therein are in the liberty of the Truth."[2] This is in relation to the act called the Test Act, passed by the General Assembly in June of the same year. Suspected persons of ques-

---

[1] *S. K. M. M. R.*, vol. ii. p. 55.
[2] Appendix, Minute of Meeting for Sufferings.

tionable loyalty to the United Colonies were required to subscribe to a declaration that the war against Great Britain was "just and necessary" and to promise to afford no assistance to the king's armies or fleets, but hearty aid in the defense of the United Colonies. A special clause provides that "in case any person so summoned shall produce a certificate from the Clerk of any Meeting of the Friends, that he is in unity with that society, or shall make the affirmation directed in an act entitled 'An act for the relief of persons of tender consciences, and for preventing their being burthened with military duty,' he shall be excused from subscribing to the said declaration or test."[1]

The South Kingstown meeting accordingly took action and made the following minute, 11th month, 1776.

This meeting is informed that through late Laws Friends are subjected to severe penalties on certain Requifitions which they may be releafed and excused from by Producing a Certificate to the chief Officers from our Clerk Setting forth that they are members of the Religious So-

---

[1] *R. I. C. R.*, vol. vii. p. 568.

ciety called Quakers therefore the clerk is directed to make and Sign Certificates to our members applying for the same where no diforder or irregularity doth appear and every such applying member is earnestly desired to Examine and see that nothing be done out of the truth that our Teftimony may be preferved pure and no reproach brought upon friends.[1]

But though the meeting was so strong in its testimony against war, it was very pitiful for the suffering which followed in its wake.

1st 1mo 1776

It is the advice of this meeting that all friends that has suffered or may hereafter Suffer on acc' of milliterry Services send the acc'ˢ and prices thereof in Value of sᵈ Sufferings to the Clerk of this meeting and for the Clerk to Transmit an acc' to the meeting for Sufferings.[2]

Thomas Hazard, from the first, was a member of this Meeting for Sufferings,[3] and was present at every meeting for the first two years, fifteen meetings in all, and very

<hr>

[1] *S. K. M. M. R.*, vol. ii. p. 51.
[2] *Ibid.*
[3] *R. I. Yearly Meeting Records*, 1776.

regularly throughout the troublous times. Nor was Friends' concern confined to their own society. Thomas Hazard was one of the signers of the address sent to both General Washington and General Howe. " As visiting the fatherlefs & the widows," it reads, " and relieving the distrefsed by feeding the hungry & clothing the naked, is the subjcct of this addrefs we cannot doubt of thy attention to our representation and request on their behalf." It informs the generals that the petitioners have been intrusted with a considerable sum of money from Friends in Pennsylvania and New Jersey, and asks leave to enter Boston to seek and relieve sufferers. John Collins, T. Hazard, Moses Farnum, I. Lawton, and Moses Brown are the signers.[1] At the meeting for sufferings of 2d month, 1776, T. Hazard, son of Robert, and Moses Brown make report that the committee have distributed the donation to the late sufferers in Boston and Charlestown, now dispersed through various towns which are mentioned, " the n° of necefsitous families & single persons being 141, & the am't distributed (at this time) £229, 4ˢ as pʳ accᵗ." These two friends had the towns about

---

[1] *R. I. Yearly Meeting Records.*

Washington's headquarters at Cambridge assigned them as their district, and the " great Bay Mare " never made a more important journey. It was perhaps of this journey that a charming story is told. College Tom, oppressed doubtless with a sense of the difficulties of his task, and the sad state of his country, mounted his horse and rode down the lane followed by the loving eyes of his wife, and the bright gaze of a young relative. As he disappeared, the girl turned to go in, when her aunt said, " Wait a moment, he has forgotten something," and presently the clatter of the horse's hoofs was heard returning. Up the lane he rode, stooped and kissed his waiting wife, and set off with good courage upon his journey.

The war pressed close home, when it came not only to Newport, but to the very borders of Thomas Hazard's farm. On the 31st of 8th month, 1778, —

The preparative meeting of So. Kingstown informs this meeting y' the Old Meeting House in s'' Town has been lately occupied as a Hofpital for the sick lately landed out of the French fleet and greatly Damaged and likewife a pale and

board fence almost wholly Diſtroyed.
Therefore Andrew Nichols Jr. and
Thomas Hazard of Rob‘ are appointed to
apply to the Barrak maſter (and Others
whoſe right and Buſineſs it is or may be)
requeſting the reparation of s⁴ Houſe and
fences or adequate Damages therefor.[1]
The committee on damages soon —

... report that they Understood thirty
pounds only of the £54 and upward which
the Damages done to s⁴ House & Fences
about the Lott were Eſtimated at were
allowed & that s⁴ thirty pounds was not
yet paid Therefore Thomas Hazard is
Deſired to apply for the same.[2]

This experience in treating with French
officers fitted him to serve on the committee
of Friends at Newport in 1781, which was
instructed to wait upon the Commander-in-
Chief of the French Army, as the meeting
deems " it incumbent to uphold our Christian testimony against our houses of worship
being used for purposes of war." The
French officers who were in possession of
the meeting-house treated the committee respectfully, " and according to aſsurance then

---

[1] *S. K. M. M. R.*, vol. ii. p. 109.
[2] *Ibid.*, vol. ii. p. 113.

given caused the house to be cleared & in a few days the key to be delivered up & the house in our quiet pofefsion." [1]

In this year he was also on a committee to draw up and sign a statement of what " may be best to transmit to posterity " as to the sufferings of friends for the Testimony of the Society. This paper has not been found, but it can hardly carry greater weight, as to the principle involved, than the minute recorded in College Tom's own hand expressing the sense of the South Kingstown meeting : —

25th 6mo. 1781.

This meeting being under a weighty concern to maintain the several Branches of Our Chriftian Teftimony and as that against war or Contributing thereto is One wherein wee at present are Tried in a more Especial Manner Therefore Tho⁵ Hazard Tho⁵ Wilbur Jnᵒ Knowles and Amos Collins are appointed to Vifit Friends in their Families and to Encourage them to have an Ear open to the Voice of Truth in their Own Hearts & to attend to its Inftruction regarding Every Tender Scroople not Only respect-

---

[1] *R. I. Yearly Meeting Records,* 1781.

ing the Payment of such requisitions as
are or may be wholly for the Purpofes of
war; But alfo where they may be mixed
And to be fully perfuaded that they move
therein Confiftant with the mind of
Truth believing that thofe who Doubt
and yet Pertake are Condemned. S[d]
committee are to make report as soon as
they conveniently can.[1]

The diary of Nailer Tom shows how
close home the trial pressed. May 8th,
1779 " Regulars landed in Point Judith "
is his laconic record. On the 21st of the
same month " The Regulars landed last
night and carried off negroes," he says. A
week later " the privateersmen took the
fish boats. I went to see them," he adds.
The next month, June 2d, while he " held
harrow for Cousin Hazard," and " Planted
our beans," " Chaddock was taken in his
fish boat by the Privateersmen." A few
days later " The Regulars landed and took
Samuel Congdon " and " burnt two houses
last night." All this happened in the early
days of June; on the 12th there was " an
alarm in the night."[2] But in spite of it

<hr>

[1] *S. K. M. M. R.*, vol. ii. p. 273.
[2] *Narr. Hist. Register*, vol. i. No. 1, pp. 39–40.

all the daily life went on, and Nailer Tom hoed corn and made stone wall for Cousin Hazard. Cousin Hazard is an important figure in his diary. He helps him make hay, bring home his wheat and rye; "Cousin Hazards bees swarmed and flew away into Knowles' garden "[1] is a fact important enough to make the item of a day. He lodges and dines with Cousin Hazard, and records the visitors there. "The three Suseys," Susey Hazard, Susey Champlin, and another cousin "staid at cousin Hazard's." "Tommy and Nancy" came to the old home, "Tommy," the second son, who is called so by all his contemporaries, having married Anna Rodman, June 6, 1780. He was the first son to leave home, going "into the verge of Greenwich meeting," the records declare, and then to New Bedford, the home of his charming wife, where he became a whaling merchant, and finally to New York. Robert, the eldest son, went to Vermont about 1790, apparently; as late as 1794, Thomas Hazard, Jr., writing to his daughter Sarah, who is visiting her grandparents at Tower Hill, says that "thy grandfather's journey into Vermont I

<hr>

[1] *Narr. Hist. Register*, vol. i., No. 4, p. 283.

fear will be too much for him at this advanced time of life."[1]   The third son, Rowland, applied to the monthly meeting, in 1790, for a certificate, as he was going to Charleston, South Carolina, on "outward bufinefs and has the profpect of Rifiding there for a time."[2]   So Thomas Hazard's house was left desolate.   In this same year also the meeting is informed that the "old Meeting Houfe is demolished by fire," and that Friends "now have no settled place to meet in."[3]   College Tom was immediately put upon the committee "to Confider of a Size Suitable to build a meetinghous where the old hous was;" but it seems an epitome of the shattered life of the countryside, so desolated by war that the very meeting was rendered homeless for the time.

But brighter days came to the farm with the coming of the sweet daughter-in-law, after whom Peace Dale is named. She came to Narragansett as the bride of Rowland Hazard during the summer of 1794, and was greeted by the large family con-

---

[1] *Extracts from The Journal of Sarah Howland,* compiled by Howland Pell, p. 84.

[2] *S. K. M. M. R.,* vol. iii. p. 22.   [3] *Ibid.,* vol. iii. p. 8.

nection with great cordiality. The few who remember her speak of her with great enthusiasm as a most sensible and delightful woman. Thomas Hazard, Jr., writing to his young daughter at Tower Hill, quaintly expresses his admiration. " I fully rely," he writes, " on thy attention to the advice & council of thy grandmother and aunt whose refined experience will be improving to thee." [1]

The long life of College Tom was now drawing to a close. He had lived to see great changes. Born in an almost patriarchal state of society, surrounded with slaves, with many relatives as his companions, with many acres under cultivation by his father, and the colonists loyal subjects of the king, he now saw the great farms divided, the country impoverished, and launched on its independent career, and, what he most cared for, the Society of Friends in Rhode Island owning not a slave among its members, and using all the force of its example as well as its preaching to exterminate the slave trade. His long efforts had borne fruit. In his latter years, Thomas R. Hazard says he used himself as

[1] *Extracts from The Journal of Sarah Howland*, p. 85.

an example of the deceitfulness of the human heart. It was a point of doctrine he had always sought to inculcate in his preaching, but he at last discovered, he said, "that he himself had ruled South Kingstown monthly meeting forty years, in his own will, before he found it out!"[1]

As Mrs. Hutchinson and her followers appeared in the very early part of our narrative, Jemima Wilkinson appears in these last years. She had her following on Kingston Hill, the Little Rest which under her despotic sway must have literally deserved its name. Husbands were parted from wives, and children from parents. She attempted to raise the dead; the Universal Friend became the author of discord. In 1784, the year which saw the culmination of so many of Thomas Hazard's hopes, she left Narragansett for her " New Jerusalem " in the Genesee Country.[2] What Thomas Hazard thought of these proceedings we do not know. It is another instance of the individualism which marked the Narragansett Country that the prophetess flourished in it so long.

[1] T. R. Hazard, *Recollection of Olden Times*, p. 108.
[2] Updike, p. 233.

But New Lights, and Ranters, and wars, and demolitions by fire, began to lose their interest to the old man so touchingly described by his daughter-in-law.

MARY PEACE HAZARD TO ROWLAND HAZARD.

SOUTH KINGSTOWN, Oct. 17, 1796.

As to thy father or mother taking charge of it (the farm) it is impossible for thy father seems to notice nothing. He is no more than a child. I do not think he can live much longer. He goes to meeting of a first day but the only way he knows when it comes is by having a clean shirt given him to put on. He does not go on fifth days because he does not know when it comes. He has at present, I believe, gotten a bad cold for his back is so lame he cannot turn himself in bed. He has been so for three or four days. Thy mother is also very poorly. There is scarcely ever a day but she is obliged to lie down three or four times. She has been the same way all the spring and summer. She has got a complaint I hardly think she will get rid of. Dr. Easton has been to see her several times but he does not do her any good. He has been over here on account of a lawsuit he has with Tommy Hazard the blacksmith and stayed here night before last. Thy mother talked with him about herself. He has promised to send her some medicine over by the first opportunity but he does not seem to have much faith in it himself. He told her she might depend upon it that if it did her no good it would do her no harm.

There were still two years which College Tom had to live, and it is almost a relief to find the entry in the Friends Meeting Records, —

Thomas Hazard Son of Robert and Sarah Hazard Departed this Life the 26th of 8th M° 1798 about 8 o'clock in the Evening and was buried the 28th of the Same Who Was in the 78th year of his age[1]

That is all; there is no word of eulogy, no mention of his long and faithful service, no statement even of the meeting for his funeral, or the place of his burial. Tradition says that his grave was made in the burial

[1] *S. K. M. M. Records* of Births, Marriages, and Deaths. "Old Book," p. 27.

ground of the old Meeting-house he loved, but the life that he lived, a life full of the faithful performance of the daily duty, full of high and strenuous endeavor for all right thinking and noble living, the life which served his own day so well, has left its impress upon succeeding generations.

APPENDIX.

SELECTIONS FROM COLLEGE TOM'S PAPERS.

1698–1795.

I. Mr. Samuell Sewall's Deed.

(Parchment, twenty-six inches by thirteen.)

THIS INDENTURE made the Twenty Eighth day of
Aprill Anno Domⁱ One thousand Six hundred Ninety
and Eight And in the Tenth Yeare of the Reigne of
our Sovereigne Lord King William the Third over
England &cᵃ. BETWEEN Samuell Sewall of Boston
in the County of Suffolke within his Majᵗⁱᵉˢ Province
of the Massachusetts Bay in New England Esqʳ
and Hannah his wife of the one part, and Thomas
Hazard of Boston Neck in the Kings Province or
Narragansett Country in New England aforesaid Yeoman on the other part WITTNESSETH that the said
Samuell Sewall and Hannah his said wife for and in
Consideraton of the Summe of Seaven Hundred
Pounds Current money of New England to them in
hand paid and Secured in the Law to be paid att and

before the Ensealeing and delivery of these presents by the said Thomas Hazard, wherewith they acknowledge themselves to be fully Satisfied and contented. And therefore they the said Samuell Sewall and Hannah his said wife HAVE given granted bargained Sold aliened enfeoffed conveyed and confirmed, and by these presents for themselves and their heires DOE ffully freely cleerly and absolutely give grant bargaine Sell aliene enfeoffe convey and confirme unto the said Thomas Hazard his heires and assignes for ever THREE HUNDRED Acres of Land of their ffarme Scittuate lying and being in the Pettaquamscot Purchase in the Narragansett Country aforeſᵈ which Robert Hannah Lately occupied; which said three Hundred Acres of Land is butted and bounded Southwest upon Land of Jahleel Brenton, Northeaſt by Samuel Wilſons Land and Northweſt by Land of the said Sewall Vizᵗ the remaining Two hundred acres of ſaid ffarme reserved to him said Sewall thereont next Sacatuckett River.   Alſo all their Shares right and Jntereſt of and in the Lands on yᵉ Neck called and knowne by the name of LITTLE POINT JUDITH NECK.   ALSO all that their Lott of Land containing by Eſtimaĉon Six hundred Acres be the ſame more or leſs lying in the Narragansett Country aforeſᵈ by the seaside there, being the Lott Nº 2 and is bounded Westward by the Lott of Thomas Mumford, and Eastward by the Lott of Benedict Arnold or however otherwise the premisses are bounded or reputed to be bounded.   TOGETHER with all and Singular the profitts priviledges wayes Easements rights Libertyes advantages benefits comodities hereditaᵐᵗˢ emoluments and appurtenanses whatsoever to the said granted and bargained premiſses

and to every part and parcel thereof belonging or in
any wise appertaining or therewith now or heretofore
used occupyed or enjoyed. AND the reverĉon and
reverĉons remainder and remainders rents iſsues and
profitts thereof. AND alſo all the Eſtate right title
Intereſt inheritance use poſseſsion Dower thirds property claims and demand whatsoev^r of them the ſaid
Samuell Sewall and Hannah his said wife and of
either of them of in and to the Same and every part
thereof To HAVE AND TO HOLD all the above and before mentioned granted and bargained premisses with
th' appurtenances and every part and parcel thereof
unto the said Thomas Hazard his heires and afsignes
forever. To his and their owne Sole and proper uſe
benefitt and behoof from henceforth and forever
more. AND the ſaid Samuel Sewall and Hannah his
said wife, and their heires, all and Singular the before
hereby granted and bargained premisses and every
part and parcel thereof with th' appurtenances unto
the said Thomas Hazard his heires and afsignes,
againſt them the said Samuell Sewall and Hannah his
said wife their heires and afsignes, and every of them,
and againſt all and every person and persons claimeing by from or under them or any of them Shall and
will warrant uphold and forever defend by these presents. AND the said Samuell Sewall and Hannah his
said wife for themſelves their heires Executo^{rs} and
Administratores hereby covenant promiſe grant and
agree to and with the ſ^d Thomas Hazard his heires
and afsignes in manner following THAT IS TO SAY
That he the ſaid Thomas Hazard his heires and afsignes and every of them Shall and may by force and
virtue of these presents from henceforth and forever

hereafter Lawfully freely peaceably and quietly have hold use occupy pofsefsn and enjoy all and Singular the abovegranted and bargained premifses with th' appurtenances and every part and parcel thereof : and all and every the rents ifsues and profitts thereof, without any manner of Lett Suite trouble vexation eviction disturbance hindrance or moleftation whatsoev^r of the f^d Samuel Sewall and Hannah his s^d wife their heires or afsignes or of any other person or persons whatsoev^r, any thing haveing or Lawfully claimeing in the said premifses or any part thereof from by or under them or any of them. FREE AND CLEERE and cleerly acquitted exonareted and discharged of and from all and all manner of former and other gifts grants bargaines Sales Leases releases mortgages Joyntures dowers Judgements Executions entailes fines forfeitures Seizures amerciaments and of and from all other titles troubles charges and Incumbrances whatsoever had made committed done or Suffered to be done or to be had made cõmitted done or Suffred to be done by the said Samuel Sewall and Hannah his said wife or either of them their or either of their heires or afsignes or any others by their or any of their meanes act consent privity or procurement att any time or times before or after the enfealeing hereof IN WITTNEfSE whereof the said Samuel Sewall and Hannah his s^d wife party to thefe prefents have hereunto Sett their hands and Seales the day and yeare firft abovewritten.

SAM SEWALL   HANNAH SEWALL

(Two seals.)

Endorsement on back.

Rec^d the day and yeare firſt within written of the within named Thomas Hazard the Summe of ffive hundred Pounds Current money of New England in part pay^{mt} of the purchase consideracõn within menc̃oned, and taken his bond or obligacõn for the other Two hundred pounds.

Sam Sewall.

Signed Sealed and Deli^{vd} in preſence of us
William Longfellow
Joseph Gariſh

Boston Aprill 28th 1698

The within named Samuell Sewall Eſq^r and Hannah his wife perſonally appeareing before me the Subſcriber one of the members of his Maj^{ties} Council for the province of the Maſsachusetts Bay in New England & Juſtice of Peace in the Same Acknowledged this Instru^{mt} to be their ffree and voluntary act & deed.

John Walley

Memorandum that on the fowrth day of May : Anno Domⁱ 1698 Full quiet and peaceable poſseſsion of all and every ye Lands within mentioned to be granted was Taken and Had by Thomas Mumford of Poynt Judith in the Naragansett Country Yeoman the Attorny of the within named Samuell Sewall and Hannah his wife by force and virtue of a Letter of attorney to the ſ^d Thomas Mumford in that behalf by them made beareing date ye 28th day of April 1698. For and in behalf of the said Samuell Sewall and Hannah Sewall. AND was afterwards by the Same authority for and in their name delivered by the fᵈ Thomas Mumford unto the within named Thomas Hazzard. To hold to him the fᵈ Thomas Hazard his heires and aſsignes according to yᵉ forme & Effect of the within written deed. In preſence of those whoſe names are hereunto ſubſcribed.

JOSEPH HULL
NATHANAEL NILES
The mark of ✕ ROBERT
NICOL

All the within and before Written Inſtruments are Recorded orderly In the 19. 20 & 21 pages of the Second Booke of Land Evidences belonging to Kingstown Nᵒ. 3 Aprill the 8th 1714.

Pᵗ   SAMˡˡ FONES Town Clerke

Endorsed on the back,
   Mʳ Samuell Sewall's deed.

II. RECEIPT FOR RENT FROM MR. BRENTON.

Newport June the 6th 1702 then received of Mʳ Thomas Hazard Six pounds current money of New England, it being in full for four Years Rent of a lott of Land in the Little neck in Pettaquamſcut from Lady Day 1698 to Lady Day 1702.

Pᵗ me JAHLEEL BRENTON.

III. LETTER FROM JUDGE SEWALL TO THOMAS HAZARD.

(Paper written on two sides of a double sheet.)

BOSTON Feby 21 1689.

MAJ^R. WALLEY

Sir, I have rec'd a letter from the Pettaquamscot Purchasers earnestly soliciting me either to meet them myself at Pettaquamscot, or Newport, or else to impower some body in my Stead to give them a Meeting for the further settlement & Division of our Lands ; that so there may be a bar laid in the way of those who are ready enough to take the advantage in this time of so much Lawlefs Liberty, to intrude themselves into the Pofsefsions & Lands of others, to the exclufion of the Rightfull Owners. My Circumftances are such that I cannot attend it myself, and I Intreat you to pardon my freedom with you in defiring you to undertake so troublesome a piece of Service for me. Necefsity in a great meafure puts me upon it, not knowing whom to impower : and the concern is not to be slighted wherefore I hope you will deny yourself so far as to engage in it. I presume they have by them a Copy of their Letter to me, which will give you an account of the businefs. I would intreat you in all respects to act in my behalf as you would do for your self were the Case your own as it is mine. Tis like they may not speak of dividing Point Judith Neck. If they find it necefsary, I have the Right of two elevenths at leaft, if not more ; and in the Little Neck by the outlet had more –en [then ?] half, if not all ; till I sold one Share to my Tenant Robt Hannah whom intreat you to Salute and encourage in my Name when you see him.   He is Son in Law to Mr Wilson one of the purchasers.   &c &c.

MR. THOMAS HAZARD, What is above written, and that on the foregoing fide, is a true extract copyed out of my Letter to Major John Walley deceafed, when he dwel'd at Briftol ; as it ftands enterd in my Booke of Letters.   I am

<table>
<tr><td>I have fent you one of my Leafes to Robert Hannah.</td><td>Sir, your friend & Servt SAMUEL SEWALL.</td></tr>
</table>

I have fent you   Sir, your friend & Servt
one of my Leafes   SAMUEL SEWALL.
to Robert Hannah.
  Bofton ; Novr 5th
  1716.
(Addressed) For
            Mr. Thomas Hazard
                  At Kingston
                        Narraganfet

IV. OPINION OF THE KING'S ATTORNEY GENERAL
     IN REGARD TO A QUAKER GOVERNOR.

(Written on three sides of a double sheet.)

Cafe
  The Colony of Rhode Island by Virtue of their Charter granted them by King Charles Anno 1663 Annually Elects their own Govern^r. & Inferior Officers both Civil & Military.
  Qu^r.   Whither One of the People called Quakers upon being chosen Govern^r of the said Colony is Oblidged to take a Solemn Oath to the Acts of Trade considering our Charter and the Indulgence granted them by Act of Parliament in Respect to Oaths And whither a Solemn Engagement upon an Affirmation is not Sufficient in that Cafe.

I Have Perufed & Confidered that Clause in the Charter which Relates to the Election of a Governour and likewife that Clause which Directs that before his Entry upon his Office he shall give a Solemn Engagement by Oath or Otherwife for the due and faithfull Performance of his Duty.

I Have likewife read over the Opinion of M^r. Auchmuty which was left along with this And am of Opinion that a Quaker if duly elected Governour may act as Such without being Oblidged to take any Oath whatfoever.

The Solemn Engagement which he is *to* Oblidged to enter into by the Charter may be by Oath or Otherwife And inftead of the Abjuration Oath and the Oath of allegiance and Supremicy There are Certain forms of Affirmation or Declaration prefcribed by the Stat. 8 G. j. to be taken by Quakers in lieu thereof.

As to the Oath directed to be taken by the Governours of English Plantations by the Stat. 7 & 8 W & 8 & 9 W for the Obfervance of the Several Acts relating to the faid Plantations I am of Opinion upon Confideration of the Several Acts made in favour of Quakers That if a Quaker Governour Solemnly Affirms in the form Prefcribed by act of Parliament *That he will Obferve the Several Acts relating to the English Plantations ;* Such Affirmation will be deemed a sufficient Complyance in him to the faid Two Acts 7 & 8 W & 8 & 9 W And will exempt him from the Penalties of thefe acts.

> J WILLES Aug^st 26th 1734
> A True Copy
> Exam per J LYNDON Cler

London 6mo. the 27th 1734.

Govern Wanton

This Serves to Inclofe the Kings Attorney Generals Opinion Upon the Cafe relating to a Gov of your Colony that may be one of the People called Quakers which Opinion I think is Entirely with us I am in great Hopes and expectation That the next Letter will bring me the Agreeable Advife of what I requested of the Colony respecting the Augmentation of my Salary which I really deferve confidering the Paines I take to Serve the Colony with faithfullnefs who Am Thy afsured Friend.

R. Patridge

We have no Warr yet

30th D. Pray Acquaint my Friends Goulding Wanton & Coddington I have this Day rec the Gold Dust per Wimple, and in my Next fhall advife them of it and what Price I sell it for and that I have got £200 Insur'd on the Guns per Roufe Potter   R. P.

A True Copy

Exam per J. Lyndon Cler.

V. Attestation of Thomas Foxcroft and Charles Chauncy.

(Paper written on three sides of a double sheet.)

We the Subfcribers, Teaching Elders or Pastors of the first gathered (com.ly called the Old) Church in Boston New England being desired to give our Attestation to what we know of Mefs.rs *Wm Brenton, John Hull & Samuel Wilbore* ancient Members of Our said Church and whose Names are mention'd among the *Petaquamfcut* Purchases.

This is to Certifie all whom it may Concern

That in the said Churche's Book of Records in Folio (carefully preserved) We find the following entries made fairly written At the head of Page 4th Stand these words " *Members admited into Boston Church* " — and underneath the body of said Page is written " *In the 8th Month* 1633 *William Brenton* " with others. In the next page we find this Entry " *Members further Admited upon the* 1st *of the* 10th *Month* 1633 *Samuel Willbore* &c And in the 26th page still under the head of Members admitted in this Entry " *The* 15th *Day of the* 8th *Month* 1648 (*by Elder Oliver*) *John Hull the son of our Brother Robert Hull* " &c.

That Our said Church was from the beginning (Anno 1630) accounted One of the Strictest Congregationall Churches in all New England : That the Ancient Custom of the said Church has been to admit her Adult Male Members (1) By an Examination of them per the Elders both as to their Doctrinall Faith and Experimental Piety &c (2) by their being openly propounded by the Elders sometime before hand in the Publick Assembly : (3) By their Exhibiting a Relation of their said faith & Experience to the Church in Publick : (4) By the Vote of the Brethren of the Church in publick : & (5) By a Publick entring into an Exprefs & Solemn Covenant with God and with the Church ; according to the known ancient & usual Practice of Churches Congregationall.

That our said Church was wont from the beginning to Exercise a strict watch and Discipline over her Members : that her Ancient Records Report to us Numerous Instances of Church Censures both of Excommunication & Admonition pafsd upon her faulty Members

together with the Faults perticularly Specified   But of
the above mentioned *Brenton Hull & Wilbore* we find
no Censure or fault mentioned throughout the Records
Indeed whereas the said *Brenton & Wilbore* with
divers others of the Members of Our Church (as
't is reported) did about the Year 1638 Remove to
a Place then Called *Aquethnick* the same which is
now Called *Rhode Island* We find an Entry made in
Our said Book of Records (page 12) in the following
words

"*The 16th Day of the 12th Month 1639   Our Brethren Mr William Hibbon Captaine Edward Gibon &
Mr John Oliver were Chosen & Delegated by the
Church to go to the Island of Aquethnicke to enquire of
the State of Matters amongst our Brethren there and to
require some satisfactory Answer about such things as
appear to be Offensive amongst them.*"   Which Records
Show both the covenanted Memberſhip of the Aquethnick Brethren with the said Church and the Church's
Brotherly Affection and Concern for them upon the
Rumor of Offensive things among them but no mention do we find in the Records of any fault of the said
Brethren either before or after ; nor of any Dealing
with them.   And as for the said *Mr Hull* it is well
known he Continued with Our Church till the Year
1669 when he became one of the Founders or first Con-
stituents of the 3d gather'd Congregationall Church
in Boston commonly Called the South Church.   This
Gentleman Was the Treasurer & a Magistrate of the
Maſsachusets Colony, chosen in those times by the
Freemen of the Colony and Maintain'd the Character
both of a Congregational Man and a ſtrictly Pious
Christian to the Day of his Death Octobr 1683 Which
was before there appear'd any Aſsembly of Church

of England People in all this Country : the first, and
that a very small one, being set up at Boston about
three Years after the said *Mr Hull's* Decease.
The late Reverend *Mr Willard* then Pastor of the
said South Church, embalm'd his Memory in An
Excellent Funeral Sermon in Print ; wherein he Observes, " *This Church hath lost an Honovrable Mem-*
ber" &c And having given him a High & Just
Character one Article of which is " *The Honourable*
Respect he bore to God's Holy Ordinances by Deligently
attending upon them " &c. He Closes his Commen-
dation of Mr Hull with this Remarkable Exprefsion
among others ; " *His Constancy in all these, while*
Times have Changed — will fpeak the Sincerity of his
Profefsion "

Boston N E   THOMAS FOXCROFT
Jan^r 29 1735   CHARLES CHAUNCY

Nova Angliâ I Joseph Marion Notary & Tabellion
Publick Dwelling in Boston in New England by
Royall Authority Duly admitted & sworn do hereby
Certifie all whom it may Concern. That the Reverend Mefs^{rs} Thomas Foxcroft & Charles Chauncy
above Named are Pastors of the first gather'd (Commonly called the Old) Church in Boston New England who have Signed the foregoing Certificate by
whom Certificates of the like Nature are usually made
out and attested and accordingly full Faith &
Credit is and ought to be given to such the Attestation both in Judgment Court & without and I
further Certifie that the said Mefs^{rs} Foxcroft &
Chauncey signed the said Certificate in Presence of
me the said Notary Thus Done at Boston in New
England this 29 Day of January A D One Thousand

Seven hundred & Thirty five Anno R^i, R^{is}, Georgij
Secundi Magnæ Britanniæ Nono
  Quod attestor manu Sigilloq^e Officij
  Rogatus

JOS MARION Not^{is} Pub^{cus}
1735

VI.   WILL OF THOMAS HAZARD.

*(Six Sheets of Manuscript, acknowledgment and appeal
on the seventh.)*

I Thomas Hazard of South Kingstown in the Colony of Rhode Island &c Yeoman being Ancient and unwell but of Sound mind and Memory thanks be given unto God, Do therefore make my Laft Will and Teftament and as touching Such Worldly Eftate Wherewith it hath pleafed God to blefs me in this Life I give Devife and Difpofe of the Same in the following manner and form

IMPRIMIS My Will is That all my Juft Debts and funerall Charges be paid and Difcharged in Some Convenient time after my Deceafe by my Executor hereafter Named Out of my perfonale Eftate

ITEM I give and bequeath unto my beloved Sons, VIZ, Jeremiah Hazard, George Hazard, Benjamin Hazard, and Jonathan Hazard, the sum of Twenty Shillings Currant Money, to be Equally, Divided amongft them that is to Say five Shillings Each to them their Heirs and Affignes for Ever, they haveing all and Each of them Receiv'd their portions Allready, To be paid in Old Tenor So Called,

ITEM I give and Bequeath unto my beloved Grandfon Fones Hazard One piece or tract of Land Scituate Lying and being in S^d. South Kingstown on the back Side of the Pond, So Called, and is part of a tract of

Land I purchafed of Samuel Sewell Late of Bofton
Deceafed Containing Two Hundred and Sixty Acres
or thereabouts, and is bounded Northerly by Land of
Said Fones Hazard Eafterly by Land of John Potter
Southerly by the Sea and Wefterly by Land of Job
Cord, I alfo give and Bequeath unto my Said Grand-
son Fones Hazard Two Other pieces of Land Scituate
Lying and being in Said South Kingstown the Biggeft
piece Containing About One Hundred and Seventeen
Acres, More or Lefs, Bounded partly on Land of
James Perry and partly on Land of John Seagars,
Eafterly on Land of George Babcock, and Southerly
on a High Way, and Wefterly on S^d Perry the Other
Piece of Land Scituate Lying and being in Said South
Kingstown Containing About Thirty Seven Acres,
bounded by Land of Said Perry Northerly, and Eaft-
erly by Land of John Seagars. Southerly on the
Other piece Laft Mentioned and Wefterly on Land of
Said Perry all Which three tracts of Land, I give and
Bequeath unto my Said Grandfon Fones Hazard to
him and his Heirs for Ever and my Will is That if my
Said Grandfon Fones Hazard Should Dye Leaving no
Lawfull Iffue, that then the Said three tracts of Land,
Shall return unto my four Sons Viz Robert Hazard
George Hazard Benjamin Hazard and Jonathan Haz-
ard and Shall be Equally Divided Amongft my Said
four Sons, and return to them their Heirs and Affigns
for Ever, AND FURTHER my Will is that if my Said
Grandson Fones Hazard Should Leave any Lawfull
Iffue When he Dyeth and his Iffue Should Dye
before they Arrive at Lawfull Age of Twenty One
Years and have no Lawfull Iffue, that then and in
that Case the three pieces or tracts of Land hereby
given and Bequeathed unto my S^d Grandson Shall

for Want of Such Iſſue, the Same Shall return unto
my Said four Sons, as Above ſaid to them their Heirs
and Aſſignes for Ever

ITEM I give and Bequeath unto my beloved
Daughter Hannah Eaſton the Sum of five Shillings
Currant Money Old Tenor, to her, her Heirs and
Aſſignes for ever She haveing Received her portion
Already to be paid by my Executor hereafter Named,

ITEM I give and Bequeath unto my two beloved
Grand Daughters Merrian Hazard and Hannah Eaſ-
ton Children of my Daughter Mary Eaſton Late of
Newport Deceaſed the Sum, of One Hundred pounds
Currant Money Old Tenor, to Each of them my Said
Grand Daughters to be paid them by my Executor
hereafter Named in ten Years After my Diſceaſe, but
if it Should happen that Either of my Said Grand
Daughters Should Dye before the Expiration of S^d
Ten Years, in that Caſe my Will is, that the Survivor
of them Shall have the Whole of Said Two Hundred
pounds at the time Aboveſ^d but if it Should happen
that both my S^d Grand Daughters Should Dye before
the Expiration of Said Term and Leave no Lawfull
Iſſue in that Caſe the Said Legacy Shall be Void and
Ceaſe, but if Otherwiſe then to be to them their Heirs
and Aſſignes for Ever

ITEM I give and Bequeath unto my beloved Grand
Daughter Mary Hazard, and to her heirs and Aſſignes
for Ever the Sum of fifty pounds Currant Money Old
Tenor, to be paid in ten Years After my Diſceaſe by
my Executor hereafter Named

ITEM I give and Bequeath unto my beloved Grand
Daughter Suſannah Gardner and to the Heirs of her
Body, the Sum of fifty pounds Currant Money Old
Tenor to be paid by my Executor here after Named,

in ten Years After my Difceafe, and to be Equally Divided Amongft her Heirs After her

ITEM I give and Bequeath unto the Children of my Grand Daughter Ruth Underwood Deceafed the Sum of fifty pounds Currant Money, Old Tenor, to be Equally Divided Amongft them and paid by my Executor hereafter Named in Ten Years Affter my Deceafe, and to be to them their Heirs and Affignes for Ever

ITEM I give and Bequeath unto my beloved Daughter Sarah Eafton The Sum of Two Hundred pounds Currant Money, Old Tenor, to be paid to her, by my Executor hereafter Named in ten Years After my Deceafe But Notwithftanding What is Abovefaid My Will is That if my Said Daughter Sarah Eafton Should have Occaffion of any part of Said Two Hundred pounds before the Expiration of the Said Term of ten Years after my Deceafe that then and in that Cafe my Executor Shall pay to her any part of Said Two Hundred pounds as her Neceffities may require at the Difcretion of my Executor and if it Should happen, that She my Said Daughter, Should Depart this Life before the Expiration of Said Ten Years, that then my Said Executor Shall pay unto her two Sons, James and John Eafton, the Said Two Hundred pounds to them or to their Heirs, or so much of it as may Remaine Over and Above of What She hath Received of the Said Two Hundred pounds

ITEM I give and Bequeath unto the Children of my Grand Daughter Sarah Gardner Which She had by Ichabod Potter Dec^d, the Sum of fifty pounds Currant Money Old Tenor, to be Equally Divided Amongft them and to their Heirs and Affignes for Ever to be paid by my Executor in ten Years After my Deceaſe.

ITEM I give and Bequeath unto my beloved Son Robert Hazard the Sum of five Shillings Currant Money, Old Tenor, I alſo give unto my Said Son Robert Hazard All the Remaining part Remainder and Reſidue of my Estate of What Kind Nature or Quality Soever Not before given Away by this preſent Will, Whom I alſo Conſtitute Make and Ordaine and Appoint my Said Son Robert Hazard my Whole and Sole Executor of this my Laſt Will and Teſtament And I do hereby Revoke and Diſſannull all and Every Will or Wills heretofore made by me, Rattifying and Allowing this and no Other to be my Laſt Will and Teſtament, IN Witneſs Whereof I have hereunto Sett my Hand and Seal this Twelfth Day of November Annoque Dom, One thouſand Seven Hundred and forty Six 1746

The Mark of Thomas T Hazard   (Seal.)

Sign'd Seal'd Publiſh'd pronou'ced and Declared by the Said Thomas Hazard to be his Laſt Will and Teſtament in preſence of us the Subſcribers,

JOHN HANDſON JUR
ABIGAIL HANDſON
JOHN HANDſON

SOUTH KINGSTOWN November 27th A. D. 1746

PERſONALLY appeared before the Town Council of said South Kingstown John Handſon Jun^{r,} Abigail Handſon and John Handſon, Witneſses to the aforegoing Inſtrument, And on their Solemn Engagements declared, That they saw Thomas Hazard late of South Kingstown deceased, Sign, Seal, and Declare the said aforegoing Inſtrument to be his laſt Will

and Teſtament And that in his preſence they set
their Hands as Witneſses thereunto, And that the
said Teſtator was in his perfect Mind and Memory
at the ſame time   The said laſt Will and Teſtament
being thus proved it is approved by the sᵈ· Town
Council.

Per order of the Town Council
BENJ^{a·} PECKCOM JUN^{r·} Cler. of the
Council for the day.

From which Judgment, Benjamin Hazard of South
Kingstown in behalf of Benjamin Hazard of Newport in the County of Newport prays an Appeal unto
yᵉ Governor & Council of the Colony of Rhode
Island which is granted, he the said Benjamin first
giving Bond to this Town Council to Proſecute sᵈ.
Appeal with effect

Per order of the Town Council
BENJ^{a·} PECKCOM Jun^{r·} Cler of
the Council for the day.

The above and aforegoing Instrument is Recorded
in the 181 : 182 : 183 : 184 : 185 and 186 Pages of the
Book of Records belonging to the Town Council of
South Kingstown, &c. Nᵒ· 4 Jan^{ry·} 9th day Annoque
Dom : 1746

By Th^{o·} HAZARD Cler. of the Concl :

OPINION OF THE GOVERNOR AND COUNCIL.

*Endorsed " Copy Judgment (Govr & Council) on the
Appeal Hazzard's vs Haſzard."*

At a General Council of the English Colony of Rhode
Island & Providence Plantations in New England
held at Newport within and for said Colony on the
fourth Monday of August in the Twenty second

Year of the Reign of his most sacred Majesty George the Second by the Grace of God of Great Britain France & Ireland King Defender of the Faith &c.

Benjamin Hafzard of Newport in the County of Newport Merchant and Thomas Haszard Junʳ of South Kingstown in the County of Kings County Yeoman Appellant from the Judgment of the Town Council of South Kingstown aforesaid held at said South Kingstown on the Twenty seventh Day of November in the year 1746 Robert Hafzard of said South Kingstown Yeoman Appellee By which Judgment a certain Instrument bearing Date the Twelfth Day of the same Month called The Last Will and Testament of Thomas Hafzard late of South Kingstown aforesaid Yeoman deceased was proved and approved And Now the Parties being heard by their Attorneys and John Handson, John Handson Junʳ and Abigail Handson Wittnefses to the said Will declared on their solemn Engagements that they saw the deceased Thomas Hafzard sign seal and declare the said Will to be his Last Will and Testament and that in his Presence they set their Hands thereto as Witnefses and that the said Testator was in his Perfect Mind and Memory at the same Time ON CONSIDERATION whereof and the Arguments of the Attorney of each Party This Council do confirm the Judgment appealed from and it is hereby confirmed.

A true Copy examᵈ by

THO WARD Secʸ

VII. A Copy of a Letter from Quebeck in
Canada, to a Pr— M——r in France, dated
October 11, 1747.

(Printed on three sides of a folio sheet.)

Great Sir,

Being refident for fome Years paft in this remote
Part of the World, and my chief Employ being to vifit
the feveral Nations of *Indians*, in order to eftablifh
them in the *Catholic* Religion, which makes them loyal
Subjects to his moft chriftian majefty our royal mafter; and agreable to your Inftructions, great Sir, I
have taken Pains to fettle a Correfpondence with
fome of our Friends among the Enemy, who have
given me a large Account of the feveral Provinces,
Cities, Towns, and Villages, along the Sea Coaft,
from South-Carolina to New-Foundland! A particular
Information would be incredible to you in *France*,
that in one Century fhould fpring out of a barren
Wildernefs, fuch a Number of fine large Cities, Towns,
and Villages, peopled in fo prodigious a Manner, as
to amount to many 100,000 Inhabitants; and their
Trade in Navigation is fo furprizingly large, that will
furmount your Belief, when I tell you, That their
Shipping large and fmall, is fo numerous as to amount
to feveral 1,000 Sail, that they even cover the Seas,
and carry on Trade to almoft all Parts of the World;
and by the beft and moft authentic Accounts I have
received, the Privateers fitted out of *North-America*,
viz. Boston, Rhode-Island, New-York and the feveral
Sea Port Towns, did us more Damage this War, by
diftreffing our Trade, and taking our Treafures coming from our Sugar Plantations, than all the *Englifh*
Men of War in the *American* Seas. The Privateers

were fo numerous, and of fuch Force, from 20 to 30 Guns, that would block up our Harbours, and take a Fleet of Ships at once, richly laden with Plantation Produce, befides Silver and Gold in Abundance. The Inhabitants of *North-America* have the Spirit and Blood of our *Oliver Cromwell;* they are of the Race of Puritans that fled into *New-England* in The time of Perfecution, and they maintain an implacable Hatred againft the *Romifh* Religion; and their refolution and undaunted Courage is fuch that whatever they undertake by Sea or Land againft us, they profecute with fuch violence, that we dread 1,000 of them, more than 5,000 hired Soldiers from *Old England:* Witnefs that unparrallel'd Conqueft of our *Cape-Breton;* such a Fortrefs as we did not fear all the World! But *Oliver*-like, They faid, *They could take it, and they would take it, and* (to the Surprize and Wonder of *all* the World) *they did take it!* They are as bold as Lions, and carry all before them! Their Principles are fuch, they have no Dread in Battle: They are taught they fhall not die a-moment before their Time; fo that if 10,000 Cannons are pointed at them, they regard it not: They feem to be like the *Ifraelites* of Old 1000 will put 10,000 to Flight; and we believe in *Canada*, if 20,000 Troops had come from *Old-England*, they never would have taken that Fortrefs; for you know, great Sir, fuch an Armament never fits out of England, but great Part of the Officers are *Scotch* and *Irifh*, and many of them of our Religion; but that is a Secret, and the major Part are feldom of any Religion: and as Money is what they are after, a fufficient Number of our *Louis d'Ores* will at any Time furnifh them with a tolerable Excufe to raife a siege and withdraw. What a fine Joke did our young Hero put upon General *Cope's* Army in *Scotland*, by our taking Care before Hand to have fome of our hearty Friends in Office in that Army ; but the Fate of our Friends in *Scotland* was, the Duke had a Number of New Troops raifed by fome Proteftant Noblemen, who filled up their Regiments with fuch Officers and Soldiers, that was not in our Power to bribe, nor had we Time to corrupt them ; that the Duke's Army was like thofe *New-England* Puritans, who have their Religion fo much at heart, that to deftroy our Holy Catholic Church is their Glory ; and I believe, better Subjects to a Proteftant Prince, is not to be found on the Globe ; they feem to be united as one Man againft us, except a Number of *Scotch* and *Irifh* that fled over to *New-England*, that are of our Religion and fome lately upon that fatal Battle at *Culloden :* and I underftand fome of the latter were Officers in Prince *Charles'* Army, and I truft our true Friends will promote them ; and now, great Sir, I will firft inform you of our prefent Circumftances in *Canada*, and then the Reafon *New-England* fo furprizingly exceeds us in Number of Men, Shipping, Trade *&c.* and then a Method to weaken and impov'rifh them, and advance ourfelves upon their Ruin. As to the inhabitants of *Canada*, our principal Men are Officers and Factors; the Officers are Spiritual and Military : We of the fpiritual Order, you know, great Sir, will have the Fat of the Land at Home or Abroad; the Civil and Military are yearly paid their feveral Salaries, with Cafh fent from our Royal Mafter, with which they make a confiderable Figure, the Planters and Artificers are generally very poor, feldom having any Money but when the Soldiers are paid off, and then they get a few Livres, but are immediately obliged to go and pay it to the Factors, who trufted them for fome coarfe Clothing, and the Factor fends the Cafh to *France* again, in order for a new Supply of Goods; and the poor Creatures feldom handle a Livre more, until the Soldiers are paid off again, and I am bold to fay, all our little Farmers and Mechanics are not able to build and fit out a Veffel of any Bignefs a foreign Voyage. If they can own a Fifhing Shallop, they are brave Fellows! And were it not for the Natives, by our extraordinary Pains and Induftry, we get and keep in our Intereft, we fhould be foon drove out by thefe implacable *Oliverians*. But I muft now inform you, the true Reafon our Enemies on the Sea Coaft, fo abundantly furmounts us in Men, Shipping, Trade, *&c.* as our Friends inform me: They fay, When thofe Puritans firft came over to *New-England*, they were distreffed, as we now are, for want of Money, and could not fit out a Ship nor Veffel no better than our Poor; but as Neceffity is the Mother of Invention, they got into a Method of making Paper Money, and it foon obtain'd a Currency, fo that in a little Time, the feveral Provinces got into the Practice, and furnifhed the Inhabitants with large Sums, at an eafy Lay, that in a fhort Time they were enabled to tear up Trees by the Roots, and to fplit the Rocks in Pieces, clear their Land, Fence it in, plough, fow, reap and mow, build Houfes, Ships, and Veffels of all forts, load them with Mafts, Spars, Boards, Staves, Oyl, Bone, Fifh, Tar, Turpentine, Iron, Beef, Pork, Butter, Cheefe, Wheat, Flour, Rice, Tobacco, Skins, Furs, *&c.* So that in half a Century they covered the Seas with Ships and Veffels, and fent them to foreign Markets, and in Return, over and above what Produce they wanted, they bought vaft Quantities of

Gold and Silver, and fent that Home to their Mother
Country to pay for what Neceffaries they wanted, having no use for the fame, fo long as Paper Currency
anfwers for a Medium of Trade. The making Paper
Money I am told has been of fuch general Advantage,
that they fend Home in hard Cafh, many £100,000
per Annum and there are very few poor amongft them.
The Farmers and Tradefmen of all forts, are jointly
concerned with the Merchant in building and fitting
out Ships and Veffels, and concerned in owning and
fitting out Privateers this War, fo that we need not
wonder the Seas were fo full of them out of *North-
America*, when all the Inhabitants of all Ranks and
Degrees are unanimoufly agreed to ferve their King
and Country, and diftrefs us, and all by the Help of
that pernicious Paper Money, that makes them rich
and powerful, able to do Wonders by Sea and Land.
I am told, the fmall petty Colony of *Rhode Island*, has
200 Sail of Veffels belonging to it, and had above 20
Sail of Privateers of large Force this War; and if the
Governments are fuffered to go on making Paper
Money, they will drive us out of this Part of the
World, without ony Help from their Mother Country.
And I muft tell you, great Sir, if Half the Force that
took *Cape-Breton* had come directly to *Quebeck*, we
fhould have furrend'red, for our chief Concern was
about packing up our Alls and vamping off, having a
Rumour of their coming; and we dreaded thefe Puritans, knowing there were none of our Religion amongft
them; and they were not to be bribed with *Louis
d'Ores*, as the *European* Officers often are: But the
Scheme I propofe, great Sir, is, I have certain Information, That great Numbers of the rich Merchants
have a Defire to have a final Stop Put to Paper

Money, by Reaſon the Planters and Mechanics run ſo much into Trade and Navigation, that they cannot endure their fellow Functioners ſhould grow rich by the ſame Advantage as they got their Eſtates by.

It ſeems moſt of the rich Merchants in the ſeveral Governments were originally mean Farmers and Tradeſmen, as Shoemakers, Taylors, Copperſmiths, Carpenters, and the like : But what Need we care what they were, or what they are, if we can accompliſh our Ends by their Help ; and to bring this about, great Sir, we muſt employ our Friends at *London* and elſewhere, and adviſe them to make our *Scotch* Friends in the ſeveral Towns in *New-England* popular, by putting them into Buſineſs, as Maſters of Ships, and by Conſigning large Quantities of Goods to others, which will make them popular and powerful ; ſo that they may get into Favour with ſuch Merchants as are against Paper Money, and then by any Art or Craft, get a number to ſign a Petition to go Home to the Parliament of *Great-Britain*, in order if poſſible to put a Stop to the Currency ; and if ſuch a Petition ſhould come to *London*, ſigned as before mentioned, you muſt enjoin our true Friends in and about *London*, to ſpare no Pains nor Money to get the Petition to paſs ; and if we bring this Scheme about, and ſtop a Paper Currency, I am bold to ſay, inſtead of their having a hundred large Privateers out of *North-America*, it will be a Wonder if they have Twenty ; for I am told, the Farmers and Tradeſmen have put their Land in Pledge for the Paper Money they fit out ſo many Veſſels with ; and the Merchants that have got the Paper Money in their Hands for the *European* Goods, deſign, as ſoon as it is ſtopped, and to be called in, to take the Lands that are in Pledge from all the common People ; ſo that all the lower Clafs will become like our Poor, to be well off to own a Fifhing Shallop. I would advife our *Scotch* Friends, as soon as the Paper Money is ftopp'd and to be called in, to collect all that they poffibly can of that, that is outftanding ; by this Method they will come in for a large Share of Lands, and fo become little Lards ; and it may be, in half a Century, we may have their feveral Clans to affift us as we have in the Highlands. The next Method I propofe, is to reduce the richeft Merchants among them, and oblige them to leffen their Trade ; and that is, *great Sir*, you muft write to our feveral rich Planters at our Sugar Iflands, and advife them to employ a Number of our polite *Frenchmen*, and fend them into the feveral Sea Port Towns on the Continent, *viz. Bofton, Rhode-Ifland, New-York, Philadelphia*, and wherever we can carry on Trade ? and thefe Men muft get in Favour with fome confiderable Merchant in each Town, to furnifh them with a fufficient Number of Veffels, in order to bring over our Produce, fuch as Rum, Sugar, Molaffes ; in fhort, we muft wink and connive at any of our Produce, to carry on our Scheme ; but let Rum be the chief Article, for by our manufacturing that, we fhall make double Profit, and deprive our Enemies of that Advantage. And thofe Men thus employed muft improve the *Englifh* Merchants to fell our Produce for them, who will readily do it for Part of the Gain. And in order to procure Silver and Gold ; for our Planters muft not take any Thing in Return but Cafh ; and by this Method, we may procure all the hard Money that is ftirring amongft them ; for when Paper Money is once ftopped, there can be no Medium of Trade ; and their Trade will be fo reduced, that there will be but little of that ; and thofe *Englifh* Traders that are not concerned with our Friends, will foon have no Ufe for their Veffels ; and being often obliged to fell at a low Price, our Friends muft be employed to buy them as Opportunity offers.   If this Method, *great Sir*, is induftrioufly and faithfully purfued and carried on, we fhall unavoidably impov'rifh, diftrefs, and confound them : All the lower Clafs will no more be able to pay for Clothing from their Mother Country, but muft be contented to live as they did of Old to wander about in Sheep Skins and Goat Skins, and to dwell in Caves and Dens of the Earth ; and thofe of the higheft Clafs will be obliged to leffen their Trade, fell their Veffels, and no more be able to fend Home to their Mother Country, fuch Quantities of Silver and Gold. Then no more *New-England* Invafions, no more beating down our Walls at *Cape-Breton ;* and when we have another War, we fhall not only have their Money, but their Veffels, and their Men being poor, muft feek Shelter in fome foreign Land.

I conclude, great SIR, *Your obedient Servant and faithful Subject to His Most Chriftian Majesty our Royal Mafter.*

Mc· O—— NE——L.

VIII.   SUSQUEHANNAH COMPANY RECEIPTS.

(Written on small pieces of paper.)

Received of Robert Hafzard Esqr of South Kingstown in ye Colony of Rhodisland two Spanifh Milled Dollors in Complyance with ye vote of ye Sufquehannah Company at their meeting Held at Hartford November ye 21st 1754.

Received p^r me   SAM^L GRAY Com^{ie}.

Received of Robert Hafzard of South Kingftown in Compliance With ye vote of ye Sufquehannah Company this Day Paft at Hartford two Spanifh Milled Dollors   Received p^r me

Hartford November

ye 21st 1754

Received of Robert Hazzard Dec^d p^r ye hand of Thomas Hazzard three Shillings a tax Voted by ye Sufquahana Comp^y three Shillings on Each proprietor in full for s^d tax which was Voted to be paid to Collo John H Lydins

p^r me JERE CLEMENT Com^tee & attorny
for S^d Lydenis.

Receiv^d March the 4th 1768 of Thomas Haffard as heir at Law to Robert Haffard Deceased Three Shillings Lawfull money being the one third part of the money Voted (by the proprietors of the Sufquehannah Purchafe) to be Raifed on Each Right at the adjournment of s^d Proprietors meeting the 6th of January last, I Receive the same by vertue of an order from the Clerke of the s^d Proprietors.

p^r EZRA DEAN.

I Jonathan Hazard of Said Town County & Colony of Rhode Island &c yeoman Do Constitute Thomas Hazard of same Town County & Colony yeoman to appear at the Meeting of ye Sufquehannah Company to be held at Windham by adjournment on the sixth of this Inftant There to act and Do any Thing or Things relative to the Purchafe of s^d Company which Shall be as binding & effectual as if acted & done by

me being Perfonally Prefent as Witnefs my Hand the
Day first above Written

JONATHAN HASSARD.

Ateft

ROL^D ROBINfON.

To the Company or proprietors of the Sufquehannah Purchace or to thofe of them that may be Con-
vened at their meeting at Great Windham (as adver-
tised) the 6th day of this Inft. Jany 1768 I hereby
Certify by thefe prefents that I have and do hereby
Conftitute and appoint my Friend Thomas Haffard of
South Kingstown in the Colony of Rhode Island to
be & appear at the Said meeting, and there for me and
in my name to appear act and do all and Every matter
and thing, whatever that Shall be thought Requifite
and Needfull for the further Eftablishment and good
of the Said Purchafe, & that I will hold what the Said
Thomas Haffard Shall do for & Concerning me in
Said afair, as good and Valid to all Intents and Purpofes as tho I were Perfonally Prefent, — In teftimony
whereof I have hereunto Subfcribed my name this
4th day of January. A. D. 1768.

S. HASSARD .

IX. AN APPRENTICESHIP PAPER, 1768.

(Printed Form, italicized words written in.)

THIS INDENTURE WITNESSETH, THAT *Benjamin
Haszard Son of Richard Haszard late of South Kings-
town in the County of Kings County in the Colony of
Rhode Island &c. yeoman deceased,* hath put *himfelf* and
by thefe Prefents, doth voluntarily, and of *his* own free
Will and Accord, and with the Confent of *Nicholas
Easton of Newport in the County of Newport in the*

Colony of Rhode Island &c. Esq. Executor of the last Will & Testament of the said Richard Haszard & who by said Will is impowered to put out the said Benjamin Haszard Apprentice put and bind *himself* Apprentice to *Benjamin Hall of Newport aforesaid Esq. And to Abigail Hall his Wife* to learn *the* Art, Trade, or Myftery *of a Cordwainer and* after the Manner of an Apprentice, to ſerve from *the Day of the Date hereof* for and during the Term of *ten Years eleven Months & seven Days* next enſuing, to be compleat and ended. During all which ſaid Term the ſaid Apprentice *his* ſaid *Master & Mistreſs* faithfully ſhall ſerve, *their* Secrets keep, *their* lawful Commands gladly obey : *he* ſhall do no Damage to *his* ſaid *Master or Mistreſs* nor ſee it done by others, without letting or giving Notice thereof to *his* ſaid *Master or Mistreſs he* ſhall not waste *his* said *Masters or Mistreſs's* Goods, nor lend them unlawfully to any. *he* ſhall not commit Fornication, nor contract Matrimony within the ſaid Term. At Cards, Dice, or any other unlawful Game, *he* ſhall not play, whereby *his* ſaid *Master or Mistreſs* may have Damage, with *his* own Goods, or the Goods of others : *he* ſhall not abſent *himself* by Day or by Night, from *his* ſaid *Masters or Mistreſs's* Service, without *their* Leave ; or haunt Alehouſes, Taverns, or Play-houſes ; but in all Things behave *himself* as a good and faithful Apprentice ought to do, towards *his* said *Master & Mistreſs* and all *theirs* during the ſaid Term. And the ſaid *Master & Mistreſs* do hereby promiſe to teach and inſtruct, or cauſe the ſaid Apprentice to be taught and inſtructed in the Art, Trade or Calling of *a Cordwainer* by the beſt Ways and Means *they* can *And to find and provide for said Apprentice good & ſufficient Meat Drink Apparel Washing and Lodging suitable for such an Ap-*

prentice during said Term And at the Expiration thereof to give unto said Apprentice all his then wearing Apparell And to teach said Apprentice to read write and Cypher as far as the Rule of Three within said Term And in Consideration of the s.d Master & Mistre∫s finding for s.d Apprentice his Apparell the s.d Nicholas Easton hath paid unto the said Benjamin Hall the Sum of four hundred Pounds old Tenor

IN TESTIMONY whereof, the Parties to the∫e Pre∫ents have hereunto interchangeably ∫et their Hands and Seals, the *nineteenth* Day of *January* in the *eighth* Year of the Reign of Our Sovereign Lord *George the third* King of *Great Britain, &c. Annoq; Dom. 1768.* Signed, Sealed, and Delivered,   *Benj.am in haszard*

   in the Pre∫ence of

     Richard Thomas   (paper torn)   *Easton*
     Lemuel Baley

X. A LEASE FROM STEPHEN CHAMPLIN TO HIS MOTHER, SIGNED BY BOTH.

(Manuscript, College Tom's hand.)

THIS INDENTURE made the fifth day of February in the Twelfth year of the Reign of George the Third by the Grace of God of Great Brittain King Anno.q Domini One Thousand seven hundred & Seventy Two Between Stephen Champlin of South - Kingstown in the County of Kings County, in the Colony of Rhode-I∫land, &c. of the One part, and Mary Champlin of the Town County & Colony aforesaid Widow Woman & Relict of Stephen Champlin late of said Town decea∫ed of the other part, WITNESSETH THAT the said Stephen Champlin for and in Con∫ideration of the yearly Rents & Covenants hereinafter reserved to be done paid and performed by the said Mary Champlin her Executors, Administrators or Afsigns, Hath Demifed, Granted, Sett, and to farm Letten And by thefe presents, Doth Demife, Grant, Sett, and to farm Lett unto the said Mary Champlin

ALL that great Room in the Southeaft corner of the houfe where she now liveth in Point Judith in said Town which is Given to my brother Thomas Champlin in yᵉ Will of our Father Late Deceaf'ᵈ and also the the (*sic*) Bedroom (in the Northeast corner of said Houfe) & the bedroom in the Chamber over the same with full & free Liberty to Pafs and repafs to and from the same either in her Own Perfon or Others at her Plea-fure, together with a convenient Place at the Door of sᵈ Houfe sufficient for Firewood and also a Priviledge in the Well for Water, and appurtenances thereunto belonging To HAVE AND TO HOLD the said three Rooms in the said Dwelling Houfe with the Rights and Priviledges herein before demifed unto the said Mary Champlin, from yᵉ Twenty fifth day of the Third month called march for and during and unto the full end & Term of Five years from thence next enfuing and fully to be compleat and ended (If she the said Mary Champlin shall so Long Live) att and under the Yearly Rent of One Pepper Corn to be paid unto the said Stephen Champlin his Heirs and Afsignes always upon the Twenty fifth day of yᵉ third month in every year of the said Term And it is Agreed by & between the the (*sic*) said Parties, that in Case, the said Mary Champlin shall dye before the Expiration of this Term, Then the remainder of the said Term shall im-mediately Ceafe & Detirmine And the said Stephen Champlin shall immediately enter upon the said De-mifed Premifes and hold the same, notwithftanding

this Prefent Demife and Leafe or anything therein
Contained. IN WITNESS whereof the Parties first
first above named to thefe Prefent

have sett their Hands and Seals the day and year
above Written
Sign'd Seal'd and Deliver'd
In Presence of us STEPHEN CHAMPLIN (Seal.)
  THᵒ HAZARD of ROBᵀ. MARY CHAMPLIN (Seal.)
  ROBERT HAZARD

XI. MANUSCRIPT IN THE HAND OF THOMAS HAZARD SON OF ROBERT.

To all People to whom these Prefents shall come
whereas Stephen Champlin late of South Kingftown
in the County of Kings County & Colony of Rhode
Island &c Yeoman deceafed Did in & by his Laft Will
and Teftament in writing bearing date the Twenty
firft day of July one Thoufand seven hundred Seventy
and. one 1771 among other Gifts and Legacies Bequeathed to my Brother Robert Champlin his Heirs
and Afsigns for ever One Certain farm or Tract of
Land lying and being in Point Judith in sᵈ Town
Called the Potter Farm and alfo by said Will Ordered
my said Brother Robert Champlin to Pay his four Sif-
ters Four Hundred Dollars each, as may more fully
appear by said Will, Which farm is Leafed by an Oral
Leafe Two Years of which leafe is yet to come from
the twenty fifth day of March next enfuing the date
hereof to Samuel Congdon of said Town & Nicholas
Gardner of exetor son of George Gardner Now Know
Ye that I Stephen Champlin son and Heir at Law to
said deceafed & Executor to said Will as alfo mentioned as Refeduary Legatee therein Yeoman For and
in Confideration of and allowance made me by my
Mother Mary Champlin Widow in a Leafe bearing

even date herewith of her Right of Dower & Power of thirds in the Farm where She now lives in Point Judith in said Town and for the Love Goodwill & affection which I have and Do bear towards my said Brother Robert Champlin and for the Better enabling him to Pay his said fifters their Several Legacies bequeathed as aforefaid and for Promoting & eftablifhing a lafting Peace unity & Harmony throughout our Whole ffamily Have given, granted, releafed and forever Quitclaimed and by thefe Prefents do freely, fully, and abfolutely give grant, releafe, & for ever Quitclaim unto him the said Robert Champlin his Heirs and Afsignes for ever all that my Right Property Claim & Demand either in Law or Equity in by & through either & all my aforefaid Capacities of in and unto the Rents & Profits that shall and may arife out of said Leafed Lands during the Two years as aforefaid To Have and to hold the same to him the said Robert Champlin his Heirs and afsignes forever so that neither I the said Stephen Champlin nor my Heirs or any other Perfon in the name Right or Stead of us or any of us shall hereafter have, Claim Challenge or demand any Right, Eftate Title Intereft Property or Demand of in or to the same, But from all and every action & Suit brought or to be brought for the same or any Part thereof shall & Will be foever Excluded & Barred by these Prefents In witness whereof I the said Stephen Champlin have hereunto sett my Hand and seal the fifth day of February one Thousand seven hundred & Seventy Two.

Signed Sealed & Delivered
in the Presenc of us
Tʜᵒ Hazard son of Robᵗ   Stephen Champlin (Seal)
Elizabeth Hazard

XII. Letter from Matthew Griswold to Governor Wanton.

(Written on two sides of a folio sheet.)

For
  The Honourable
Joseph Wanton Esqr
  Att Newport
Govr of the Colony of
  Rhode Island &c　　　Lyme June : 19th : 1773 —
    Thefe —
S^r

Your Favour of the 15th Ins^t is come to hand : Shall pay all due attention and lay it before the Judges of our Sup^r Court at the next Interview wee have.

Tho, am not able to say that as a Court wee can properly Interpofe in the Matters you Refer to.

The People Claim^d as Slaves are Esteem^d with us as the Proper Objects of the Care and Protection of the Government in Common with Other Inhabitants. If any outrage undue Violence or Inhumane Severity is used it is Esteem^d the Duty of the Informing & Peace officers of the Colony to Interpofe & give Relief upon proper Application made to them.

As to the Matters of Slavery our Common Law Courts are Open and wee have had Sundry Instances within my Observation of actions bro^t wherein the Points in Question & upon which the Caufe Turn^d was whether the Perfon Claim^d as a Slave was Legally so or not. Some Obtain^d others Did not According to the Evidence & attending Circumftances of Each Individual Cafe. — Our People

who have Demands of that kind Claim it as a Right
to have a Day in Court; a fair Chance to prove
their Special Property (if any they have) I apprehend Those Trials were Estem^d open & fair — Yet it
seems Thofe Things are not greatly Favour^d in Law:
by People of Consideration here Inasmuch as the
Negroes who have been Manumitted in this Colony:
being Ignorant of the Art of Honeft living have
Frequently become Strowling vagrants have United
with Thieves & Burglars & prov^d very Troublesome
and Dangerous Inhabitants. I sho^d be Concern^d that
any People Sho^d be opprefs^d by unlawful holding in
Servitude. Justice ought to be done to Every one.
If any material of Importance Sho^d further Occur
upon further Confideration & Consultation Upon this
affair Shall give Your Hon^r the trouble of Another
Letter.

I am with Great Esteem & Respect Your Hon^{rs}
Moft Obedient Humble Servt
MATTH.^w GRISWOLD

XIII. COPY OF A MINUTE FROM QUARTERLY
MEETING.

(Manuscript.)

We desire you may be more particular and explicit
in your answers for the future, and that you would
remind the several monthly meetings of the same,
they having frequently come and at this particular
time in too general a manner, not serving to give so
clear and perfect an account of your State as the Importance of the Cafe requires. We desire not to be
too Cenforious, whether Indifferancy in the Cafe or
an unwillingnefs to exprefs the weaknefs failings and

Imperfections of your State or whatever may be the Cauſe thereof we know not.   But we befeech you that in anſwering the Queries you give the utmost Care to render the same in as plain full and Concise terms as may be.

DANIEL UNDERWOOD.

(Reverse Side)

Meetˢ for Sufferings adjourned untill the Second Second day of the 8ᵗʰ month 1775.

MOSES FARNUM	NATHAN DAVIS
MOSES BROWN	JACOB MOT JR.
JEREMIAH HACKER	THOMAS STEAR
JOSEPH MITCHEL	JOHN COLLINS
THOMAS HASSARD	THEOPHILIUS SHOVE JUN
ISACK LAWTEN	SAMUEL GOLD
THOMS LAPHAM JR	JOSHUA DEVOL
GEORGE ARNAL	PHILIP WANTON
JEREMIAH ASTEN	JOSEPH SOUTHWICK
JOHN ROGERS	EBEN CHACE
BENJAMIN ARNAL	DAVID BUFAM
JONATHAN MACY	JOHN CASSE
BARZILLA TUCKER	CALEB RUSEL.

XIV. COPY OF A MINUTE OF THE MEETING FOR SUFFERINGS HELD AT PROVIDENCE Yᴱ 13TH 8ᵀᴴ MO 1776.

This Meeting again taking under Consideration a Certain Act of the General Assembly lately passed called the Test Act, and also an Act passed in the 7th Mᵒ last (so far as they relate particularly to Friends) wherein it is provided that if any Friend bring a Certificate from the Clerk of the Monthly

Meeting to which he belongs that he is in Unity such Friend shall be excused from certain requisitions & exempted from the penalties mentioned in said Acts. It is the conclusion of this Meeting that it may be safe for any Monthly Meeting to grant Certificates to any Member applying for the same, for the purpose afores^d after the necessary inquiry made & due regard had in said Certificate to the State & standing of said Member; Nevertheless it is earnestly recommended to all such applying Members to enter deeply into themselves & not implicitly follow the sentiments of others but see that their proceedings therein are in the liberty of the Truth, & the Clerk is desired to send a Copy of this Minute to the Monthly Meeting of Rhode Island & other Monthly Meetings as occasion may require.

XV. RELEASE OF GUARDIANSHIP.

(*Manuscript.*)

Know all Men hereby, That I Robert Hazard of South Kingston in the County of King's County, Yeoman (Son of Richard Hazard) Have and do hereby for and in Confideration of the Sum of One hundred & forty five pounds six shillings & eight pence half penny lawful money wh I have this day rec^d of Thomas Hazard of s^d South Kingston, the receipt of wh I do hereby acknowledge, difcharge & releafe the said Thomas Hazard from all and every demand of any nature kind or quality whatever wh I have against him, as well for the time during wh he was my Guardian, & rec^d the profits of my Estate as all other demands wh I have againft him, (not meaning hereby to difcharge my former Guardian Enoch

Hazard for any demands I have againſt him) In Witneſs wherof I have hereto set my hand this twenty-six
day of April A. D. 1776.

    Robert Hazard Son of Richard.

Witness. —

  F. J. Helme.

XVI. Constitution of the Providence Society
  for Abolishing the Slave-trade.

(Printed on one sheet. No date.)

It having pleaſed the Creator of mankind to make
of one blood all nations of men, and having, by the
diffuſion of his light, manifeſted that, however diverſi-
fied by colour, ſituation, religion, or different ſtates of
ſociety, it becomes them to conſult and promote each
others happineſs, as members of one great family: It
is therefore the duty of thoſe who profeſs to maintain
their own rights, and eſpecially thoſe who acknowledge the obligations of Chriſtianity, to extend, by the
uſe of ſuch means as are or may be in their power, the
bleſſings of freedom to the whole human race; and in
a more particular manner to ſuch of their fellow-crea-
tures as by the laws and conſtitution of the United
States are entitled to their freedom, and who by fraud
or violence are or may be detained in bondage. And
as, by the African ſlave-trade, a ſyſtem of ſlavery, re-
plete with human miſery is erected and carried on, it
is incumbent on them to endeavour the ſuppreſſion of
that unrighteous commerce; to excite a due obſer-
vance of ſuch good and wholeſome laws as are or may
be enacted for the abolition of ſlavery, and for the
ſupport of the rights of thoſe who are entitled to freedom by the laws of the country in which they live;

and to afford fuch relief as we may be enabled to thofe unhappy fellow-citizens, who, like the fons of Africa, falling into the hands of unmerciful men, may be carried into flavery at Algiers or elfewhere.

From a conviction of thefe truths, and the obligation of thefe principles, and from a defire to diffufe them wherever the vices and miferies of flavery exift, and in humble reliance on the favour and fupport of the Father of mankind, the fubfcribers have formed themfelves into a Society under the title of *The Providence Society for abolifhing the Slave-Trade.* —— For affecting thefe purpofes they have adopted the following rules :

1ft. The Society fhall elect, by a majority of votes to be taken by ballot, a Prefident, a Vice-Prefident, one or more Counfellors, a Secretary, and a Treasurer, who fhall refpectively continue in office for one year from the time of their election, and at the expiration of every year fucceeding, there fhall be a new election of officers in the fame manner.

2d. The Prefident fhall have authority to maintain order and decorum at the meeting of the Society, and to call a fpecial meeting at any time, with the advice of three of the Standing Committee herein after named.

3d. The Vice-Prefident, in the abfence of the Prefident, fhall have the fame authority as the Prefident : and in cafe the Prefident fhall die or be difplaced, the Vice-Prefident fhall officiate until a new Prefident be chofen.

4th. The Secretary fhall keep a record of the proceedings of the Society, in a book to be provided for that purpofe, and fhall caufe to be publifhed, from time to time, fuch part of the proceedings, or refolutions, as the Society may order, or the Prefident with the Standing Committee between the meetings of the Society may think proper to direct.

5th. The Treafurer, if required by the Society, fhall give fecurity for the faithful difcharge of the truft repofed in him, and fhall keep regular accounts of the monies received and paid, obferving always to pay no money without an order figned by the Prefident, or a majority of a quorum of the Standing Committee, who are prohibited from drawing, between the ftated meetings of the Society, for a larger fum than ten pounds, unlefs efpecially empowered by the Society at a previous meeting.

6th. If any of the officers above named fhall refign or be difplaced, the Society fhall fill the vacancy in the mode prefcribed by the firft article; and if the Prefident and Vice Prefident, or Secretary, or Treasurer, be abfent at any of the meetings, the Society may elect one to officiate *pro tempore*.

7th. The Society fhall meet once in every quarter, that is to fay, on the 3d. fixth day in the 2d, 5th, 8th, and 11th months in every year, at fuch place as fhall from time to time be agreed upon, in order to receive the reports of the Standing Committee, and devife the ways and means of accomplifhing the objects of this inftitution.

8th. That nine members, with a Prefident or Vice-Prefident, conftitutionally affembled, be a quorum of the Society for tranfacting bufinefs.

9th. Every member after fubfcribing thefe rules fhall pay into the hands of the Treafurer two-thirds of a dollar, and at the commencement of every quarter one-fixth of a dollar; and all donations to the Society fhall be made through the Prefident, who fhall pay them to the Treafurer, and report them to the Society at the next quarterly-meeting.

10th. Any citizen of the United States, who fhall be recommended by two-thirds of the Standing Committee to a quarterly-meeting, fhall be balloted for, and if approved by two-thirds of the members prefent, he fhall be declared a member. The Committee of feven fhall have Authority to receive fuch members as may offer and fubfcribe before the next quarterly-meeting, this rule notwithftanding.

11th. Two thirds of the members prefent at a quarterly meeting fhall have power to expel any perfon whom they may deem unworthy of remaining a member, and no perfon fhall be a member who holds a flave, or is concerned in the flave-trade.

12th. It fhall be the bufinefs of the Counfellors to explain the laws and conftitution of the States, which relate to the emancipation of flaves, and to the flave-trade. And, when it becomes neceffary, to urge the due execution thereof, and their claims to freedom, before fuch perfons or Courts as are or may be authorized to decide on the fame.

13th. A Standing Committee of feven members fhall be appointed to tranfact the bufinefs in general, four of whom are empowered to act ; whofe duty it fhall be to take the moft effectual meafures to accomplifh the objects of this inftitution agreeable to the direction and at the expence of the Society, and to report a particular account of their proceedings at the next quarterly-meeting, at which time two of their number fhall be releafed from the fervice in the order their names ftand on the minutes, and the vacancy filled up by the fame or two others appointed in their room, and in like manner a difmiffion and appoint-

ment of two fhall take place at each fucceeding quarterly-meeting.

14th. The foregoing Rules fhall be in force without
alteration fix months, after which period they fhall be
subject to fuch alterations as two-thirds of the members prefent, at a quarterly-meeting, fhall agree upon.

XVII. WILL OF THOMAS HAZARD SON OF ROBERT.

*(Written in his own hand on two sides of a large quarto
sheet of paper.)*

BE IT REMEMBRED this Nineteenth day of the
Twelfth Month in the Year of our LORD one Thousand
Seven Hundred and Ninety Three that I Thomas
Hazard of South Kingstown in the County of Washington and State of Rhode Island &c. Yeoman being
of a Sound disposing mind and memory and in a
pretty good State of health for which and all Other
favours I desire to be very thankfull, and calling to
mind the mortality of my body and knowing that it is
Appointed once for man to die do in the fear of GOD
make and Ordain this to be my Last Will and Testament that is to say first I will that all those Debts I
do owe in Right to any persons with my funeral
charges be well and truly content and paid in a convenient time after my deceafe by my Executrix hereafter Named out of my personal Estate and as touching Such Worldly Estate as it hath pleased GOD to
blefs me with in this life I give and Dispose of the
Same manner and form following.

IMPRIMUS I give and bequeath to my beloved Wife
Elizabeth Hazard the use and improvment of the
west end of my dwelling Houfe that is to say Two
Rooms above Stairs and the two rooms under them

and previledge to get Water out of the Well So long as She Shall Remain my Widow, I also give to her Two Cows and my great Bay mare so Called, and my Chafe with the previledge of its Standing in the Chafe House I alfo give her the keeping of the two Cows & horfe or great bay Mare to go in the Chafe during the time She Remains my Widow I also give her my House hold furniture Except what I Shall otherwife mention and give away in this Will, I also give her my Silver Watch and the keeping of the three creatures the mare to be kept in the Stable in the Winter Seafon & the Cows to be kept well to hay, I alfo give to my said Wife One Hundred pounds Lawful money to be raised out of my perfonal Estate by my Executrix hereafter Named, all which gifts and Legacies to her are in Lieu of her Right of Dower and power of thirds of in and unto my Estate.

ITEM I give and Bequeath to my Beloved Son Robert Hazard and to his Heirs and Afsigns forever all that part of my homestead farm in South Kingstown which lyeth to the Eastward of the Country Rhode Containing about One Hundred and fifty Acres more or lefs together with my Rights on a Sedge Island so called said Lands being Bounded Westerly on the Country Rhode Northerly partly on Elisha Watfons Land and partly on Job Watfons Land. Easterly partly on Pettyquamscet River including my rights on a Sedge Island & partly on a Cove Southerly on Walter Watfons Land, I alfo give him one feather bed and furniture with all my Notes I have against him, and my Will is that he shall keep the Creatures as given to his Mother and Allow her the previledges as aforesaid out of what I have given him.

ITEM I give and Bequeath to my beloved Son

Thomas Hazard the Note I hold against him for five Hundred and Thirty Eight pounds, and one feather bed and furniture.

ITEM I give and Bequeath to my beloved Son Rowland Hazard and to his Heirs and Afsigns forever all my Lands lying in South Kingstown above the Country Rhode or to the Westward of said Rhode Containing about One hundred and fifty Acres more or Lefs With the Buildings thereon Standing the Same being Bounded Easterly on the Country Rhode Southerly partly on land lately belonging to John Case Deceased and partly on Jeremiah Niles's land Westerly on said Niles's Land Northerly partly on said Rowland Hazards Land and partly on Job Watfons Land I alfo give to my Son Rowland Hazard Two feather beds and furniture and all my Notes against him.

AND all the Remainder of my Lands and Real Estate where ever the Same may be I give to my Said Three Sons and to Their Heirs and Afsigns forever to be equally Divided among them I alfo give to my said three Sons Each of them Two Silver Table Spoons.

AND all the Remainder of my personal Estate I give to my aforesaid Wife and Three Sons to be Equally Divided among them.

And Lastly I hereby Nominate and appoint my Beloved Wife Elizabeth Hazard to be my whole and Sole Executrix of this my Last Will and Testament Rattifying and Confirming this only to be my Last Will and Testament hereby Revoking and disannulling all former Wills & Executors by me heretofore made IN WITNESS and Confirmation Whereof I have hereunto Set my hand and Seal the day month and Year first Within Written.

THOMAS HAZARD.

Signed Sealed published pronounced and Declared by Thomas Hazard the Testator be be (*sic*) his Last Will and Testament in the prefence of us as Witnefses.

ANDREW NICHOLS
ROBERT KNOWLES. fon of JOSEPH
ANDREW NICHOLS Junr.

BE IT REMEMBERED that at a Town Council held in South Kingston the 10th September A D 1798. Personally came Messrs Andrew Nichols & Andrew Nichols Junr. and on their Solemn Affirmation declare & say that they Signed their Names as Witnefses to the preceeding last Will & Testament of Mr Thomas Hazard Dec^d. together with Mr Robert Knowles and the Testator Signed his Name in their presence & they Signed as Witnefses in his presence & in presence of each other at the same time, and that said Testator was then in his perfect mind and Memory. Whereupon said last Will and Testament being thus proved it is approved of as and to be the last Will and Testament of said Testator.

Signed by Order of said Town Council
JAMES HELME Council Clerk

Recorded the foregoing in the Council Book N°. 6 belonging to South Kingston Pages 416. 417 and 418. Sepr. 18. 1798.

JAMES HELME, C. C^rk
50 Cents. — T. Hazards Will

XVIII. Rhode Island Currency.

Quotations from the letter of Governor Richard Ward to the English Board of Trade, January 9, 1740, showing the value of different issues of paper money in silver.[1]

Year			
Year 1710 (First Issue)		8 Shillings in bills.	
" 1715 First Bank		12 " "	
" 1721 Second Bank		16 " "	
" 1728 Third Bank	one ounce	18 " "	
" 1731 Fourth Bank	of silver	22 " "	
" 1733 Fifth Bank	equalled	25 " "	
" 1738 Sixth Bank		27 " "	
" 1740 Seventh Bank		27 " "	

Old Tenor Bills.

Table fixing the value of old tenor bills at different periods, for the use of the courts, made by the General Assembly June, 1763.[2]

SPANISH MILLED DOLLARS.

							£	s.	d.
1751	1 Spanish Milled Dollar equal to						2	16	00
1752	"	"	"	"	"	"	3	00	00
1753	"	"	"	"	"	"	3	10	00
1754	"	"	"	"	"	"	3	15	00
1755	"	"	"	"	"	"	4	5	00
1756	"	"	"	"	"	"	5	5	00
1757	"	"	"	"	"	"	5	15	00
1758	"	"	"	"	"	"	6	00	00
1759	"	"	"	"	"	"	6	00	00

[1] S. S. Rider, *R. I. Historical Tracts*, No. 8, p. 55.
[2] *R. I. Colonial Records*, vol. vi. p. 361.

		£	s.	d.
1760	1 Spanish Milled Dollar equal to	6	00	00
1761	" " " " " "	6	10	00
1762	" " " " " "	7	00	00
1763	" " " " " "	7	00	00

Scale of Depreciation of Continental Bills of Credit.[1]

A. D.		SPANISH MILLED DOLLARS.	DOLLARS PAPER CURRENCY.
1777	January 1....100 equal to.........		105
"	July..........	"	125
1778	January......	"	325
"	July..........	"	425
1779	January......	"	742
"	July..........	"	1477
1780	January......	"	2934
"	April........	"	4000
"	August 15....	"	7000
1781	February.....	"	7500
"	May 15......	"	8000
"	May 30......	"	16000

[1] Condensed from tables in *R. I. Colonial Records*, vol. ix. pp. 282 and 424.

SUNDRY PRICES AND VARIOUS ENTRIES

TAKEN FROM THE ACCOUNT BOOK OF THOMAS HAZARD
SON OF ROBERT, DURING THE YEARS 1750 TO 1784
INCLUSIVE.

1750.

	£	s.	d.
Oats per bushel (March)...............		12	00
Oats per bushel (May).................		15	00
Potatoes per bushel...................		10	00
Butter................................		5	6
Hay half a load.......................	10	00	00
Fatt Goose per pound..................		1	6
Wool per pound........................		8	00
Tea per pound.........................	3	4	00
1 yoke of oxen........................	140	00	00
1 horse...............................	50	00	00
Veal per pound		1	6
Mutton hind quarter per pound.........		2	00
Lamb per pound........................		2	00
White Flannel per yard................		15	00
Striped " " "		16	00
Felt Hatt..	1	00	00
½ of an hundred of Sugar..............		65	00
Sugar per pound.......................		4	9
Handkerchief..........................		14	00
Callaminco per yard.................		18	00
Indigo................................	7	4	00
Flax Seed per bushel..................	2	00	00

Mr Jos.ʰ Torrey D.ʳ

To my Plow oxen & Two hands ½ day to			
Plow..................................	2	00	00

	£	s.	d.
To Carting of Hedgewood ½ day 2 hands cart & 4 oxen......................	1	10	00
To my Cart & oxen going up to George Gardners Mill for Boards.............	2	00	00
To the Hire of my mare for his son to ride to Brandford in Connecticut..........	2	00	00

1751.

	£	s.	d.
Corn per bushel......................		25	00
Potatoes, per bushel...................		15	00
One 3-year-old horse..................	105	00	00
Veal per pound.......................		1	6
Land let per acre.....................		13	6
Calf skin............................		25	00
Tow per pound.......................		3	6
Fatt Goose per pound.................		1	6
Butter per pound.....................		7	00
Lining Cloth per yard................		4	4

Richard Hazard D.ᵣ

	£	s.	d.
To 6 yards of Devonshire Cersy at.......	6	00	00
" ½ yd of Shalloon at................		24	00
" ¼ yd of Fuston at..................		34	00
" ¼ yd of ozenbridgs at..............		12	00
" ⅛ yd Cotton Velvit at..............	7	00	00
" 4 yards of Tape at..................			06
" Two dozen of Buttons at............		10	00
" 2 Sticks of Twist at................		5	00
" ½ oz of Silk at.....................		40	00
" 1 Yoke of oxen *Fatt*................	120	00	00
" Sheep *Fatt* each...................	2	00	00
" Hides and Tallow (per pound).......		1	6

	£	s.	d.
To Weaving *Duroy* per yard..............		5	00
"　"　Blanketing　"　"　..............		5	00
"　"　Flannel　"　"　..............		3	00
"　"　Tow Cloth　"　"　..............		3	00

1752.

	£	s.	d.
Corn per bushel......................		25	00
Potatoes per bushel...................		20	00
Butter per pound.....................		7	00
Milk per quart.......................		1	00
Cheese per pound.....................		3	00
Meal per pound.......................		1	00
Hoggs per pound......................		1	6
Wool per pound.......................		8	00
Leather for double soled shoes..........	3	10	00
Linen handkerchiefs...................		22	00
Stockings		35	00
Day's work of Robin...................		15	00
Pickle pork per pound.................		3	00
Beef　　　"　　"　..............		1	10

1753.

	£	s.	d.
Potatoes per bushel..................		20	00
1 Milch Cow and Calf.................	60	00	00
Cheese per pound.....................		3	00
Tea per pound........................		62	00
Nutmeg per ounce.....................		12	00
Pepper per ounce.....................		12	00
Cinnamon　"　......................		5	00
3-year-old horse.....................	150	00	00
Sheep skins each.....................		5	00
One yoke of oxen.....................	160	00	00

	£	s.	d.
Handkerchief		22	00
Weaving Linen per yd		7	00
" Tow		4	00
" Ticking		7	00
Pork per pound		2	6
Milk per quart		1	6
A Man's Saddle	33	00	00
Hay per Hundred weight		20	00
Carting wood per load		20	00
One Live Goofe		16	00
Wine per gallon		40	00
Rum "		44	00
Loaf Sugar per pound		12	00
½ hundred of Sugar	18	00	00
Currants per pound		8	00
Raisons		8	00

1754.

	£	s.	d.
Apples per bushel		12	00
Veal per pound		1	6
Wood per cord standing		50	00
Dressing Boots		12	00
Milk per quart		1	00
Handkerchief		22	00
Hind quarter of lamb per pound		2	00
1 three-year-old bay Mare with white nose	70	00	00
Load of *Mash* Hay	10	00	00
One old Brass Kettle W^t 14^{lb} ½ per pound		8	00
Butter per pound		7	00
Sheep per head	3	10	00
Choclat per pound		14	00

1755.

	£	s.	d.
Corn per bushel......................		30	00
"　　" 　　...................		35	00
Potatoes per bushel...................		18	00
One brown Steer Calf.................	8	00	00
One Yearling Bull....................	14	00	00
Cheese skim milk per pound...........		1	6
"　　New milk　　" 　...........		3	00
Oats per bushel......................		16	00
1 old black *Troting* mare..............	55	00	00
Load of hay..........................	20	00	00
1 yoke of oxen.......................	130	00	00
Weaving *Sarge Worsted* per yard........		6	00
"　　　Worsted.....................		5	00
"　　　Tow Cloth per yard..........		4	00
"　　　Half *Duroy* per yard..........		6	00
"　　　Linnen per yard.............		5	00
"　　　plain Cotton and Linnen.......		5	00
"　　　Striped　" 　　" 　......		5	6
"　　　Flannel plain................		3	6
"　　　" 　　Striped..............		4	00
Spinning (Amy Shearman) a day........		20	00
Hay making a day		20	00
White washing "		23	00
Flask of oil.........................		26	00
Nutmeg per ounce....................		28	00
Veal per pound......................		2	00
Pillion	6	00	00
Bridle..............................		50	00
Stirrup Leathers.....................	1	04	00
Sheep per head......................	3	10	00
Cotton wool per pound...............		22	00
Indigo per ounce....................		13	00

	£	s.	d.
Wool per pound............		9	00
Milk per quart.............		2	00
Days work.................		30	00

1756.

	£	s.	d.
Corn per bushel..........................		30	00
Corn per bushel 5th mo................		35	00
" " 6th mo...............		40	00
Oats "		15	00
" " 3rd mo...............		20	00
Milk per quart.........................		1	6
" " 4th mo.................		2	00
Stockings..............................		36	00
Thread per skien......................		1	3
Making shirts, each...................		25	00
Shoe buckles..........................	1	5	00
Man's work per day...................		12	00
Wool per pound........................		12	00
Day's work (Indian James Daniel).......		30	00
Making shoes..........................		16	00
Pair of shoes..........................	1	10	00
Leather enough for a large pair of Double Sole Shoes...........................	3	00	00
One pair of *Breetches*		50	00
Chex per yard.........................		26	02
Veal per pound........................		2	00
Lamb "		2	6
Tallow "		8	00
Making Heels for Womens shoes........		4	00
Tea per pound.........................	3	00	00
Cheese per pound......................		5	00
Women's Work per week...............		20	00
Flax per pound........................		6	6

£   *s.*   *d.*

	£	s.	d.
Hatcheled Flax per pound (Sarah Pew, Spinster)...........................		10	00
Women's shoes........................	2	15	00
Wool per pound........................		12	00
Carting a load of wood.................		30	00

1757.

	£	s.	d.
Corn per bushel 3rd mo................		40	00
" " 5th mo................		50	00
" " 6th mo................		60	00
" " 9th mo................		55	00
Oats per bushel		20	00
" " 12th mo................		25	00
Sow and pigs	25	00	00
Beef hides per pound..................		5	00
Women's household work per week.......		25	00
Pair of shoes	6	00	00
Tallow per pound.....................		9	00
Veal " "		3	00
Women's work per week		25	00
Calves per head	7	10	00
Pork per pound		7	00
Young Cows (good beef)...............	80	00	00
Salt per bushel......................		20	00
Cheese per pound....................		5	6
Butter per pound		15	00
Milk per quart......................		2	00
Edmons Ointment		20	00
Candle wick per pound		16	00
Stockings per pair		50	00
Ell wide Bearskin full Cloth per yard	7	10	00
Kersey Cloth " per yard	6	00	00
Worsted Drugget.....................	3	00	00

	£	s.	d.
Trimming for a coat................	5	19	9
Making a jacket		55	00

1758.

	£	s.	d.
Corn per bushel 6th mo.............		50	00
" " 10 mo.............		55	00
Oats per bushel		25	00
Turnips per bushel................		30	00
Side of veal 42 lbs...............	6	6	00
Tanning per pound		5	00
Hay per hundred weight		45	00
Making a pair of shoes		30	00
Women's work per week		25	00
Shoe buckles......................		20	00
Cersey Cloth per yard.............	6	00	00

£21 10*s.* Lawful Money turned in old Tenor @ £5 10*s.* the dollar.

£7 10*s.* old Tenor equals 11*s.* 6*d.* Lawful Money.

1759.

	£	s.	d.
Corn per bushel		60	00
Rye per bushel		60	00
Potatoes "		30	00
Turnips "		25	00
Apples per bushel		30	00
" " 10 mo		25	00
Wool per pound		25	00
Butter per pound		7	00
Mowing a day	3	00	00
Farm labor	1	00	00

Then agreed with William Wallsworth to work with me six months if I like to

£   s.   d.

hire him after one month for £12 Lawful money. But if I should not like to hire him after one month is expired then I am to give him for said one month Thirty shillings Lawfull money it being Connecticut Prock so called no interest to be reckoned thereon.

	£	s.	d.
2 Spanish Mill^d dollars in old Tenor	12	00	00
5 Shillings Lawful Money in old Tenor	4	11	10
Veal per pound		5	00
Sole leather for a pair of shoes		35	00
One calve skin	4	00	00
One *Fatt* Sheep	12	00	00
Hay per hundred weight		50	00
Veal per pound		6	00
Mutton "		6	00
Women's work per week (Sarah Pugh)		25	00
Chex per yard	3	00	00
Flannel "		40	00
Crocus per yard		20	00
White flannel "	6	00	00
One Comb		2	00

1760.

	£	s.	d.
Apples per bushel		40	00
Turnips per bushel		30	00
Butter per pound		16	00
" " 6th mo		15	00
Mutton per pound		6	00
Cheese per pound		8	00
One Fatt Sheep	12	00	00
Spinning Worsted per skien		6	00
Man's Saddle	45	00	00

	£	s.	d.
Carting one load of goods to Franklin's Ferry	10	00	00
Eggs per dozen		7	00
Hog's Fatt in a Tub per pound		12	00
Lamb per pound		6	00
Mutton "		6	00
Molasses per gallon	3	00	00
Cheese per pound		8	00
Fat Sheep per head	12	00	00
Veal per pound		5	6
1 Load of good Hay for 13 days' mowing			

1761.

	£	s.	d.
Corn per bushel		80	00
Oats "		50	00
Pork per pound		1	6
Pork pickled per pound		10	00
Sole leather for shoes	1	15	00
Thread per skein		3	00
Wool per pound		15	00
1 horse whip	6	00	00
1 doz. buttons		12	00
Hay per hundred weight	4	00	00
Half a day's Carting	5	00	00
Herds grass seed per pound		30	00
Butter per pound		17	00
Tow Cloth per yard		42	6
Pins per ounce		10	00
One pair of Shoes	6	00	00
Fat Sheep per head	10	00	00
Beans per peck		20	00
Beef per pound		4	6
Pork per pound		7	6

	£	s.	d.
Tow cloth per yard......................		8	oo
One Cow & Calf..	150	oo	oo
Cheese per pound......................		8	oo
One ox...............................	225	oo	oo

1762.

	£	s.	d.
Corn per bushel........................		100	oo
Barley per bushel		8o	oo
Mare and colt.........................	130	oo	oo
Veal per pound...........		6	oo
Cheese per pound......................		12	oo
Sarge per yard........................		14	oo
Wool per pound.......................		23	oo
" "		18	oo
" "		25	oo
Sheep per head........................	12	oo	oo
One pair of shoes......................	6	oo	oo
" " "	8	oo	oo
Thread per skein.......................		3	oo
Making one *Gound*....................		20	oo
One Winter Milch Cow & Calf..........	150	oo	oo
Eleven dollars equals..................	77	oo	oo
Binding for a *Pettycote*.................		15	oo
Hay per hundred weight...............	4	oo	oo
Salt Pork per pound....................		12	oo
Veal " (side)...................		6	oo
" " (hind quarter)		5	6
Two oxen beef hides & Tallow 1398 lbs			
at 4*s.* 9*d*.........................	322	o	6
One Fat Lamb.........................	5	oo	oo
Fifty Sheep & Lambs at £9 the pair.....	450	oo	oo
4½ lbs of Sole Leather paid by 2½ days'			
work (Daniel Knowles)............ ...			

1763.

	£	s.	d.
Barley per bushel.....................		90	00
1 Fatt sheep.........................	9	00	00
Veal per pound.......................		5	6
" "		5	00
Mutton per pound.....................		6	6
Beef "		5	6
" "		6	00
1 Calf skin..........................	8	00	00
Wool per pound.......................		20	00
1 Hatt Beaver........................	40	00	00
Leather for a pair of shoes	5	00	00
Sole leather for a pair of shoes..........		50	00
Weaving Flannel per yard..............		8	00
Weaving one *Coverled*...............	10	00	00
Lamb per pound......................		7	00
Calve Skin...........................	8	00	00
Butter per pound.....................		25	00
Pickled pork per pound		12	00
Tow cloth per yard...................		32	00
Salt per bushel.......................		90	00
¼ ⅛ & ⅛ of *ozenbridges* at 38*s*...........		17	00
Thread per Skein.....................		4	00
Woman's work per week...............		50	00
18 lambs at £6 per head..............	108	00	00
4 Sheep at £12.10....................		50	00
One Black mare......................	220	00	00
Two Fatt Horses.....................	660	00	00
Cheese per pound.....................			
" "		10	00

(or 6*d*. lawful money.)

1764.

	£	s.	d.
Corn per bushel		80	00
Barley per bushel		80	00
Herd's grass seed per quart		25	00
Cheese per pound		12	00
Tobacco "		9	00
Gardening (John Dye) per day	3	00	00
Shoes made by John Shearman	9	00	00
Veal per pound		5	00
" " hind quarter		5	6
Pickled pork per pound		12	00
100 feet of white pine boards	12	00	00
Pair of stockings	4	00	00
" " mitts		25	00
Two Hoogh^{ds} of Cyder Con^t 7 Barrels at £5	35	00	00
4 oz Indigo	3	15	00
Calve skin Vamps for a pair of shoes	2	10	00
2 Bushels of Lime	3	10	00
Paper per quire		34	00
Mohair per stick		10	00
Flax per pound		16	00
Wool "		25	00
Tow cloth per yard		30	00
Side of Lamb weight 8^{lbs}	2	8	00
Lamb skins	5	10	00

26th — 4th mo. To one Ten shilling Bill Lawful Money dated ye 12th of ye 5th month 1760 Turned into old Tenor 14 pounds. (280 shillings = 10 — 1*s*. = 28*s*.)

Received of Jos^h Torrey by the Hand of his wife 14 Spanish Mill^d in gold & silver to buy a cow for him in Connecticut. Returned 8 dollars some cop^r 1 cow to s^d Torrey.

£ *s. d.*

13th 8mo By five Shillings Lawful Money &
the Int 7^d½ it being dated the 20th third
month A. D. 1762 in old Tenor five
Pounds Ten Shillings & 6^d (£5.10^s.6^d.)
For recording the will of Robert Hazard..   4 00 00

1765.

Corn per bufhel......................	100 00
Barley "	80 00
Weaving Tow cloth per yard...........	8 00
" Linnen......................	12 00
Beef per pound.......................	4 6
" " 11th mo................	5 00
Shoes	9 00 00
Cheese per pound.....................	4 00
Cow and calf at........20 Spanish Silver	
Mill^d Dollars.	
Cheese per pound.....................	8 00
Skim Cheese per pound................	4 00
Flax per pound........................	20 00
Wool per pound.......................	38 00
Two cows Weighing (Beef Hides and Tal-	
low) 1133 ^{lbs} at 5*s*..................	283 5 00
Filling one Barrel with Cider...........	4 00 00
Pickel Pork per pound................	10 00

1766.

	OLD TENOR.			LAWFUL.		
	£	*s.*	*d.*	£	*s.*	*d.*
Corn per bufhel 6th mo.....		80	00			
" " 7th mo.....					3	9
Oats "					1	6
Flax seed per bushel........					3	9

	OLD TENOR.			LAWFUL.		
	£	s.	d.	£	s.	d.
Veal per pound...............		5	00			2½
Beef......................		4	00			
New England Rum per gallon		70	00			
1 yearling steer..............				2	8	00
Housewifery per week.........		50	00			
Tea per pound..............	8	00	00			
Wool per pound.............						14½
" "						9
Butter per pound............		16	00			
Sugar per pound............		15	00			
Weaving *Caliminco* per yard..		16	00			
Molasses per gallon........		36	00			
Cheese per pound..........						3¾
Skim milk Cheese per pound						2¼
Sheep Skins................		40	00			
Spinning Worsted per Skien..		7	00			
" *Lining* yarn " .		8	00			
Pickeld Pork per pound.....		12	00			
" " "		10	00			
Filling one Barrel with Cider.	7	00	00			
9 Sheep & Lamb skins.......	12	00	00			
Tow per pound..............						4½
One pair of shoes..........		160	00			
Cranberries per quart.......		6	00			
Carting with Team & one hand per day.............					4	4
Two pair of oxen to plough per day.................					2	3
One Barrel of Sugar 9 dollers						
One pound of Indigo 1½ "						
62 Cheeses 62 "						
One doller to be considered at	8	00	00			

OLD TENOR.   LAWFUL.

£ *s.* *d.*   £ *s.* *d.*

Settled accounts with Daniel Knowles and credited ye full Ballance of Twenty Pounds old Tenor (being first turned into Lawful money @ 23*s* & 1/3 amounting to 17*s*. 1*d*. & 3/4 Lawful) on a note of hand I have against him.

George Ireish.

18th 6th mo. To one Dark Coloured Natural pacing Horfe with some white in his Face, at fifty-five Silver Spanish mill^d Dollers. I am to take 1 hoggshead of Molafses, 1 barrell of sugar at £70 old Tenor per Hundred, the Molafses at the value of 36*s*. old Tenor. A Doller being considered at the value of Eight Pounds old Tenor, the Remainder in Tea at ye Rate of Eight Pounds old Ten^r and in Indigo at the Rate of Twelve Pounds old Tenor to have one-Half of ye remainder in Tea, & ye other in Indigo.

1767.

	OLD TENOR			LAWFUL.		
	£	s.	d.	£	s.	d.
Corn per bufhel.............		80	00		3	00
" " 2 mo.......		90	00			
Apples per bufhel..........						9
Barley per bufhel...........	3	10	00			
Oats "		45	00		1	6
Salt "		80	00			
Onions per bushel.........					3	00
Wool (old Wool & Dagglocks) per pound...............						4¼
Gammon per pound........		12	00			
Fifh per pound.............		2	6			
One Sheep...............	12	00	00		9	00
Mutton (hind quarter) per pound..................		6	00			
Veal per pound............		6	00			
Pork "		7	00			
Beef "		4	6			
Hogg's Fatt per pound......		14	00			
Weaving linnen per yard....		15	00			
" Tow coverlid......	8	00	00			
To cutting and carting half a load of wood.............	6	00	00			
1 old Horfe to Rowland Robinfon...................				3	15	00
Received in full for ye old Horfe	100	00	00			

10½ days' work & 4 days, mowing paid by 8 bufhels 3 pecks of corn, 1 Fatt Lamb, and 1 Spanish Mill^d Dollar.

	OLD TENOR.			LAWFUL.		
	£	s.	d.	£	s.	d.

Cheese 20 pounds the Spanish Dollar.

12th mo. 2nd day.

William Congdon son of Jos[h] Dr.

To one Bay Horfe five years old @ 500 lbs. & one half Hundred w[t] of sugar such Sugar as was Set at 8 Dollars the Hundred Clean & of a bright Colour.

Peleg Peckham credit. One Piece of Gold of ye Value of 8 Doll[rs] & 4 Dollers in Dollers by ye Hand of thy Wife (for cheese).

	OLD TENOR			LAWFUL		
One Ewe lamb.............	6	00	00			
3 Piftereens at.............						7½
Flower per pound..........		5	00			
Molafses per gallon.........		55	00			
One yoke of oxen..........				9	00	00
Cheese 20 pounds y[e] Spanifh *Doller*..................		8	00			
New England Rum per gallon					2	3
Load of Hay.............				2	6	00
Hay per Hundred weight....					1	2½
Side of Leather...........					2	3
Plowing Andrew Nichols' *Lott*					5	00
Tallow per pound..........						5½
Sugar "		15	00			
Sheep skins...............		25	00			
Lamb "		20	00			

	OLD TENOR. £ s. d.	LAWFUL. £ s. d. qr.
One Lamb...................		5 3
Stone Lime per bushel........	4 10 00	
1 Thimble..................	6 00	
Cheefe new milk...........	9 00	

1768.

	OLD TENOR. £ s. d.	LAWFUL. £ s. d. qr.
Corn per bushel	80 00	3 00
Oats per bushel	40 00	1 6
Barley per bushel..........	80 00	3
Wool per pound	32 00	
Flackseed per bushel........		4 6
Flax per pound...........	16 00	
Tea per pound	6 00 00	4 6
Sugar per pound...........	13 00	6
Chocolat per pound	42 00	1 6
Wine per gallon...........		3 00
West India Rum per gallon ..	80 00	
New England " " ..	52 00	
Weaving *white Flaning* per yard	8 00	
Cheese per pound..........	8 00	
Shoes per pair.............	2 00 00	
Soles for shoes	25 00	
To John Shearman for making and repairing Shoes for ye Family ye year past, and his finding some Women's Hats....................	75 00 00	
1 Steer...................	20 00 00	15 00
2 Earthen Boles. One Jack Knife & dozen of pipes		1 11
1 Yearling Steer	50 00 00	1 17 6
1 Steer, a Neat Beaft........	65 00 00	2 8 4¼

	OLD TENOR.			LAWFUL.			
	£	s.	d.	£	s.	d.	qr.
To Two Johannes in Gold to the value of 16 Spanish Mill^d Dollers				4	16	00	
1 Fat Lamb................					5	3	
1 quarter of Lamb						14	
Pickel Pork per pound......		12	00				
" " " 5 mo..						5½	
6 Pound old Ten. equal......				4	6		⅛
Lime per bushel	4	10	00	3		4½	
Fiſh per pound		3	00				
1 Sythe Snead					1	6	
1 old Sythes per pound......						2¼	
Molaſses per gallon		55	00				
" " 8th mo		46	00				
Veal per pound						2½	⅘
19^{lbs} of Flax @ 7⅘ of a Farthing....................					11	4⅘	
Spinning 80 skeins of Linen Yarn per skein		8	00	1	4	0	
Carding and Spinning 75½ skeins Tow per skein......		7	00	1	00	00	
Weaving 30 yds Tow Cloth per yard		8	00		9	00	
Weaving 42 yds Diaper @ per yard		10	00		15	9	
Boiling & Washing the yarn that made s^d cloth	3	12	00		2	6	
To Carting with my Team one Load of Goods from J. Franklin's ferry to s^d Peleg's (Peckham) houſe					9	00	
By 28^{lb} of Rice 1/4 & 1/16 of							

	OLD TENOR.			LAWFUL.			
	£	s.	d.	£	s.	d.	qr.
Callico 1 Earthern Bole 1/2^{lb} of Allum Some Red Worfted Quality 3 Needles 2 Skeins of Thread 1/4 yrd of Cambrick The whole £13. 8. - 3^d 1/2 old Ten					10	00	3
By 18/old Tenor..........						8	
John Gardner (on ye Hill weaver) in South Kingstown credited By weaving 1 Coverlead at		8				6	
Mowing a day.............						3	
To Two Johannes in Gold to ye Value of 16 Spanish Mill^d Dollers Joⁿ Garton Prefent				4	16	00	
Keeping Cows per week......		40					

1769.

	OLD TENOR.			LAWFUL.			
Oats per bushel	40	00			1	6	
Apples per bushel.........	15	00					
Salt per bushel 4	00	00			3	00	
Load of hay...............40	00	00					
to be paid in carpantry per day 5	00	00					
Sheep skins with wool on 6	00	00					
" and lamb skins ...40	00	00		6	00		
Candles per pound..........	20	00				9	
Cheese per pound	10	00					
Plumbs (3 pounds)..........	36	00		1	4		
Molasses per gallon.........	46	00					
1 Saddle Cloth 12	00	00					
1 Hunting Saddle...........60	00	00					

	OLD TENOR. £ s. d.	LAWFUL. £ s. d.
To 1 Book Entitled the Prin-ciples & precepts of ye Chris-tian Religion &c.	10 00	4½
(Josh. Hull credited)		
By making one Hetchel at 3 shillings old Ten^r per Tooth 320 Teeth..........		16 00
By one fire Pann...........		3 00
Some Sole & upper Leather @	120	4 6
Tallow	4 9	
(Benedict Oatley.)		
By £9 old Tenor. he said it was to Buy Corn with.....		6 9
To 1/2 lb of Candles @ 20*s* old Teno^r		4½
To 3 lbs of Pickle Pork @ 10*s*.		1 1½
633 weight of young Swine @	4	4 11 1
1 days carting with my Team		9
Lamb per pound	6	
Mutton "	6	
250 Clout Nails............	35	
By 1 pair of shoes set on ye hipt mare he *found Iron* for 1 *shoe*		1 10½
By shoeing my Horſe & my old mare, each a pair of shoes before @		1 6
To the Happy man &^c a half sheet @	2 coppers	
1770.		
Corn per bushel	80 00	3 00
Oats per bushel	40 00	1 6

	OLD TENOR.			LAWFUL.		
	£	s.	d.	£	s.	d.
Flaxseed per bushel.........					3	9
Wool per pound		30	00			
Cheefe per pound...........						$4\frac{1}{2}$
Skim Cheefe per pound......						$2\frac{1}{4}$
Veal per pound.............		6	00			
Beef per pound..............		4	6			
Lamb "		7	0			
1 Heifer at 9 dollars				2	14	00
Bafs Fish scal^d and gutted per pound...............		3	00			
Fish "		2	6			
Pork per pound.............		7	0			
£8 old Tenor @ 9*d*					6	00
3 Spanifh Mill^d *dollers*					18	00
Tallow Tried per pound... .		12	00			
Butter per pound		20	00			
1 Horfe .... 25 dollars						
Keep of a horfe per week		40	00			
" " cow "		40	00			

Coll^l John Potter D^r.

	OLD TENOR.			LAWFUL.		
To 5 veal Calve skins Del^d thy Negro Hager when she had 20 of wool for Thee at 30*s*. old Ten..............				1	2	6
Filling one barrel of Cyder...					6	
Twelve Pounds old Ten @ 9^d					9	
Tailoring per day (Andrew Nichols)...................					2	3
Haying per day............					3	
10 lb old Iron when I sent my Hand Irons to be repaired @					3	
One pair of Vamps for Shoes		50				

	OLD TENOR.			LAWFUL.		
	£	s.	d.	£	s.	d.
15 pounds of Flax per bushel		16			9	00
Salt per bushel					3	4½
Fat Sheep each.					7	6
Chocolate per pound		40				
Mutton per pound.		6				
To Carting wood y^c 3 day & fifth day of this Instant y^c 11th mo	12	00	00		18	00
To my Team & hand one day to Move thy Goods to the Ferry at	16	00	00		12	00
Beef hides & Tallow per pound		4	6			

1771.

	OLD TENOR.			LAWFUL.		
Corn per bushel		80	00		3	00
Oats "					1	6
Apples per bushel.		35	00			
Veal per pound.		6	00			
Beef per pound.		5	00			
To carting one day	12	00	00		9	00
Chocolate per pound		40	00		1	6
Sugar per pound.		15	00			
1 pair of Shoes at.	9	00	00		6	9
1 Fatt Horse @ 40 Dollars . . .				12	00	00
1 Fatt Steer @ 16 Silver Dollars				4	16	00
Half Soles and heel lifts.		20	00			
Sole leather per pound		30	00			
1 day's work at putting in Glaſs & Winder Caſements @. . . .	4	00	00			
6 days work at mak^g my Cart & boaring 8 yoakes at 3^s					18	
2 days work at Carpentry @ 3^s					6	

	OLD TENOR. £ s. d.	LAWFUL. £ s. d.
(Powel Helme credit)		
9th 3rd mo Recd 7lb of Choco- late toward keeping ye Cod- dington Horfe		
9th 4th mo To 7 weeks & six days keeping ye Coddington Horfe at 1lb of Chocolate per week		10 6
9th 4th mo Credit by thy In- structs my Robert in the art of Navigation in Part, @ 5s 8d which is in full		5 8
Keeping a horse per week....		1 4
1 acre of Land Plowd & Howd to Plant Corn at	28 00 00	11 1
Dagg Locks per pound	10	
Plumbs per pound...........	18	
Lamb "	7	
Salt Hay per Hundred	40	

1772.

	OLD TENOR. £ s. d.	LAWFUL. £ s. d.
Corn per bushel 3d mo		3 00
" " 8th mo.....		3 9
Oats per bushel	40 00	
Molafses per gallon	46 00	
1 h o2 5 3/4lbs of Sugar per.. hundred.................		42
(By my Stillyards 114½lb)		
Cheese per pound	12 00	
Weaving Flannel per yard....	8 00	
Salt per bushel.............		3 4¼
1 pair Shoes		7 6
Hogg's Fatt per pound	14 00	

	OLD TENOR.			LAWFUL.		
	£	s.	d.	£	s.	d.
To Filling 1 Hodg^{hd} with Cyder per barrel...........					5	3
Keeping a horse per week....					1	6
1 days work at repairing ye Dragg....................		4				
(Joseph Hull Junr) Credit By making & Sett^s one shoe I found Iron & mending 2 Pair of Bridle Bits @ 2s old Ten each		4				
Tow per pound.............		9				
Mutton "		6				
Beef "		5				
Veal "		6				
1 days Work with my Cart & oxen Carting wood........					9	
One Load of Hay Weighing 2230 Weight				2	5	00
3 Hundred 1/4 with ye Ropes that Bound it of Hay @....					2	3
1 Three year old Heifer @ 10 Dollers						
2 Fatt oxen @ 63 Dollers						

1773.

	OLD TENOR.			LAWFUL.		
Corn per bushel.............					3	9
Barley per bushel..........					3	00
Lime per bushel............					3	9
Tar per gallon.............					1	3
To Making one pair of Cloth Shoes & Sole Leather & Thread.................	5	00	00		3	00

	OLD TENOR.			LAWFUL.		
	£	s.	d.	£	s.	d.
Sheep at....................	10	00	00	1	12	6
Hay per hundred weight....	3	00	00		2	3
Beef per pound.............		4	00			
Cheefe per pound..........						6
Butter per pound..........		22	00			
Pork per pound.............		8	00			3½
Tow "						4½
One pair of shoes..........					5	00
To Carting wood 2 days.....	240	00		18	00	
Tar per quart..............		8	00			4

To Carting one Load of Cole
  from Thos Sweets @......   9 00

To Carting one Load of Cole
  from Ministerial Farm @..   9 00

Rowland Robinfon D^r

1st 2^d mo To 111 Sheep @
  £10 (and he ought to Pay
  for keeping them 3 weeks).   1 12 6

25th 3mo Rec^d 3 Balls 30 Dollars 1 Barrel of Flower 7¾
  Dollars

15th 4th mo Rec^d 100 Dollers
  one Doller lefs 16 old yet
  Due. Paid in ye whole for
  the Sheep.

     John Hazard D^r

11th mo 22^d day To Two beef
  Hides by thy Boy 1 being a
  Bull's & y^e other Cow's
  Hides.

16th 12th mo To 3 Beef Hides
  1 being an ox Hide the

	OLD TENOR.			LAWFUL.		
	£	s.	d.	£	s.	d.

other Two Cow Hides & 2 Boar Skins.

17 Settled 3 Calves Skins in which Settlem^t Coufin Hazard is Debtor to me 40/ old Ten^r and Receiv^d 2 Sides of Sole Leather Weighing 23$^{lbs.}$

1774.

	OLD TENOR		LAWFUL	
Corn per bushel............			3	9
Barley per bushel...........			3	oo
Potatoes per bushel.........	35	oo		
Tar per gallon.............	32	oo		
Sole leather for a pair of shoes...................			1	6
Pork, pickled, per pound....	12	oo		
Day's work carting wood....			9	oo
1 Silver Dollar @..........			6	oo
Keeping a horse per week...			1	6
To my Team & 2 Hands Carting one Load of Sand from little Neck Beach to Tower Hill....................			6	oo

Gideon Fowler D^r

To one silver Doller @......			6	oo

Robt & Tommy Prefent.

Joseph Congdon Junr Creditted since we Settled
To Shoeing Horfes By Seting five pair of Shoes on 5 Horfes @ 7$^d\frac{1}{4}$........... 3 oo

4th 8th mo By Repairing one

	OLD TENOR.	LAWFUL.
	£　s.　d.	£　s.　d.

Staple for a forebridge of
a Cart & Shuting together
the Iron for the End of the
Tongue of the Cart nine
nales to nale it.......... 　　　　1　6

13th 9th mo by Shoeing my
great Bay mare afore only. 　　　　1　¼

By Shoeing Rowland's
Horfe afore only I found
the Shoes.............. 　　　　　　7¼

(Turn over 4 leaves & look
to the Right Hand)

In ye year 1774 Rec^d of Oliver
Kinnion 12¾^{lb} of Fish &
gave him an order upon
Joshua Sweet s^d Fish at 3*s.*
old Ten^r p^r p^d 1 18 00

S^o Kingston &^c Jeffrey
Watfon Jr. D^r　10th mo

1 Vol. of Sewel's Hiftories at 　　　　18 00

& 4 coppers Expense on it. 　　　　　　2½

C^t By 6 / sent to Philadelphia
when Subscriptions were
Sent there.............. 　　　　　6　0

Received Two Dollars & four
Coppers of Jeffrey Watfon
Junr in full............. 　　　　12 00

S^o Kingstown 12th 12th mo A D 1774
Brought from the 231st Page
John Torrey D^r
To keeping his Horfe from the
17th of the 9th month to the

	OLD TENOR. £ s. d.	LAWFUL. £ s. d.

29th of the 11th month viz
7 weeks @ 1s 6d pr week... — 9 00
John Torreys Horfe came
to me to Winter the 2nd day
of the 12th month again.

1775 John Torrey took his
Horfe away having been
with me at Pasture fifteen
Weeks Two days from the
2d of ye 12th mo 1774 @   (A blank left.
See Settlement in 1781.)

To Carting one Load of
Sand @................ — 6 00

1775.

	OLD TENOR. £ s. d.	LAWFUL. £ s. d.
Corn per bushel...........		3 00
White beans per bushel.....		4 6
Cheese per pound..........	6 00	
New Milk Cheese per pound.	12 00	
Veal per pound............	5 00	
Salt Pork per pound........	12 00	
Beef per pound.......... ..	4 6	
(Andrew Nichols Junr.)		
To carting Load of *Eal Grass* to thy house & Collecting it from my shore..........		2 3
Mowing a day............	4 00 00	
Farm labor...............	40 00	
Spinning linen per skien...	8 00	
Tallow per pound..........	16 00	

6th mo. Receivd Two Dollars
of Rowland Robinfon to-

	OLD TENOR.	LAWFUL.
	£ *s.* *d.*	£ *s.* *d.* *qr.*
ward Some I Lent Him 10th mo 22 in Paper Bills by ye hand of my ſon Robt		
This acc^{t} is Carried forward to 157		
Lent Brother Rowland Robinſon in the 3rd month Last		19 6 00
My Wife lent his Wife in her last Sickneſs............		6 00 00
I over paid him 5*s* per Gallon for 67 Gallons of Molaſes which amounts to........		12 7 ¼
C^{r} given to the above acc^{t} againſt Rowland Robinſon		1 18 1 ¼
In the 6th mo Last Receiv^{d} ..		12 00 00
10th mo Receiv^{d} in Paper Bills one 10*s* Bill & one 12*s* Bill		1 2 00 00
		1 14 00 00
To 1 pair of oxen 3 times to ye ferry & to Littlerest @..		(blank.)
To 1 pair once to ye Ferry @		"
To 16^{lb}¾ of Cheeſe @.......	12 00	7 6 ½
(Other entries of oxen's work with no price.)		
13th 4th mo Receiv^{d} the above acc^{t} againſt Powel Helme in a Settlement with him		
T Hazard of Rob^{T}		
Shoeing the old black mare before..................		1 8 ¼

	OLD TENOR.			LAWFUL.			
	£	s.	d.	£	s.	d.	qr.

Shoeing the great bay mare before.................... 1 8 ¼

Shoeing Tommy's Horſe before.................... 1 8 ¼

 John Gould Credited

9th mo 2d Day To his wife's Spinning 24 Scains of linnen yarn at 8/ old Ten.

 Settled this acct with John Gould

5th mo 5th day Benj Perry Dr To 1 Veal Calve Skin delvd pr Quaſh

6 day To 1 veal Calve Skin delvd to thy own hand

6th mo 6th day To one Calve Skin Sent by Son Rowland

16th To one Bull Hide, died at Giddeon Clarkes, sent by Tommy

20th To one Calve Skin deliverd it myself

7th month 11th day To one Large Veal Calve Skin ye day I set out for the Quarterly Meet. Sent per Rowland

    1776.

Corn per bushel............ 3 00

Turnips per bushel........ 1 2½

White beans per bushel..... 6 00

	OLD TENOR. £ s. d.	LAWFUL. £ s. d.
Leather for a pair of shoes..		3 00
Caps & Taps for a pair of shoes..		1 00
Double Fold Linen per yard		8 00
New Milk cheese per pound.		5
Beef " .	6 6	
Wool per pound.............		1 6
Cloth for a coat per yard....		9 00
One Hoe...................		3 6
Valentine Ridge for Combing *Warsted* per pound.......	14 00	
Tow cloth per yard.........		2 00

South Kingstown &c 7th mo 5th day.

Eunice Nichols Tailorefs D^r

To 13th of Sheeps Wool @ Entered here by miftake turn over 5 Leaves look to the Right Hand for her acc^t (Having turned over 5 leaves)

Unice Nichols D^r

		LAWFUL. £ s. d.
26th 6th mo To one bufhel of Indian Corn at 3/.......		3 0
5th 7th mo To 13^{lb} of Sheeps Wool at		15 0½
9th to 2^{lb}¾ of Veal @ 6/.....		1 2
8th mo 26th day To 2 of Tow @ (by thy Father) 4^d.		8 00
To 1½ yard of Double Fold Linnen @ 8/............		12 00
To Leather for a pair of Shoes £5 old Ten............		3 9

<table>
<tr><td></td><td colspan="3">OLD TENOR.</td><td colspan="3">LAWFUL.</td></tr>
<tr><td></td><td>£</td><td>s.</td><td>d.</td><td>£</td><td>s.</td><td>d.</td></tr>
</table>

10th mo 3rd day To 5^{lb} of Mutton at 7 Shillings old Ten^r.   1 3½

1777 3rd mo To 30^l of Flax
@....................   (blank)

To 2^{lb}¾ of Sheeps Wool being
s^d unices Ballance........

    Benj^a Perry Credited

2^d mo. 25th day By Two Calve
Skins one a very Small one

20th 4th mo By 1 Side of Sole
Leather................

21st 5th mo Rec^d 5 Calve
Skins being my ⅔ with 2
Rec^d heretofore out of 11
Calve Skins Deliver^d in y^e
year 1775

    James Helme Credited

1st mo 22^d day for writing my
Will 12 00

21st 2^d mo Rec^d of Thomas
Robinfon Thirty one Shil-
lings Lawful Money to Lay
out in Flax

3rd mo 14 Day Sent Thomas
Robinfon 30^l of Flax, and
Since Settled the Remain-
der of s^d 30/ with Him

        T Hazard

    John Smith D^r

9th mo. 20th day To 1½ bufh-
els of Corn @ ....   (blank)

	OLD TENOR.			LAWFUL.		
	£	s.	d.	£	s.	d.

John Smith Paid ye above Charge of 1½ bufhels of Corn in his Wifes whitening linnen Cloth for my Wife When they Settled.

1777.

	OLD TENOR			LAWFUL		
Corn per bushel............	4	00	00	3	00	
Butter per pound...........					9	
Cheese per pound..........					6	
Making a pair of Bretches...					9	00
"　　"　　" for Tommy.................					6	9
Board Nails per thousand...					20	00
Two hundred Weight Grofs & 9^{lb} Neat of Hay @ 3/.....					6	3

Benj Perry Cr.

12 mo 3rd By 3 Sides settled W^t 37^{lb} Perry had 22^{lb} ½ & I had 141^{lb} ½ of the Hides delivered him in 1775 & 1776 and one side unfettled not being Suffi-ciently Dried the Weight to be Known by ye other Side when it shall be Dried & Coufin Perry hath rec^d 5^{lb} ¼ of what is settled more than his Part.

23rd 1st mo 1777 Settled 6 Sides with the one Men-tioned above not Suffi-

	OLD TENOR.			LAWFUL.		
	£	s.	d.	£	s.	d.

ciently Dried yᵉ Weight
Known by [that] of its mate
side

South Kingstown &c Look on
  yᵉ Left hand one Leaf Back
Chriſtopher Potter Credited
  To Making Shingles the
  Winter paſt No 4073 @ 5/   1 00 4½
6ᵗʰ mo 5ᵗʰ day Numbered the
  Cheeſes made this year in
  the Cheeſe House 17 and
  Two in the Preſses the
  Whole 19
Benj Hazard Son of Richard
  left my Houſe on yᵉ 18ᵗʰ of
  2ᵈ mo 1777
24ᵗʰ 6ᵗʰ mo Sent to Paul Green
  Ten Calve skins Two of
  them Eat much with Rats
  Two Swine Skins four Beef
  Hides all to be Tanned &
  the Calve Skins Curried for
  one Third the Hoog's skins
  to be Dreſsed for Saddle
  Leather.
7ᵗʰ mo 7ᵗʰ day To Two good
  Veal Calve Skins
29ᵗʰ To 2 large Calve Skins
  Sent by Tommy
Look at yᵉ Bottom at the
  Right Hand.

OLD TENOR.　　LAWFUL.

£　*s.*　*d.*　　£　*s.*　*d.*

Supplied the Widow Alice
Gould by order of the
Meet[s] for Suffering as fol-
loweth (Viz[t])

12th mo 8th day To one pair
of Shoes at 33/. . . . .　　　　1　13　00

9th To 7 yards of Tow & lin-
nen 18/. . . . .　　　　6　6　00

The above articles are Settled
by receiving pay from y[e]
Meeting for Suffer[s]

1778.

17th 3rd month. BE IT REMEMBERED, that it is
agreed between Thomas Hazard son of Robert, and
Sier Averit, in manner following (Viz.) That the s[d] Sier
shall work at Husbandry, that is to say, at Howing,
Ploughing, Walling, Ditching, Fencing, Mowing, Haying and milking &[c.] For the full Term of Eight Months,
to begin on the 18th Instant, and to be compleat and
ended on the 18th of the eleventh month following,
& to make good to s[d] Hazard, all lost Time, in Proportion of the Value of Labour at the seafon of ye
year when it may be Loft, either by Sicknefs or otherwife.   And the said Hazard, doth covenant and agree
with the s[d] Sier, to Pay Him at the end & Expiration
of Said Term, & making up of lost Time, The full
sum of five Dollars p[r] month, That is to say, Forty
Dollars For the Term of Eight months as aforesaid.
The Value of which money is hereby agreed on
between the Parties hereto to be determined and
Settled at the Expiration of the Term afores[d,] by a

Liquidation of the articles hereafter enumerated, (Viz.) Pork at 3¾*d*. p^r Pound, Beef at 3*d*. p^r Pound, Cheese at five Pence p^r Pound & Indian Corn at 3 shillings p^r . Bushel.

As Witness our Hands the day & year first above written.

(Signed) Th° HAZARD of Robt.
Witness — ANSTIS BROWN. SIER AVERIT.

Colonel John Willson D^r

3^d mo 14th day To 14^lb¾ of Cheefe a 6/ and 4½ bushels of corn (no price)

22nd of 12th month, Col. John Wilson settled accounts this day with Thomas Hazard of Robert, and there is due to him on balance, 4 pounds of cheese.

As witnesseth my hand. (Signed) JOHN WILSON.

12th day of 2nd month 1780, in settlement of account this day received satisfaction for the above 4 pounds of cheese of Col. John Wilson.

(Signed) THOMAS HAZARD.

Of Cheefe made this year 1778 Viz No 74 the 27th of the 7th mo with that made this day Thos Hazard of Robt

1st mo 28th day Received of Rowland Robinfon Seven Pounds Ten Shillings in Paper Bills.

8th mo 4th Coufin George Hazard son of Richard Borrowed of me 37 Paper Dollars

26th 8th mo Rec^d a note of George Hazard for s^d Dollars

                                               LAWFUL.
                                            £ s. d.

26th 3rd mo 3 yards of Tow Cloth in one
     Frock............................   4   6
1 pair of old Stockings   1   0
To mending one pair of Shoes & Thread at   1   6
One Knot of Thread @................   2¾
Making Shirts Each old Tenor 40*s*
1 pair of Leather Breeches 36/..
Sarge per yard................£7 00 00
Shoes per pair................ 6 00 00

                    1779.

                                           LAWFUL.
Making one Coat 15 00
1 pair Knee buckles   1   4 00
Mowing per day.........   3 00

(Memorandums of corn, butter, veal, molasses, wool,
etc., occur in this year with no prices attached, and
the accounts seem to have been settled by barter as
in the previous year, and as in the following agreement.)

   1779.   4th month 23rd day.

Settled accounts with Thomas Hazard of Rob't, and
there is due to said Hazard, the full Ballance of
Spinning 54 and ½ scains of linen yarn, which she is
to spin by Promiss under her hand.

                          ANSTRESS CRANDOL.

   1779.   7th month 3rd day.
               Anstress Crandall, credited.
By spinning 54 and ½ skains of yarn.

3rd mo 3^d day agreed with Siah Averit to Labour at Hufbandry for Eight months at 5 Silver Dollars p^r month

Turn over 4 Leaves

(Having turned over four leaves a long account is seen.)

Sier Averit Continued from 4 Leaves Back	£	s.	d.
To one sheep skin for a Leather apron @	1		
To Repairing thy Shoes & Soles		2	3

These are the only items carried out. Tow cloth Thread, making *Breches* and shirts, shoes, stockings.

To 9 sheets of paper at three Several Times

To one Knife at 10 Dollars

To 1 pair of Shoe Buckles @ 12 dollars: 3 pence: hard money

To Doctor Torrey 6/ in the old way

To 10 Dollars for his Sicknefs & Trouble

(All are entered, but not carried out. At the very end, crowded at the foot of the page, comes the receipt.)

3rd mo 31. 1780 Settled with Thos Hazard for 16 months work in ye Two Seafons past last & Received of Him the full Ballance of Fifty five Pounds Ten Shillings Lawful money as Witnefs my Hand

(Signed) SIAR AVERIT

3rd month 9th day George Hazard Son of Richard Entered into & occupied part of my houfe above the Rode & is to Give me 9 Dollars p^r annum to be paid in Labour at Hufbandry the Enfuing Seafon at 3/ p^r day for mowing & 1/6^d for Howing & Haying.

1780.

In evident despair at the trouble of managing so many kinds of money the last accounts in the book are boldly in Old Tenor, with no attempt at other reckoning, though there are many items with no prices attached.

11th mo 21st Daniel Howland D^r

To one Hundred Weight of New Milch Cheefe @ (no price)

9th 7th month 1781 Rec^d a Note of Hand for the above acc^t of s^d Howland.　He paid the Note.

(Entries of corn, mutton, veal, tallow, beef, one turkey, molasses, wool, are made in Valentine Ridge's account but with no prices.)

10th mo 27th on Settlement with Neighbour Ridge & there is due £30 5*s.* 6*d.* old Tenor.

1781.

7th mo 31 John Torrey credited by his acc^t for weaving 43 yards of Flaning & 28 yards of Broad Cloth & weaving.　On Settlement of all acc^{ts} made with Thomas Hazard this day there is due to Him the Ballance of Seven Pounds, Fourteen Shillings at the Rate of Four Pounds p^r Bufhel for Corn.

(Signed) JOHN TORREY.

John Watson D^r

5th mo 9th day To 1 peck of beft Rock Salt @ (no price) Rec^d of John Watfon pay for ye Peck of Salt except 3 Coppers.

William Congdon D^r

	£	s.	d.	qr.
To Two little Books @			9	00

	£ s. d. qr. in ye Old Tenr way
To 10lb of sugar @ 7d ¼qr	8 00 00
To 13lb of Good Mutton H. Q. @	4 12 09

11th mo 27th Oliver Smith a Negro Boy came to My Houſe with his Miſtreſs Elizabeth Smith aged 8 years the 7th of the 8th mo this Preſent year who is to work for me for his Bringing up untill he may have an advantageous opportunity to go apprentice.

1782.

11th 8th month Numbered the Cheeſes in the Cheeſe House & ym in the Preſses one of which made this day the whole amount to 70 in all THO HAZARD

Made a Double Curded Cheeſe on the 22nd day of the 9th month & afterwards until the 6th mo 24

	£ s. d. in ye old Ten way.
To 1*s*. 6*d*. in Hard Money	2 00 00
Corn per bushel	80 00
Veal per pound	6 00
Butter per pound	20 00
To 2 Dunghill Fowles @ 20/	2 00 00

1783.

5th mo 24th William Congdon's ox was Brought to Paſture @ (no price) Drove sd ox away the 10th of the 6th month in sd year having been here 2 weeks & 3 Days. Robert Hazard my Son Recd Pay for Keeping the ox of William Congdon.

1784.

9th mo we had of Son Rob[t] Corn for the Piggs as followeth meafur[d] myself 1½ Bushels Jack 1 bushel Abigail 3 Pecks Oliver half a bushel. 26th 9th mo Nicholas Gould had 24[lb] of Pickle Beef Son Rob[t] about 14 Quarts it being all

27th Nicholas Gould had half a Bufhel of Indian Corn @ (no price)

CONTRACTS FOR LABOUR.

1757.

Priamus a Negro Boy Came to live with me at my Houfe, the week after y[e] General Election Held at Newport for General officers for the Colony of Rhode Ifland in the year one Thoufand Seven Hundred & fifty seven, being six years old the octob[r] following the s[d] Election, which was held in May before.

1759.

6th of 1st mo A: D: 1759. Mary Dick began to Work and is to Work untill y[e] 1st of y[e] 4 mo @. 30/ P[r] Week & from that Time untill y[e] end of y[e] eleventh month @ 40/ P[r] Week that is to Say 8 months of y[e] year at 40/ & 4 at 30. And She is to have Two pair of Shoes in y[e] year at £4 the Pair. She to do Houfehold Work & y[e] Dairy both Butter & Cheefe & other Bufinefs When Necefsary.

1759   2[d] 4th mo.

Then agreed with William Wallfworth to work with me Six months if I like to hire him after one month for Twelve Pounds Lawfull money (But if I should not

Like to hire him after one month is Expired then I am to Give him for said one month Thirty Shillings Lawfull money it being Connecticut Prock so Called no interest to be reckoned thereon.

24th of ye 2nd month.   Anno Domini 1761.

Daniel Knowles, fon of John Knowles of Richmond-ton, began to work with me at Hufbandry and hath agreed to Labour thereat from the day abovefd for ye full Term of one year, and to make up all Lost days after the end of sd year and I am to Give him therefor when said time be fully ended, the full sum of Three Hundred Pounds old Tenor

THO HAZARD fON OF ROBT

fo Kingstown ye 24th of the 4th mo 1761 agreed with John Bull to Work for me from ye 19th Inst for ye term of Six months he is to make good all Lost day in which he may be out of my Bufinefs by sicknefs or otherwife & I am to give him therefor at the Expiration thereof £240.

5th month Calld May, 1762.

Jonathan Maxfon of Richmond began to Work at Hufbandry for fix months with me he to make Shoes in Wet Weather if it shall beft agree with my Conveniency, and when said Term be fully Compleated I am to Pay him Two Hundred & Eighty five Pounds old Tenor & keep him one Horse during sd Term.

4t 4th month 1763.

Joseph Davis of Westerly began to Work for me at Husbandry, and in Wet weather to Labour at Carpentry &c. for the Term of Six months, he to make good all Lost Time at ye Expiration thereof and I am to Pay him for his Labour to be done in s^d Term, after Rate of £50 p^r mo.

12mo 27 day 1763.

Then agreed with Henry Hill to Labour for me at huſbandry & at any kind of Buſineſs to be done at Farming for the Term of Ten months to begin on ye 2nd day of ye 1st month next in ye year 1764. And at ye Expiration of s^d Term he Paying all Lost days I am to Pay him the sum of £400 Pounds old tenor or the Value thereof in any kind of Bills or money current at s^d Time.

1763.

Michael Dye began to Work with me who is to Work 8 months making good all Lost days if any Should be through Sickneſs or other unavoidable cause & When the Same is compleated as Covenanted, I am to give him therefor £400 old Tenor, or an equivalent in Dollers at £7 Pr Doller, to be at my election.

THₒ HAZARD ſON OF ROBᵀ

1st day 9th month 1763.

Hir^d John Mash for one month (he to pay lost days) when it is Compleated to give him Thirty five Pounds for his Labour

The 16th of the 8th month. Then Took of John Mash Junr Eighteen Spaniſh mill^d Dollars & one Piece of Gold Call^d an eight Doller Piece or half Johannes To lay up for him as he is Drawn & going in the Engliſh army against the French.

The 6th day of the 11th month.   Delivered to said John Mash Junr the Eighteen Dollers and piece of Gold above mentioned.

The 14th of the 3rd month Call^d march A: D: 1764:

Covenanted & agree^d With Jos^h Davis of Hopkington to Labour for Seven Months to begin on ye 26th Ins^t he to make up Lost days if any there should be and When s^d Term Shall be Compleat & ended I am to allow & Pay him as a Confideration therefor the Sum of Three Hundred & Sixty Pounds old Tenor or an equivalent in any other medium Current in the Colony of Rhode Ifland.

S^o KINGSTOWN ye 24th of Sixth month A: D: 1766 Then agree'd with Mary Chafe for one year from the date hereof at ye Value of 50/ old Tenor Pr Week for the Summer Seafon & forty for the Winter Seafon She is to Work at Houfewifery Spinning &c.

1778 S^o KINGSTOWN &c.

Jacob Barney Came to my Houfe the 19th of ye 5th month & Went to work the Next day at Hatting (vizt) on the 20th and is to Work four months @ Journy Work & he is to Teach my Son Tommy the Hatters Trade & alfo another Lad if I require it & Provide one and I am to Pay Him the Common journy man's Wages in the usual way (according to the N^o of Hatts he Shall make in s^d Term) by the Hatt & to find him his Board for his instruction of the Lad or Lads as afores^d.

1778. S⁰ KINGSTON &ᶜ· 17ᵗʰ 3ʳᵈ mo.

BE IT REMEMBERED that it is agreed betwen Thomas Hazard ſon of Robᵗ And Sier Averit in manner following (Viz.) That the sᵈ Sier Shall work at Huſbandry that is to Say at Howing Ploughing Walling Ditching Fencing Mowing Haying and milking &ᶜ For the full Term of Eight Months to begin on the 18ᵗʰ Instant, and to be compleat ended on the 18ᵗʰ of the eleventh month following & to make good to sᵈ Hazard all loſt Time in Proportion of the Value of Labour at the seaſon of yᵉ year When it may be Loſt either by Sickneſs or otherwiſe. And the said Hazard doth covenant & agree with sᵈ Sier to Pay Him at the end & Expiration of Said Term & making up of lost Time The full sum of five Dollars pʳ month That is to say Forty Dollars For the Term of Eight months as aforesaid. The Value of which money is hereby agreed on between the Parties hereto to be detirmined & Settled at the Expiration of the Term aforesᵈ by a Liquidation of the articles hereafter enumerated, (Viz.ᵗ) Pork at 3ᵈ ¾ Pʳ Pound, Beef at 3ᵈ Cheeſe at five Pence Pʳ Pound & Indian Corn at 3/ Shillings Pʳ Buſhel as Witneſs our Hands the day & year first abovewritten

     (Signed) THᵒ HAZARD of Robᵗ

Witneſs — ANSTIS BROWN.   SIER AVERIT.

1781 11ᵗʰ month 27ᵗʰ day.

Oliver Smith a Negro Boy came to my Houſe with his Miſtreſs Elizabeth Smith, aged 8 years the 7ᵗʰ of the 8ᵗʰ moᵗʰ this Preſent year, who is to work for me for his Bringing up untill he may have an advantageous opportunity to go aprentice.

1789   18th day 4th month A. D. 1789.

Agreed with Jack Sanford, a Black man, to Labour with me at Huſbandry & He is to milk through the Seaſon & take care that all the Cows are well Milked for the full Term of Seven months from the Last day of the third month now last Past, & will be compleat & ended the last day of the Tenth month in this Present year & he is to make up all Lost Days, which He may Looſe through sickneſs or any other unavoidable Contingency.   And I on my Part am to Pay or Cause to be Paid to him the Value of Three Dollars p^r month, in articles and Produce off the farm, at the Following rates (vizt) Corn at 3s. p^r Bushel, Cheeſe 4$d\frac{1}{2}$ per pound & other articles at a proportionable Rate, in the old way & in Cloathing as may be agreed, if He needs any   All which is to be Due & to be paid at the Expiration of said Term as Witneſs

(Unsigned)

(A small sheet not bound in the Account Book.)

This may Certify that Thomas Hazard of So Kingstown in the County of Waſhington and State of Rhode Iſland yeoman hath let unto Thomas Gould (a black man) for the year enſewing a certain priviledg containing the lower rooms of the hous where said Gould lived last year except a priviledg in one half the seller and the priviledg of paſsing in at the door next the Rode to the firſt stairs leading up into the Chambers in said hous Likewise one-Quarter of an Acre of ground for a garden, Being the same ground s^d Gould occupied for a Garden laſt year, For which previledg said Thomas Gould agreeth to

pay unto the said Thomas Hazard aforefaid two
pounds Eight Shillings in Labour for the rent thereof
one year, which is to commence on the 25th day of
the third M° AD 1794 and to end on the 25th day of
the third M° in the year AD 1795

In prefence of   his
JOB WATSON Jnr as witnefs   THOMAS X GOULD
                                          marke

RECORD OF BIRTHS.

Sarah Hazard Daughter of Thos Hazard and Eliza-
beth his Wife was born the 10th day of the month
Called January (it being ye 1st day of ye week) old
Stile in the Year of our Lord one Thoufand feven
Hundred and forty Seven (1747)

And Departed this Life the Twenty Sixth day of
may on the Seventh day of the Week about Eleven
o-Clock at night in the Year of our Lord one Thoufand Seven Hundred and fifty Three New ftile being
five years four months and five days old.

Robert Hazard fon of Thos Hazard & Elizabeth his
Wife Born the Seventeenth day of The Tenth month
Called October about fifty minutes after one o:Clock
in the morning in the year one Thoufand Seven Hundred fifty & Three

Thomas Hazard fon of Thomas & Elizabeth his Wife
Born the Thirteenth day (being ye 5th day of ye Week
about 9 'oClock morning) of the eleventh month Called
November & in the year of our Lord one Thoufand
Seven hundred & fifty five and Departed this Life the
fifteenth day of the Third Month in the year of our

Lord one Thoufand Seven Hundred and fifty Six about 10 morning oClock yᵉ 2ᵈ day of yᵉ Week

Thomas Hazard fon of Thomas & Elizabeth his Wife Born yᵉ 15ᵗʰ of yᵉ 11ᵗʰ mo Called november 5ᵗʰ of yᵉ Week about Nine o'Clock in the Evening A: D: 1758 being the 2ᵈ fon of that Name

Rowland Hazard fon of Thoˢ Hazard & Elizabeth his Wife Born the 4ᵗʰ day of the 4ᵗʰ mo Callᵈ April being the Second Day of the Week about Ten o'Clock in the forenoon according to the World's Accᵗ one Thousand feven Hundred and Sixty Three

1781 Sarah Daughter to Thoˢ Hazard Junʳ & Anna his Wife & Grand Daughter to the abovesᵈ Thomas Hazard & Elizabeth his Wife was Born the 18ᵗʰ day of the 9ᵗʰ month about yᵉ middle of the Day.   1781.

A REGESTOR OF DEATH'S.

My Father Robᵗ Hazard Died yᵉ 20ᵗʰ of yᵉ 5ᵗʰ mo. 1762 at about half after one in yᵉ morning ; After an Illnefs of Ten Weeks & four days eleven Hours & an half which he bore with a becoming Patience Aged Seventy Three Years

THᵒ HAZARD fon of ROBᵗ decd

My Grand Father Thoˢ Hazard Departed this Life yᵉ 21ˢᵗ day of yᵉ month Callᵈ November in the Year one Thoufand Seven Hundred & forty Six, aged 88 or 89 years.   This accᵗ taken from a memorand. found amongſt my Fathers Papers after his Death.

THᵒ· HAZARD fon of ROBᵗ decd

Brother Richard Hazard Departed this Life on ye 30th of ye Ninth month Calld Septembr aged 31 years 10 month & Ten days He died on ye 5th day of ye Week about 38 minuts after Four in ye afternoon after an Illness of Twenty days 1762

Wm Robinson son of Rowld & Mary Robinson died ye 19th day of the 7mo being ye 5 day of ye Week at near 12 at night

Lathan Clarke son of Samuel & mary of Conanicut departed this Life the Seventh of ye fifth month 4th day of ye Week about the dawning of the Day 1760

Martha the Widow of sd Latham & Daughter of William Robinson by his first Wife (Vizt) Martha daughter of John & Sarah Potter departed this Life ye 7th of ye 9th month about 9 of ye Clock in ye Evening 1760.

Venibee departed this Life the 3rd of the 1st mo 1759

Dick drowned ye 22d of ye 4th mo 1759

1767 Susannah Hazard Widow of Richard Hazard abovesd & Daughter of George & Mary Hazard (of Boston Neck in So Kingstown late deceasd) departed this Life on the 28th of ye 4th mo. Calld april about 9 oClock in ye evening aged

1771 Stephen Champlin Departed this Life the 22 of the 7th mo. Calld July the first day of ye Week about Sun Sett.

Mary Champlin Widow to the above s^d. Stephen departed this Life the 13th of the 3rd month A. D 1773 aged

Sarah Hazard Widow of Robert Hazard late deceased, departed this Life the 1st day of the 2^d month Call^d February 1772 about half after Eight oClock in the evening being the 7th day of Week. Aged 77 years the   of the Eight month Call^d Auguſt 1771.

The 12th of the 7th month Called July A. D: 1732 Grand Father Richard Borden departed this Life.

The above acc^t of Grandfather Borden's Death was taken from an acc^t Left by Father Hazard & found on a looſe Paper amongst his Papers after his Death

TH^o HAZARD of ROB^T